THE BORDELLO GIRL

Hilary Murray

1

AT EXACTLY ELEVEN O'CLOCK THIS morning my great-aunt woke, stared wide-eyed as if witnessing something completely unexpected and then, with a long and contented sigh, departed this world.

Sitting at her bedside I thought I was ready. Thought I had every emotion in check, after all she was well into her nineties. But I didn't. It was as if my throat had closed over and I couldn't breathe. And suddenly I was weeping. Heavens! What would she have said to that! After reaching for the box of tissues and blowing my nose, I glanced around the private ward as if expecting to see - what? A ghostly figure floating towards the ceiling? Of course there was nothing of the sort. Just the usual cream painted walls and floral pink curtains half drawn over tropical shutters.

After that everything became very much a process. The duty nurse - lilac scrubs and salted hair scraped back into a large tortoiseshell clip - led me from the room to start the formalities. There was no one else. No family. No children or grandchildren living close by. Only me, and that was by chance after a failed marriage had led me to pack up my worldly goods and shift to Australia's Far North, a decision that turned out to be more of a challenge than I'd thought. I'd always had a vague idea of the existence of a distant relative in the area but I'd no plans to get in touch back then. It was an additional complication I simply didn't need. So it was a surprise even to me when I did. Perhaps I was feeling adrift and in need of a little grounding, a sense of who I was and the roots I had sprung from.

"Please don't call me great-aunt," she said firmly on our first meeting. "It makes me feel as though I've already got one foot in the grave. Why don't you call me Thea and I will call you Laurie. There, now we're friends."

My great-aunt was a lively, well-read, robust woman and, it turned out, one of life's rarities; someone completely at peace with the hand fate had dealt her.

"A good life," she said sipping on a glass of Madeira after one of our regular lunches. "It's all you can wish for. A good and happy life."

And yet from the little I knew it had not always been that way. Of her two sons, the eldest had been killed in the final months of the Second World War while Bill had long ago made his life in the United States. As far as I knew he'd not returned to Australia for God knows how many years, and at this point I was wondering if he would even bother coming back for the funeral.

I'd let myself into Thea's house, taking a moment in the hallway to let the silence wash over me. It was strange to think there was no one to welcome me, or call out, telling me to join her in the kitchen.

She had known this moment would come of course, and had asked me to take care of everything. We were in her cosy front room and she had just settled a pot of Earl Grey tea and two delicate china cups and saucers onto the low table between us.

"You can give my clothes to the Sallies," she'd said, as if we were discussing nothing more contentious than the weather. "Of course, they might consider them a little outdated but they might be pleased with some of the glassware."

I'd glanced at the old-fashioned, lead-lighted cupboard.

"Are you sure? Didn't you tell me some of it's from Ireland?"

"One or two pieces are. Why don't you have those?"

"I will. But I'd rather you had the use of them a while longer."

She'd smiled. "We all have to go sometime. And when I do, there is something else I need to ask of you."

"Oh? What's that?"

Thea was pouring tea.

"I have things that are precious to me. Items I can't bear to throw away. You must do that."

"Of course."

I was imagining redundant furnishings or unwanted books. The usual bric-a-brac found in an elderly person's loft or spare bedroom. But there was something in her tone that made me hesitate.

"What sort of things?"

Thea was already opening the carved wooden trinket box she kept on the side table.

"This," she said, waving a small brass key, "will open the bottom drawer of my writing desk. There's a box inside. Of course it's all ancient history. But I think I'd like someone to know the truth."

That threw me.

"Then why don't we do it together?" I suggested. "Now if you like?"

"No. It can wait."

I flashed my eyes as if we were co-conspirators. "Will I find the deeds to a fabulous fortune?"

"Would I be living here if that were the case?" she countered dryly.

I could see her point. The house was definitely on the small side and the garden even more so when compared to the vast property she and my great-uncle had owned in the highlands. I'd seen it first-hand one morning, when following her directions, I'd driven her up and parked on the verge near the gate. She'd gotten out of the car and bunching her hands into her jacket pockets, she'd gazed across the front paddock towards the house in the distance.

"I loved him with all of my heart," she said when I joined her.

She'd taken my hand then and I felt the fragility of her bones.

"It never dies, you know. It never goes away."

There is nothing worse than having to trawl through the belongings of someone who has recently died. Even more so when that person is close, and standing in the middle of Thea's front room I was already siding with those who would much rather leave things exactly as they were, as if the person would one day be coming back.

But I did not have that luxury.

I'd called Bill from the hospice and broken the news of his mother's death. It was late evening in California and I'd heard a women's voice in the background asking who was calling. This was not the first time we'd spoken as I had been keeping him up to date from the moment Thea had gone into care. But now it was different and there was a tremor in his voice as he told me he would get the first available flight in the morning.

With so much to be getting on with, it was all a bit overwhelming so I decided to take the easy option. To make myself a coffee and start with the bottom drawer of Thea's writing desk.

It was time to satisfy my curiosity.

The key was where Thea had left it, in the trinket box and kneeling on the carpet I soon had the drawer open and the box she'd mentioned, nothing fancy, just plain cardboard and similar in size to a large shoebox, on the floor in front of me.

I had no idea what I expected to find, and perhaps that was why I hesitated, running my fingertips over the mottled lid as if to delay the moment. In fact the contents were disappointingly ordinary. Two bunches of letters tied up with ribbon, a large official-looking envelope, a cream and gold wedding invitation, an old passport - hers it turned out and bearing the name Crawford. Her maiden name I guessed. And there were other things. An old and crumbling pressed rose, a toy car and a small, leather covered photograph album. Turning the stiff pages I studied the gray-toned images of a young man in uniform. Tom, her eldest child - he'd been so afraid the war would be over before he was old enough to join up. I found the telegram sent by the War Office and his birth and death certificates in the large envelope, along with the copy of the purchase contract for the property in the highlands and the birth and death certificates for my great-uncle. Strangely there was no marriage certificate, nor Thea's own birth certificate, and I would need one or the other in order to complete the information required by the registrar.

Oh well, I thought, no doubt they'll turn up elsewhere.

Picking up the smaller bundle of letters, the one bound in blue ribbon, I turned it over in my hand. The return address was that of an Australian battalion and I didn't need to be told that these were her son's and perhaps crammed with places he'd seen and people he'd met? Or had he already seen action and were his thoughts sober? Even then he would try to reassure her. She was his mother after all.

The other letters were bound in white ribbon and I wondered uneasily if they were intensely private love notes from my great-uncle? But the writing on the topmost envelope had a feminine style to it, though not that of someone proficient in the art. Turning up a few right-hand corners at random I checked the postmarks. More than a dozen or so, they were all in chronological order.

Given there was nothing else in the box I wondered what Thea had been referring to when she spoke of my learning the truth?

It could only be the letters and suddenly I found it hard to breathe. If I slipped the bow, separated the envelopes, if I read the pages inside, what would I find?

I was gnawing on my bottom lip, something I always did when confronted by uncertainty.

Surely the contents couldn't be too terrible, for if they were, I simply wouldn't read them. I'd grown very fond of my great-aunt and nothing was going to spoil my memories.

I bit down a little too forcefully and winced.

For heaven's sake! Why should I be expecting the worst?

Easing back against the sofa and stretching out my legs I tugged on the ribbon. The long tails were creased from having been tied for so long and before lifting the first envelope from the pile I ran each one between my fingers.

Then I carefully extracted the folded sheets of lightly scented writing paper.

June 1924

Auckland
New Zealand

2

IT WAS THE SAME EVERY time, Silas thought, rolling off his wife and onto his back. Sheer indifference followed by silent reproach. What was wrong with the woman? It wasn't as if he didn't try to get the whole thing over as quickly as possible. Nor, since he was not that inconsiderate a man, did he insist on bothering her every night.

Staring up at the narrow shaft of moonlight he waited for the final scene to play out. For if his removing himself from her might be likened to the lowering of the conductor's baton then the dragging down of her cotton nightgown was the indisputable closing of stage curtains.

Seconds passed, and whilst her breathing was measured, he sensed she was as much waiting as he was. But for what, he wanted to know? For God's sake, just do it and then they could both get some sleep.

Instead she had to punish him.

Why? He was no different from any other man. He had needs of course, and whilst he'd no expectation she'd have a true understanding of the urges contained in a man's loins, surely she could manage a little more enthusiasm, especially since in all other aspects he was a good husband. He didn't beat her. He didn't hold her in disregard. Nor did he treat her like a servant; though God knows it would come to that if something weren't done. So how could he be at fault?

And then the mattress gave a little and he closed his eyes in relief at the rolling and shuffling that followed.

Finally, he thought, turning away.

How had it come to this? He'd never experienced this level of disappointment with his first wife, so why should it be so vastly different with the second?

He listened to her steady breathing. A little too steady in fact, so she too was awake. Nothing would be said and unable to bear the tension any longer, he grasped the bed covers and swung his bare feet to the floor.

The house was still and as quiet as the grave, and his study colder than expected since the fire in the grate had been banked up with lumps of house coal and a thick covering of ash to ensure the remaining embers burnt through until morning. Silas shivered, and before settling his lean frame into his chair, tugged his robe tightly about him.

Stacked neatly and precisely on his desk were his ledgers. A little to the right, as befitting a man for whom that hand dominated, were his pens and ink. The large blotting pad was equal parts from front and sides. It was the way he like things. Precise with nothing out of place. Even the room's solitary adornment, an ornately framed photograph, had been fixed exactly centre of the narrow chimney breast.

The image, taken on their wedding day, had been Theodora's wish. He'd been less enamored with the idea but given her begging and pleading he'd eventually consented, though it must be said with a distinct lack of enthusiasm. And things hadn't improved on arriving at the studio. Confronted with her choice of backdrop for the sitting; a bower of summer flowers and an idyllic pastoral view, his heart had sunk. But once again he'd held his counsel and stood erect and serious while Theodora, her ankles crossed demurely and her dress adjusted to fall in soft folds, was posed on a chair at his side.

Now the portrait mocked him, and although disappointed with the way his marriage was turning out, he had to admit it could have been worse, for in a world still coming to terms with the economic devastation of war, it was being reported that some women were casting aside all reason and openly defying convention. Even going so far as demanding the right to think and act with the same freedom as men! Thankfully his wife was more circumspect, and that was in her favour. And then there were her circumstances. Had she not been without family he doubted he would have considered a betrothal at all given the substantial difference in their ages.

Opening one of the ledgers and about to unscrew the lid from the bottle of black ink, Silas's shoulders slumped once more.

For hadn't that been the entire point?

How else was he to have sons so late in life unless his bride was of childbearing years? It had never been a consideration before. Indeed, he'd spent his own youth channeling his energy into his financial affairs. But on reaching his fifth decade, and with his hair thinning and his joints starting to complain, the need for heirs became at first apparent, and then urgent. And that was why, since the night of their wedding, he and his young wife had been copulating regularly. It was therefore not beyond the bounds of credibility that, even without living issue, there should have been signs of a successful conception at least once in the last four years.

But there was not.

Which left only one conclusion, that far from having the fruitful womb he'd been relying on, his young wife was barren.

There was another good reason for him to think so.

Having invested heavily in the marriage, he'd naturally taken it upon himself to follow up on his concerns, and discovered that, in layman's terms, she suffered from a condition known as lack of ardour. There were cures for this of course, and any number of pills and potions could be purchased over the counter at any chemist shop, though some were patently quackery. Failing that, there was vibrotherapy, or the mechanical massaging of the female genital area by a medical doctor.

Every option had been considered and dismissed, simply because these remedies took time. Weeks, months, years even. And at his age that was something he didn't have.

Then a chance remark in the most unexpected of places conjured up the possibility of a solution. Even then there were no guarantees. Whenever were there in life? The one thing Silas was certain about though was that if he was successful in putting forward his case, the result would certainly bring about a change in his wife's attitude. For better or worse.

Either way, it was a gamble Silas Crawford was prepared to take.

3

PLACING THE THIN CHEROOT BETWEEN her lips, Kitty Malloy reached for the table lighter and if Silas was affected by the vision of a pale and shapely arm, it was her ability to inhale a goodly amount of aromatic smoke that truly impressed him. And that, it appeared, was the intention. He could see it in her eyes and in the way she drew on the cigar, swirling the smoke around her mouth before expelling it in a manner that could only be described as derisive.

"Another brandy?" she was asking.

A bead of sweat ran down his neck, and after glancing at his empty glass, he made a show of crossing one leg over the other and brushing a hand down his trousers.

"Don't mind if I do."

It was rare for him to find a woman daunting, but with her severely bobbed hair and disgraceful way of dressing his hostess was exactly that. He knew she thought him a creature to be brought to heel. Someone to be humiliated even, and to his shame he felt a fluttering response in the pit of his stomach. Thanks to her business, Kitty knew too much about men; and that included their habits and their foibles and their needs. It made her all the more disquieting; as did talk of the wealth she had amassed by providing the necessary means of relief. Silas had heard the rumours - and he'd no reason to doubt them - of houses owned and rented to the lower classes, and of bonds and other paper assets stashed away in a bank vault. He'd also heard of the considerable endowments to the Catholic Church, and even at that moment found it incredible that a woman of her kind could ever imagine she could buy herself out of sin.

Kitty had picked up a small brass bell.

"And your wife? She is in complete agreement?" she asked, once the brassy peal had died away.

The corner of his eye twitched. It was an irritating occurrence of late and one he felt undermined his natural authority. As a distraction he picked at a speck of lint. Of course it was disappointing to be sitting in Kitty Malloy's bawdy house discussing the unhappy subject of his wife. But the problem was hardly of his making. In fact, he should be commended for taking such a positive course of action, even one as unorthodox as this.

"She is."

His smile was intended to reassure.

"I find that rather extraordinary."

"Madam," and he removed a second and equally imaginary piece of lint, "a sheltered upbringing does have its merits. But clearly it is to my wife's detriment that she has not been advised on, and perhaps even exposed to… how shall I put it…" Silas allowed a moment to imply he'd spent many hours in consideration of this very dilemma. "… more worldly behaviours."

When her plucked and penciled eyebrow arched, he almost wilted, but before he could continue the door opened and a whore - he knew of no other description given the girl's sashaying walk and the all-too knowing smile aimed in his direction - entered. Tearing his eyes away offered little relief when he inadvertently met Kitty's own once more. But matters only got worse when responding to his hostesses pointing cigar, the whore bent to gather the brandy balloon from his fingers and gave him not only a highly suggestive wink, but also an unencumbered view of two delightfully rounded breasts.

His throat bobbed in an ineffectual swallow. More than anything he wanted to grab the girl and bury his face in such delightful abundance.

"So," Kitty began, once the cause of his distraction had moved away to fix his drink. Silas barely heard. Staring at the rolled down stocking tops he was wondering whether it would be appropriate to make use of the house facilities after the interview given he was already on the premises - an idea that was reinforced when the girl returned with his recharged glass.

All it took was a touch that lingered a little too long and a glance from under heavily kohled eyelids to make up his mind.

"Thank you Nelly." Kitty was leaning forward and lodging her cheroot on the rim of her ashtray.

"Shall we conclude the arrangements?" she said, watching the door close once more. "And then perhaps you might like to enjoy the comforts of the house? As my guest, of course."

Silas tried for an air of nonchalance, for deep down he would have preferred to maintain his dignity and refuse the offer. But it was too late for that. The fire in his belly had been stoked and he was already imagining the wonderfully depraved and unspeakable deeds he could demand of the girl.

"Why not?"

"Then we are in agreement," Kitty said. "I will expect your wife on Thursday."

"Indeed."

Silas was both pleased and relieved at the ease with which the business had been concluded. Thanks to Kitty's need for a housekeeper to oversee certain domestic requirements, in a few short month's Theodora's virginal posturing and inherent coldness would be a thing of the past since it would soon become obvious, even to her, that a conjugal union between husband and wife was a reasonable expectation and not a penance. After that, there was no reason she shouldn't bear the sons he desired. Of course, placing one's wife in a house of ill repute might not be a conventional remedy for such an ailment, nor would it find social acceptance amongst his peers. But when had he ever cared for the good opinion of others'? And anyway, wasn't his plan for them both to leave Auckland for good once he'd returned from his business abroad?

"I do have to say," Kitty continued almost as an afterthought, "that your request is most unusual as I'm no doubt you are aware. It will be an interesting experiment."

Silas gave a slight nod as if in acknowledgement of such insightfulness.

"You said your wife was a virgin on your wedding night?"

Again Silas nodded.

"And young?"

"Not even twenty years of age."

Already salivating at the thought of what might be waiting for him upstairs, Silas was less concerned with Theodora's pre-marital condition and more concerned with finding a polite way of drawing the meeting to a close. "Ours is a marriage of little more than convenience," he said, managing at last to fully concentrate on his hostess. "It is also one of great disappointment. I do believe however, that the end will justify the means."

His tone was intentionally grave.

"Indeed," and here Kitty paused once more.

Silas waited, wondering what was to come.

"Mixing with my girls should suffice in theory," she was gazing somewhat thoughtfully into the distance, "and as we have agreed, she will be of good use in a number of quarters. Overseeing the laundry, arranging supplies, a spot of bookkeeping perhaps."

One look at her expression told him access to any of her trading accounts was unlikely, and he was hardly surprised.

"She is still young, you say?"

"Twenty-three."

"Hmm, and no doubt losing the first bloom of youth. Oh, I'm just thinking aloud," Kitty was waving her hand as if it were nothing of concern. "Perhaps given her maturity there should be an element of practice if we are truly to deliver the results you wish for?"

"Practice? I'm not sure I understand."

"You were thinking mere theory would suffice?"

"I…?"

Silas was too stunned to realise his mouth had fallen open.

"Nothing too exciting of course." The bracelets on Kitty's arm were chinking again. "But in order to ensure a complete turnabout in her attitude we may need to take things to that extent. Wouldn't you agree? My concern is that at her age any unresponsiveness might already be a little too embedded."

Silas cleared his throat.

"It was not my intention, nor had I given thought to such a scheme."

"Well I suggest you do. After all, if she painted landscapes or portraits one would hardly expect her to be able to create anything of magnificence without at least sketching the outline first, regardless of how much she read up about the subject."

"I see. Well, when you put it like that…"

It had never crossed his mind to have his wife take part in the physical activity of the place. Not even for one minute. Good God! The woman was a veritable ice-maiden. But perhaps that was Kitty's point. And if those sessions were to be limited to just the once or twice, and more importantly discreet; then would there be any harm if the outcome were to be as beneficial as suggested? On reflection he doubted it. Indeed, she might even learn a few skills, and that was worth considering.

"So you think it would be helpful?"

"I do. In strict moderation of course, so much better we embark on a thorough tutoring rather than disappoint."

"Indeed."

"And once she has resumed her place in your household, I'm sure she will demonstrate a far better willingness and understanding."

Silas's brow creased for the first time. Did he detect a note of sarcasm? But having retrieved her cheroot from the ashtray it seemed as though Kitty had other things on her mind.

"As for the financial arrangement," she continued, putting the cigar to her lips once more "you will pay the agreed amount for my trouble and in return I will supply food and board. And on the odd occasion she may receive a gratuity? The usual percentage to the house, and the rest…?"

Kitty was exhaling a steady stream of aromatic smoke.

Silas hardly cared. He certainly had no need of a few desultory pennies.

"Let her keep it. No doubt she'll have costs to cover. Clothes, fripperies. That sort of thing."

"Perfect. In that case, I look forward to Thursday."

4

THEA FROZE AT THE SOUND of the front door opening. Silas was not usually home this early and according to the clock on the mantelpiece it was not yet four. Hell and damnation! Why had he chosen that very day to do so, for here she was, caught up in the novel she'd borrowed only a few hours earlier from the public lending library. He would not be pleased. Not that he had an issue with her reading. No, it was *what* she was reading that was the problem, for she'd discovered a perverse thrill in solving fictional murders and the books she selected and hid from him were the works of authors such as Agatha Christie and Dorothy Sayers with her dashing sleuth Lord Peter Wimsey.

Unfortunately Silas did not see things in the same way and had pointed out - rather forcibly, it must be said - that novels offering all too graphic descriptions of crimes, and abhorrent ones at that, were hardly a suitable read for a woman. *Ridiculous* she'd wanted to say; didn't he know times had changed? Couldn't he see the strides women were taking in the world? They were certainly not the actions of a weaker sex. And all she was doing was reading. Why, had things been different, she might have joined the movement too. But after four long years of marriage she knew better than to do or say anything to inflame the situation. Instead she quickly bookmarked the page and slipped the offending item behind a cushion.

"Silas," she said, rising from her chair and greeting her husband when he appeared in the doorway. "You are early. Nothing wrong I hope."

"Not at all my dear, in fact, today I have concluded a very satisfactory piece of business."

"How very gratifying for you."

"Oh, it certainly was."

If she wondered at his overly casual tone there was no time to dwell on it, for she had only the few moments he'd stepped away to discard his hat and gloves on the hallstand to glance into the mirror hanging over the fireplace. And thanks Heavens she did, for three pins had somehow worked loose from the thick roll of hair at the back of her neck. Cursing his refusal to let her have a shorter, more up to date style, she gathered up the resulting wisps and jabbed both them and the pins back into place. He could be so very stubborn at times - unless he was the one being troubled. How different it would be if *he* was the one forced to spend hours each morning arranging the mane of hair, that if left to its own devices, would have tumbled unkempt down her back. But it wasn't just that. She wasn't yet twenty-four, but thanks to his old-fashioned notions she was looking more and more like forty-four these days. Damn it all. Why had no one warned her that marriage could be such a trial?

Returning with the evening newspaper, Silas settled into the winged-back chair on the other side of the fireplace, and following his lead Thea too resumed her seat clasping her hands in her lap. For a moment there was only the rustle of pages being shaken open and turned until he asked, somewhat formally, how she had spent her day.

Thea deliberately avoided any mention of leaving the house. It was better that way, since there would then be no need to lie when he requested more information on the books she had borrowed. Instead she replied with a part-truth, that she had spent the morning in the kitchen with cook discussing the re-provisioning of the larder. Thankfully her response sufficed, and with a deliberate flourish Silas turned another page of his newspaper.

"I will be dining out this evening," he said, casting his eye down the page, "perhaps you would be so good as to inform the staff."

"Of course."

It hardly came as a surprise, since the times he dined at home were becoming less and less frequent these days. Thea was not privy to where he went on these occasions, nor indeed whom he might be meeting, but in truth she didn't care. Anything was better than three courses of stilted and forced cordiality. Left to her own devices she would take supper on a tray right here in the sitting room and listen to a play or concert on the radio.

She had no idea what the servants thought of her marriage. Cook had been in situ for years, though not long enough to serve the first Mrs Crawford. Ada had been employed after her fiancé failed to return from the Great War. Both kept their thoughts to themselves, as of course they should, while Albert, the elderly odd-job-man come gardener saw little of what went on inside anyway. He lived out, as did Silas's chauffeur.

If only she had friends. Girls or wives of her own age she could meet for tea or invite to her home. But she'd little chance to make such acquaintances since moving to the city. And now she was married and

restricted by her husband there was even less opportunity.

The truth was she was bored witless. In fact it had
reached the point where her only desire was to get
through the long drawn out day with her sanity still
intact.

But the nights Silas visited her bedroom were
worse.

She would feign sleep, but to no avail. He would
pull back the bedcovers, and in a voice that sounded
strangely unlike his own, insist she lift her nightgown.
Then, breathing heavily, he would do the most
despicable thing to her most private of places. The first
time it had happened she had lain as still as she could,
her eyes shut tight, willing it all to be over as quickly as
possible. And she had bled, which had been mortifying
- even more so knowing the stain would be discovered
when the bed linen was changed on Friday. After he'd
removed himself from her she'd been left with a sticky,
viscous substance between her thighs, and an intense
and painful need to urinate that had not cured itself for
two long days. That was why she'd pleaded to be
excused such doings in the future, but his response had
been frosty.

It was the duty of a wife to tend to her husband's
needs in every way, he'd told her.

Thankfully those needs were quickly met these
days, and she was even more grateful that they no
longer were accompanied by the continual urge to use
the lavatory.

Knowing Silas's behaviour was unnatural she was
glad her mother was no longer alive, for the poor
woman would have been distraught to know what went
on behind closed doors. That her son-in-law made use
of his distention to poke and prod between his wife's

legs in order to join them as one would have shocked her to the core, and that reinforced Thea's idea that while Silas may have some standing in the community at large, he was certainly not a gentleman.

Unlike her father.

A surveyor and assessor of land, James Daniels had branched out, investing in a local company with a small fleet of freighters that journeyed back and forth across the equator bringing goods to New Zealand that the country couldn't provide for herself. Thanks to substantial quarterly dividends, the family had prospered, and in nineteen seventeen they'd moved up from the Garden City of Christchurch to the teeming metropolis of Auckland and a large imposing home on a ridge overlooking the waters of the Hauraki Gulf. But in less than twelve months both he and her mother were dead, lost to the deadly Spanish 'flu' epidemic, and left alone in a city she barely knew, and with no one to whom she could turn, Thea didn't know whether to be grateful or despairing that the horror that claimed so many lives had passed her by without so much as a look.

Silas Crawford, a business acquaintance of her father's, hadn't spared his words when he put it to her on the dreadful day they had laid her parents to rest, that with no one else in New Zealand, her situation in the far-flung reaches of the Dominion was precarious, to say the least.

Her solicitor had advised the same, although with a little more tact.

Aware that while not exceedingly wealthy, she was now of considerable means, the senior partner of Russell, Phelps and Morris, Solicitors and Notary Public, suggested she might consider returning home to England. That is if a family member could be found to take her in. An aunt perhaps, he'd suggested cheerfully. Confronted with the prospect of domiciling herself in a country she hadn't seen since babyhood Thea had responded tartly that she had no intention of going anywhere, and that at almost nineteen she was quite capable of fending for herself.

Mr Russell's amazingly bushy eyebrows had almost reached his hairline at that, but after much to-ing and fro-ing a compromise was reached. Thea would remain in the family home, at least until she came of age, but she would employ a companion, a woman of good character to act as chaperone. A very relieved Mr Russell arranged for the post to be advertised, and after conducting interviews and scrupulously following up on references, appointed a person he considered suitable.

Unfortunately Thea wasn't as enthusiastic with his choice, and to a girl whose upbringing had been based upon open thought and discussion, Elizabeth McKinley's personality was a revelation. Though less than a dozen years her senior, the dour Scot had a pinched look, a religious fervour and an uncompromising belief in the trials of the flesh. In fact, much of the modern world was anathema to her. Her young employer on the other hand, believed all change was for the better, and that the Golden Era - for that was how the up-and-coming decade was already being hailed - would have a far-reaching effect on the status of women.

Elizabeth McKinley was rigid with disapproval. Even Thea's reassurance that she had no intention of wearing excessive make up or accepting dates with men she hardly knew did little to help matters. But having been encouraged to think for herself by liberal-minded parents, Thea had no intentions of being browbeaten by anyone, least of all a paid companion.

She made it plain that her father had shared thoughts and ideals with her, both political and economic. He'd also discussed the future of the family business, even going so far as to encourage her to try her hand on his secretary's expensive Underwood typewriter. In the not-so-distant future, he'd said, women would be as valued an employee as a man and that in turn would lead to a few select females being at the very helm itself. That was when she'd understood that as his only child he was hinting that such a position would be hers for the choosing, should of course she find the idea more rewarding than the more conventional route of a husband and children. It had been an exhilarating moment. Not that it was possible anymore, but that was why, tired of the overbearing Miss McKinley, Silas Crawford's offer of marriage seemed the answer to her prayers.

Even so, she was cautious on two counts.

Her first concern was the difference in their ages. He was considerably older than her. Would that matter? The other was that she would be his second wife and she had serious doubts that she was truly qualified to fill the first Mrs Crawford's shoes.

Mr Russell had no such qualms and to her surprise wholeheartedly recommended the union. The gentleman in question was financially secure, she was reminded with a certain diplomacy, and so it was not as if he were in need of her money. And then there was something else to take into account, and this was where Mr Russell had leaned forward. The bonds of holy matrimony remained far less restricting than the ones society imposed on young, unwed females. Even in these modern times.

He'd sat back once more, resting his elbows on the rubbed and worn leather chair arms that spoke of many years of use.

"Have you any further doubts, my dear," he continued on a more somber note, "four years of war has left the country with a shortage of young men of marriageable age. A terrible legacy indeed."

Thea had lowered her head respectfully, recalling that like so many others, he too had lost a son in that terrible conflict.

And so, on a cold and blustery day, Thea and a rather stern-looking Silas were joined together in front of a handful of guests. All but one were seated on his side of the church. Only Mr Russell was on hers, and as she made her vows he beamed proudly as if she were indeed his kin. But despite his earlier assurances, it didn't take long to discover that far from embracing the new decade, her new husband's principles were very definitely from another era. One in which wives were considered little more than chattels, so that while he enjoyed a successful and fulfilling life outside of the home, she was expected to remain very much within. Perhaps it was inevitable then that over time, and with nothing else to absorb her, Thea withdrew into her books; her fashionable murder-mysteries and whodunits, until the only body she wanted revealed on the fictional mortuary slab was that of her miserable husband.

Silas made his announcement at breakfast on Wednesday.

Ada had left the room only moments before, having placed the covered dishes of scrambled eggs and bacon in the centre of the table. Thea was filling her cup with her preferred Darjeeling tea, and as she returned the silver teapot to its stand, her husband made a show of folding his morning paper and placing it to one side.

"I have decided to spend some time abroad," he said, draping his napkin across his lap and reaching across to lift a lid.

Thea's teacup paused halfway to her mouth.

"How delightful."

"There will be a fair amount of travelling as I intend to visit associates and colleagues in Paris as well as London and Berlin."

Surprise was quickly replaced with a rush of excitement. Europe! Cultural cities of historical significance, and more. So much more! There would be tours and a lively round of social events. The theatre, the arts, and oh, the fashions! She had read that on the other side of the equator hemlines were becoming daringly high. But Silas would not appreciate such levity, and especially not at the breakfast table. She let her breath out slowly.

"That would be most interesting. I understand that Germany is looking to become very industrialised."

"Exactly my reason for going," he said drily.

She tried to temper her excitement. She might be leaping to conclusions after all since he hadn't exactly said she would be going too. But at worst, if she were to be left behind, at least she would have her life back for a while.

"I will be shutting up the house," he said, placing his knife and fork on his plate and turning to gaze around the room. Thea did the same, wondering if he too was seeing the heavily patterned wallpaper and overly fussy drapes that were at least twenty years out of date. If she were to accompany him, and if he were willing to grant her a little time out of his busy schedule to visit the amazing furniture and décor emporiums springing up in those great cities, why then, they could bring back the latest designs and ideas; fabrics even, to transform the house into a modern delight.

So many *if*'s, and she opened her mouth to speak. But Silas was already holding up his hand.

"You, I'm afraid, will not be coming with me."

Shocked by the absoluteness of his statement Thea could only stare.

"But I have made arrangements for you in my absence," he continued, retrieving his fork and spearing another morsel of food into his mouth.

"Oh. But Silas…" About to plead her case, she stopped. His hand was up again, and this time he was shaking his head as well.

"It is done and there is no point in being disagreeable," he said, pre-empting anything she might say. He touched his napkin to his moustache.

"You may pack whatever you feel is necessary. Either way, please be ready first thing tomorrow morning."

5

HUNCHED IN HER CORNER, Thea was unusually quiet. Trips in their motorcar were something she looked forward too, given the opulence of the vehicle with its plush leather and walnut interior, but with little idea of her destination that morning she found it hard to raise any enthusiasm. And it seemed even nature was conspiring against her, for while autumn might be just around the corner, the days were still gloriously sunny. Auckland would never get as cold as home her father had once told her or as chilly as Canterbury. Perhaps that was why so many of their neighbours had chosen to plant palms and other tropical flora. Not that she cared at that moment.

Rather she was going over and over her predicament.

Of course, accommodation might have been arranged in one of the city's more respectable hotels, one offering safe and respectable lodgings for unattached female guests. It made perfect sense when weighed against the cost of maintaining their large house over winter. Or, and this was her greatest fear, had Silas been in contact with the dreadful Miss McKinley, intending to shackle them together once more? Not having seen nor heard from the woman in years, she had no idea where she was living, though from memory recalled the mention of a house and an elderly mother in the genteel suburb of Mount Eden.

Hardly any more appealing was the notion she was to be foist upon one of Silas's relatives. A number had turned up for their wedding and she believed there were more scattered about, mostly in other parts of the country. But given they weren't heading in the direction of the railway station that idea could probably be discounted, and thank Heavens for that.

If only he'd not left her high and dry by refusing to answer any of her questions. And then she was frowning. For having left the leafy avenues and sudden profusion of downy magnolia buds, they'd motored past the Domain, the planned location of the new city museum, and turned onto the road that whilst leading down to the port and Silas's own destination later that day, also continued on to the less salubrious parts of the city. The wharves and docks, the breweries and timber yards, the factories, tanneries and gas works. And if that were not bad enough, on the surrounding slopes and in the gullies were the shacks and cottages of the lowest class of worker; the Maori, and the poorest and most disenfranchised of European immigrants. Freemans Bay; a place to be feared since the sanitary conditions were known to be dreadful, and there was always talk of plague and tuberculosis. It was beyond comprehension that Silas would have business in such a place. Thankfully that turned out to be so, for they had turned once more and skirting the deplorable slums, continued along another ridge, this one wide enough to allow liveried vehicles to park and unload in front of emporiums. And the properties on either side were of better construction too. Timber-clad stores had given way to brick and plaster buildings in the very latest neo-classical design. Hand painted signs on hoardings and grand facades were in abundance. A millinery, a drapery, a shoe store, a haberdashery, and on the corner, with its windows bursting with pyramids of tins, packets and boxes, a large grocer and purveyor of fine foods.

There were residential streets too, some being home to families of moderate means. Single level dwellings; the houses and gardens while small, were tidy. Other roads showcased larger, more substantial dwellings, and peering out as they turned down into one such road and pulled up at the kerbside, Thea spoke for the first time.

"Is this where I am to stay?"

Considering its proximity to the busy thoroughfare, the leafy street showed little sign of life. That is, apart from two women making their way down the hill. But when they stopped to stare at the car, Thea frowned. There was a time when the sight of an expensive motorcar would create interest, but that was long ago. Now the streets were filled with automobiles, trucks and buses, and nobody bothered in the slightest. So what was the attraction?

Stepping onto the pavement she gazed around.

Most houses were of individual design with established front gardens and shady verandahs running the full width of both upper and lower floors. Even, in some cases, around the side. That said they were still not as desirable as the home she had left that morning. Silas was tapping his foot on the pavement and she gritted her teeth. What would those women make of such discourtesy? Regardless, it didn't do to upset him when he was in a mood, and so, straightening her shoulders, she followed him up the front steps - and then almost fell back in fright. Even before Silas had chance to raise the brass knocker, let alone allow it to drop, the door had swung open and a man of Maori blood, a bald-headed mountain of a creature with ripples of flesh where his neck should have been, was on the threshold.

"Good day Sir."

It wasn't just the sheer size of the man, but that his face was devoid of any normal skin colouring, being instead an inky blue-black mass of swirling, spiralling tribal tattoos from which only his eyes and mouth could be determined. Yet his manner was surprisingly deferential.

Entering the house, Silas merely nodded.

Thea's first glimpse of the interior was that it was lavish in the extreme but not in a style chosen by a decorator of any taste. The spacious hallway was the colour of burgundy wine and carpeted in a vast red and blue Persian rug. The lighting was heavily shaded. Even so she could hardly miss the life-sized statue of a man and woman, entwined and naked with not even an artfully draped cloth between them. Though even that paled beside the gilt-framed portraits of women in various stages of undress. And there was a particular scent. Perhaps a type of incense or exotic perfume given the heavy, oriental muskiness.

Thoroughly unnerved she turned to her husband but he'd already passed through another door, and a glance at the man-mountain indicated she should do the same.

Thea gave him her most haughty stare. Did he think she was stupid? Anyone could see this was not a place for a woman who cared for her reputation.

She would wait in the car until Silas had finished his business, whatever that might be.

But even as she turned for the door the man-mountain was scowling and shaking his head.

It seemed she had little option.

Having removed his hat, Silas was waiting impatiently.

"My wife," he said, when Thea finally stepped into the room.

She saw the woman immediately. Having turned from her desk and with one arm resting on the back of her chair, her expression was one of open curiosity.

Thea returned the stare with equal interest. The knee-length sleeveless dress and the long ropes of pearls were very much the latest fashion, though she'd never seen so much uncovered flesh before luncheon nor so much lipstick and rouge. Conscious of her own more demure outfit, she decided the woman must be American and a jazz-crazed flapper at that. It would explain the house too, since she'd read that such people were outrageously decadent in all ways. But for the life of her she couldn't think how Silas and this woman were acquainted.

Regardless, she refused to be intimidated, and taking her time she cast her eye about the room. Pale walls, sleek chrome lighting and glamorous furniture, it was as if in leaving the hallway she'd walked into a completely different world. It was an effort to contain her envy, for it was *exactly* the furniture she would choose, if only she had the chance.

"You like my art?" No American accent, instead there was a hint of Irish brogue.

Silas too, seemed to be interested in her response.

"It has merits," she replied, glancing at the large work dominating one wall. She'd already guessed the identity of the stylised woman lying naked on the rumpled sheets.

"Merits?" The woman was clearly amused.

Silas had settled on the only piece in the room that was a complete mismatch; a velvet chaise longue and

Thea could imagine no other reason for it being there other than perhaps it had been retained for sentimental reasons?

"What do you think? Can you do something with her?"

Thea felt a wave of fear rush through her as the woman sauntered over to a side table, and opening a silver box, took out a thin cigar, clamped it between her lips and lit it. And then she had to fight hard to contain her amazement, for other than in a Hollywood film, she had never seen anything like it.

"I'm sure we can; one way or another."

"Good," Silas replied. "Then I look forward to somewhat of a transformation on my return."

"Silas, would you mind telling me what is going on?" she managed as the room seemed to close in. He was leaving her here?

"Certainly my dear, this is Miss Kitty Malloy and she runs a very profitable business. Would you care to guess what that might be?"

Thea had no idea, but the challenge in her husband's voice left her with very little doubt that whatever it was, it was unwholesome and odious, and that was enough for her.

"No, I would not, Silas. In fact I would like to leave now."

But not only did her husband remain seated, if anything he made himself more comfortable. Kitty too had dropped into an armchair and was fingering her creamy pink pearls.

"I'm sorry my dear," his tone was a touch cavalier, "but that won't be possible. Please understand you are here for your own good. You see, you have an unhappy condition. One that naturally only came to light after our marriage," and at this point he looked at Kitty and shook his head. "As you know, I have been patient and tried to reason with her."

"Silas?" Thea took a step forward. "What are you talking about?"

"I am talking about your frigidity, Theodora, your unnatural lack of emotion in the marital bed."

Lurching sideways she grasped at the nearest support. "How dare you!"

"Oh, I dare. In fact, I dare to the point of bringing you here in order you may be cured of your predicament."

"My predicament? *My* predicament?"

"Yes, as you so rightly say, *your* predicament. Now I trust you will appreciate the opportunity being offered you and do everything you are instructed."

"Silas, this is our private business and of no concern of anyone else," Thea said, glaring at Kitty who, whilst enjoying her cigar seemed also to be relishing the dispute between husband and wife.

"I disagree," he replied.

Thea's lip curled up. "You are surely not telling me you have brought me to a physician?"

"Of course not, this is a house of ill repute. A bordello," a small bow of acknowledgement was made to their hostess before he continued, "a place where men come to enjoy the favours of the fairer sex. At least," and he added pointedly, "those women that enjoy and encourage such pleasures."

Thea could hardly breathe for fright.

"My dear, I know you find the subject distressing. It is just unfortunate your mother did not live long enough to educate you as to the extent of your wifely duties."

Once again Silas was shaking his head, though now the gesture was a trifle overdone.

"What can I say? Happily Miss Malloy has offered to act as a surrogate in the matter. And I can think of no one else with greater credentials."

Kitty acknowledged the compliment with a tilt of her head.

Thea was reduced to begging.

"Silas, please! Let us discuss the matter privately."

"There is nothing to discuss. You will remain here and you will use the time constructively to overcome your aversions."

Thea took a deep breath.

"No, Silas. I won't do it."

"Please don't make a scene, Theodora."

Knowing she was at his mercy Thea went over and sat meekly beside her husband. "Silas, if my condition is so onerous to you, why not divorce me? I will not contest it," she said quietly.

"Out of the question."

"Please…"

"Theodora, it will be hard for both of us, but for the sake of our marriage I am willing to bear it. I suggest you should do the same."

"*Well!*"

It seemed Kitty had decided the spat was fast becoming tedious.

"Well," she repeated, this time a little less forcibly. "Now we have that out of the way, does she have any luggage?" and stubbing out her cigar in the onyx ashtray she looked questioningly at Silas.

"There are cases in the trunk of the car."

"Frank will bring them in." Kitty nodded towards the man-mountain who had remained by the door the entire time.

Silas was gathering together his hat and gloves.

"Then I can leave her in your capable hands?" he said.

"Of course."

"Excellent. In that case, I think our business is concluded."

Kitty too had risen.

"Just one thing more," she said, addressing Silas but looking at Thea, "do you wish to receive regular reports?"

"That would be appreciated."

And then, as if in afterthought, he turned back to his wife.

"One day you will appreciate the trouble I have gone to."

"Rot in hell."

Never had Thea hated anyone as much as she did right then.

"Interesting," his forefinger was touching the brim of his hat in farewell, "a spark of life already."

6

"OPEN THEM."

Frank had lugged in the two leather travelling cases, and looking to carry out his mistress's instruction turned to Thea, his hand outstretched for the keys.

"And if I don't comply?" Thea's knuckles whitened as she increased her grip on her handbag.

"That would be a pity."

There was no doubting the undisguised threat, so opening her bag and rummaging in the bottom, Thea thrust the small bunch of keys forward.

"Here," she said, with as much contempt as she could muster.

Kitty's eyes were flinty and never once left hers as Frank slipped each key around the ring, trying one after the other in the lock. Knowing she was being assessed but with little real understanding as to why, she was taken aback when Kitty nodded towards the silver box on the side table.

"Smoke?"

"I beg your pardon?"

"Do you smoke? You know... cigars... cigarettes?"

Though his head was down Thea could tell Frank was finding the exchange amusing.

"No, Miss Malloy, I do not."

"Well you soon will. And I doubt that that will be your only vice by the time your husband returns."

Suddenly Thea felt sick. Physically sick. With her ears ringing she clutched at her stomach, forcing down the acid threatening to bubble up into her throat."

"Oh for the love of God." Suddenly Kitty was exasperated. "Please don't act the eternal virgin with me. It's already wearing a little thin."

With a satisfied grunt Frank had lifted the lid of the first case.

"Get it all out," Kitty instructed him. "Let's see if there's anything that will be of use to her."

The case was manhandled onto an angle and tipped upside down, and with Thea's clothes in a pile on the floor, Frank began sifting through them.

"Oh dear, no… good grief no," Kitty was sighing and tutting as each item was held up for display. "Do young women still wear *those*? Pass them to me."

Frank had been fondling a pair of pastel pink mid-thigh bloomers.

"No wonder your husband has been forced to take such drastic action." Holding up the offending item it seemed Kitty had been confronted by her worst nightmare. "Get rid of them Frank."

Scrunching the bloomers into a ball Kitty threw them back into the pile. "Take it all to the basement. What's in the second case?"

"Appears to be shoes and bags," he said, flipping the lid and pushing aside an embroidered purse, "and books."

"Books?" Kitty was leaning forward. "What kind of books?"

Lifting one up, Frank turned it over as if it were a rare object.

"Dunno."

Thea guessed he couldn't read. She wasn't surprised since few of his kind had the opportunity or desire to attend school.

"GK Chesterton."

Removing it from his grasp, Kitty read the author's name aloud. "Any more?"

Frank passed over another two.

"Hmm, another crime novel and what's this one? Ah, Edith Wharton. Interesting." After perusing the inside flap of the cover, Kitty flipped open a page at random. "Is it any good?"

"I haven't read it yet. Do you enjoy reading?" Thea ensured her tone was nothing short of patronising.

"I do, when I have time. You must allow me to borrow this one when you've finished with it." Snapping the book shut, Kitty gave it back to Frank. "Right then, pack everything away and take it all downstairs. Oh, and get one of the girls to bring me a drink while you're at it."

She looked up.

"Better make that two."

Kitty had a sound instinct for business. It was the only way to survive in a trade that could be precarious to say the least, for if it wasn't the girls playing her up, it was the men. Or the competition. Or those she bribed. Life was never meant to be easy her ma used to say. But this was the first time she'd struck a deal to overcome a wife's dislike of sex.

But the girl had turned out to be something of a surprise and not at all what she'd been expecting. She had grit for one thing. It was also unlikely that she was frigid. In fact, Kitty would put money on the problem being Silas's technique - or lack of. But why point that out? She was a rare find, with enough about her to be delightful in time. It would indeed be an interesting experiment, for if there was one thing Kitty knew, it was that men liked novelty. And that's exactly what the girl would provide, once fully trained of course, and for the right price, regardless of any agreement to the contrary.

And with Silas Crawford out of the country, who was to know anyway?

Even so - and this was where Kitty was already weighing up her next move - if she was as reluctant as he'd said, it would take a good deal of coaxing and coercion to get the girl to show real enthusiasm for the role.

Kitty studied her. She was a little pale; hardly surprising under the circumstances, but her almost translucent complexion clearly defined her as a member of the bourgeois. However, she would need work. Her brows were far too thick and had clearly never seen tweezers. Substantial thinning and shaping would make all the difference to those luminous eyes.

"Thought you might like something special, Miss Kitty."

With a brimming glass in each hand, one of her girls was carefully backing into the room. Plainly the grapevine was already hard at work, since when she turned it was obvious where her interest lay. No doubt everyone in the house was wondering about the young woman sitting in her parlour. Oh well, they wouldn't have long to wait, and with a quick glance at Theodora, who seemed to be struggling with both Nancy's frank stare and the lack of appropriate garments, Kitty accepted a glass and took a sip.

"Hmm, it's good, Nancy, very good."

Turning to Theodora, and then to the glass placed in front of her she said, "try it."

"No, thank you."

The response was polite but firm and knowing such a blatant disregard of etiquette would become tantalising gossip the moment Nancy left the room, Kitty allowed her face to show displeasure.

But it seemed the girl was prepared to stand her ground.

"I'm sorry," she said, no less disdainfully, "but I don't touch alcohol."

Kitty recognised that behind the haughty facade the girl was a bundle of nerves. Nonetheless, it was time to impose her authority once and for all.

"You do now. Drink it."

There was a further moment of rebellion, not helped by Nancy's barely contained excitement, but then the glass was reached for and a tentative sip taken.

"Is it too your taste?"

Theodora was grimacing. "I'm afraid not."

"Really?"

"It's a little too strong, especially at this time in the morning."

Kitty nodded. "That'll be the gin. You'll get used it after a while."

"So," she said, settling back once the door had closed behind a reluctant Nancy, "let me see if I have this right. You are still young, but you don't smoke, you don't drink liquor and you don't enjoy your husband's advances. Have I missed anything?"

While Theodora's cheeks had reddened, it seemed she was not going to be baited.

"Tell me, is there anything you do enjoy?" Kitty was idly fingering her pearls, "or are you one of those creatures who find satisfaction only in more virtuous enterprises? Bible readings, bringing sustenance to the poor? That sort of thing?"

"Miss Malloy," the words were precise, "I am at a loss as to why my husband has left me here in your establishment. I can see no reason for him to do so regardless of what he may have told you about our private affairs. Therefore I am leaving. I wish you a good day."

And she jumped to her feet.

Kitty was enjoying herself.

"I'm sorry, but I can't allow that," she said, taking another sip of her cocktail. "I'm sure you understand."

"No I don't. And I am not aware of any legal right you have to keep me here."

There was a note of triumph. Wavering; but nonetheless there. It had been a long time since Kitty had met anyone prepared to defy her; in fact girls would usually agree to almost anything in the hope of working for her, and so she took a moment before replying.

"Perhaps not, but I do have a contract with your husband. And as if that isn't enough, I also have Frank."

"I see."

Kitty could see the girl was considering her next move. When it came, it was most unexpected.

"In that case what about another arrangement, one between ourselves."

Well now, Kitty thought, this could be interesting.

"Go on."

"I have money of my own and people I could stay with while Mr Crawford is abroad. What would it take for you to forget the so-called contract you have with my husband?"

Kitty was impressed. Though probably lying, the girl had far more backbone than she'd credited. Even so, it wouldn't hurt for her to think she might be thrown a lifeline.

The seconds ticked by while Kitty appeared to think over the offer. And then she sighed and shook her head, as if in trying to find a solution she'd met only with frustration.

"If only it was that simple."

"Surely that's exactly what it is?"

"On the one hand you're right. But you see it all comes down to principle."

"Principle?"

"Yes. I have a binding agreement. How could I go back on my word?"

"Oh, I think you could quite easily be persuaded to go back on your word. For the right amount of money - I would say it's just a question of how much?"

The tone was a little too condescending and the stance a little too cocky for Kitty's liking. Of course she could always take the girl's money - if she had any, that is - and let her go, and part of her was tempted. But the business she would bring in was even more appealing. She would lift the place. Give it a touch of class.

It was time to spell it out.

"You just don't understand, do you? Now listen to me. Your husband has entrusted you to my care whilst he is away. And that means you will live here, you will eat here and you will sleep here. And that is how it's going to be."

"But that's not all, is it? Your girls have interactions with men, don't they? That's what this place is all about," Theodora's voice had risen. "Isn't it? Tell me, how do you intend to achieve that with me? I'll scream the moment a man looks at me."

Finally things were going well, Kitty thought. The girl could have fainted or had an attack of the vapours. Who knew what might have taken place. Instead, she was outraged, and getting more so by the moment.

That was a situation Kitty knew how to deal with.

"Well now. Let me see," she gazed upward. "I could have you tied to a bed, gagged and blindfolded for, what, four or five hours at a time? That way you could service several men without complaint. I have to say it would be a mite uncomfortable for you but we do have to think of the needs of our clientele, and a badly behaved whore is more a liability than an asset."

Thea gasped. But then she straightened, and took a breath.

"If you care for your business at all you will let me go."

"And miss out on such a wonderful opportunity? I don't think so."

"I'll make your life hell."

"I think you have it the wrong way round." Kitty couldn't help a tinge of admiration. Even though she hadn't a hope of winning, the girl was still putting up a fight. "You know, I like a woman with spirit. And so do my customers - when it's channeled in the right direction."

"You're mad! I won't do what you want just because of a deal you have with my husband."

"Oh you will. It won't be easy, I'll grant you that. But it will be done. Look at you. You're on fire. Such passion!"

It was true. Erect and imperious, the girl was no longer merely Silas Crawford's wife, but Boadicea, Joan of Arc and Helen of Troy all rolled into one - and perfect for the theatrical extravaganzas Kitty loved to stage. She could see it already. The warrior queen,

naked apart from the sheerest skirt and winged helmet-
the other girls at her feet gazing up adoringly.

But it seemed her star attraction wasn't done.

"We shall see about that," she threw over her
shoulder, having already turned for the door. "I'm
going to the police."

"And tell them what? That your husband left you
in a bawdy house to learn a few tricks? They'll laugh at
you."

That stopped her.

Kitty got to her feet. "And if that doesn't bother
you and you still want to take it up with the boys in
blue, well you won't have far to go. We see plenty of
them in here. Especially those higher up the ranks.
Why, even the district superintendent pops by every
now and then - usually when we have someone new.
Amazing how he always seems to know."

"I don't believe you."

Standing only inches away, Kitty tilted up the girl's
chin.

"Theodora, you are going to make me a lot of
money in the next few months, so I suggest for both
our sakes you find a way to accept the situation. I can
make it hard for you. Or we can do it the easy way."

The girl was shaking, but whether in fear or rage
Kitty had no idea. Then, having failed to prevent the
solitary tear from spilling over and making its way down
her cheek, she closed her eyes.

At last they were getting somewhere.

"Come on," Kitty said, "look on the bright side.
There are plenty of girls here. You'll get to know them
well and you might even make friends. Why don't I take
you through to the salon? Not everyone will be up yet.
Some will be sleeping off last night's activities, but

others will be waiting for clients. Oh, and if I might just offer you one piece of advice?"

Her hand was already on the doorknob.

"Try to get along with them. It will make the next few months' so much easier for you."

7

THEA HAD NO IDEA WHAT to expect when she followed Kitty through the heavy drapes, but it certainly wasn't a room of lavish velvets and damasks and a bunch of girls in varying states of undress, lounging around and chatting as if they hadn't a care in the world.

Having made her way to the centre of the floor, Kitty clapped her hands for silence.

"Ladies," she said, her attention finding each girl in turn, "this is Theodora. She will be starting with us tomorrow. I will leave her with you so you can get to know each other."

Then, seemingly oblivious to the stunned silence, Kitty turned on her heel and left - though not without a shot to Thea as she passed by.

"It's up to you now."

Thea had no idea what to do. And it seemed the others felt the same. But then a girl with vibrant red hair came forward and circled her not once, but twice.

"Theodora, is it?" she asked, her manner not un-friendly but not particularly welcoming either. "Or is that what you want us to call you?"

Thea had no idea what she meant.

"Your working name?" the girl pressed, playing to the giggles of her audience. "We don't want to get confused."

"I'm sorry, but I'm afraid I don't understand."

Thea was trying to ignore the bare shoulders and diaphanous slip. Nothing was hidden, not the size and shape of the girl's breasts, nor the rosy pink of her nipples.

"Your name," the girl tried again, raising her eyebrows and turning to her audience once more.

"Thea. No one calls me Theodora. Well, not usually," she was thinking of her husband and his irritating habit of pronouncing each syllable with painstaking clarity. "Please, call me Thea."

"I see. And do I take it, *Thea* that you've not done this sort of thing before?"

There were more smothered giggles and right at that moment she wanted to die. But given that was unlikely she looked straight ahead and shook her head. The girl leaned in and ran a finger down her back, and considering there'd been no formal introduction and Thea didn't know her from Adam, it was an overly familiar gesture that shocked her.

"So what is it?" the girl pressed. "Hard times? Old man left you?"

It was as if everyone was waiting and with little other choice, Thea jumped on the second option. It was as near to the truth as anything else.

"Join the club."

The response came from a young woman sprawled on a cushion-clad sofa.

"Yeah, that's right. I'd forgotten about that," the speaker was elbowed by the girl next to her. "Went off with yer younger sister didn't 'e?"

"Don't remind me."

"Yeah. Better off wivout 'em sometimes."

Thea was thankful the spotlight was off her. Even momentarily.

Then, "You'll be fine."

Realising the assurance was meant for her she turned in the direction of the voice and nodded gratefully. She was finding it all hard to take in. The general scantiness of clothing, the heads of platinum blond hair set into finger waves, the smoky eyes and expertly painted lips. It was completely overwhelming.

"Yer local?"

Thea had no intention of divulging any private information - especially to the chatty girl on the sofa.

"Not really," she replied, "the South Island." It was partially true after all. "What about you?"

"England. East End."

Thea was astonished, and without thinking asked, "How did you get here?"

"On a boat."

Now it was this girl's turn to roll her eyes and grin at the others.

Thea found it difficult to see the joke. It wasn't pleasant being the focus of so much attention. Perhaps if she could just sit down? Recognising the girl who'd delivered her cocktail and catching her eye, she smiled weakly.

"Give her a break, Daisy," Nancy said, and Thea felt an immediate rush of gratitude.

"Yeah, sorry," Daisy came back, "just teasin'. 'Ow'd I get 'ere? Same as we all did love. Fell for good looks and a load of half-baked promises. Ain't that the truth?"

There were nods all round.

"So, you're starting tomorrow?" The redhead was circling her again.

"No." Thea had no intention of *starting* at all. Not that night, or any other.

The circling stopped. "No? But didn't Miss Kitty…"

"No." Thea said, even more firmly.

Once again the room was still.

"Then why are you here?"

Having taken a step back, the girl was staring at her.

It was an awkward moment and Thea wondered how she could explain. But it seemed the girl had arrived at her own conclusions.

"Look, you need to jump in feet first," she said, a little more kindly.

"Ain't so bad," Daisy piped up. "A bloke's a bloke and a cock's a cock. Ain't nuffink to worry about. At least, not in 'ere."

"Listen to the expert," someone else said, and once again there was laughter but this time good-natured.

"Not exactly dressed for it, are you."

This from a girl whose arm was draped around the shoulders of another, and Thea glanced down. Plainly the drop-waisted dress purchased only last month from Smith and Caughey's Queen Street department store made her stand out like a sore thumb. As did the matching felt hat.

"You've got other things?" someone asked.

"I do. But I believe they are now in the basement."

There was yet another moment of silence as this new piece of information was absorbed.

"Why are they in the basement?" she was asked by the girl who'd been circling her.

"I'm not sure."

"Hmm, well, don't worry. We'll lend you something for now. Daisy, you're about her size, why don't you see what you've got? Esme, you too. Go on. Take her upstairs. Show her round while you're at it. She might as well get to know the place."

"Thank you…" she stopped. There might have been no reciprocating introductions, but it had already dawned on Thea that even here, there was a hierarchy in place.

"Belle," the girl supplied, "and it might pay you to remember my name, because in this salon what I say, goes."

"Up 'ere's where we do the business."

The ornate staircase had been revealed only once they'd passed through a second set of floor-length drapes, and as Daisy led the way up Thea found herself concentrating on the polished mahogany treads and the richly patterned stair runner rather than the displays of photographs on the wall, for they were even more shameful than those in the hallway below.

Regrouping on the landing, Daisy then led her charges down a corridor and pointed to a partially opened door.

"See? We've got 'alf a dozen rooms like this one," and nudging Thea inside the two girls piled in after her.

Regardless of the fact she would not be using it - or any other room specifically for the purpose of entertaining men - Thea had to admit to a twinge of curiosity, but aside from the décor being more garish than anything she'd ever seen in her life, there was nothing more sinister than the usual furnishings found in a room intended for sleeping. In fact, it could easily have been one of the spare bedrooms at home.

"Now, 'ere's the rules. Once yer done and you've shown yer gen'leman out, get back smartish and tidy up. It 'as to look like this for the next customer. Get it?"

"Clean sheets in the press outside if you need them. You don't always," Esme offered shyly. Seeing the sun-touched skin and smattering of freckles across the girl's nose, Thea wondered what hardship had made a cow-cockie's daughter leave the farm. But Daisy, with her newly found authority, was already shuffling them out.

"No need to bovver wiv all of 'em," she said crossing the corridor and pushing open a second door, and then a third. Both were of a similar style to the first.

"Just remember, if a door is closed the room is occupied. Now, let's go over the uvver side. It's where we 'ave the play rooms."

And with an exaggerated wink Daisy shepherded them back across the landing and along another corridor where, after pausing for dramatic effect, she flung open a door.

"For the clients who want somefink a little special."

This room was quite different. Dark and gothic, one wall was a display of whips and riding crops and leather paddles, whilst another held restraints. Hanging from the ceiling was a pair of sturdy looking manacles, though most incongruous was the prayer kneeler in the corner, upon which, no doubt the sinner could plead for forgiveness.

"Do you mean," Thea stammered, catching sight of her shocked expression in the cheval-dressing mirror, "that men are tortured in here?"

Folding her arms Daisy winked again, but this time at Esme. "She'd be surprised wot we do in 'ere, wouldn't she."

"Yes, she would."

This truly was becoming a nightmare.

"This is Belle's domain. She's a proper expert. Knows just when to lay it on and just when to stop. Wouldn't mind having a go meself sometimes. Not that she'd let me. It's bloody good business for her."

Esme was nodding in agreement. "Men pay a lot more for Belle's services than ours."

"Oh," Thea said weakly.

"Com'on, I'll show you where we sleep."

The passage at the end of the corridor was considerably narrower, and thankfully there were no lurid adornments on the wall. But nor was there a thick carpet. Instead it was dingy linoleum.

"'Ere we are." Daisy was leaning against a door.

Crammed with furniture, none of which matched, the room contained three iron bedsteads, three chests of drawers, a couple of upright chairs that looked as if they had last seen service in a kitchen, and an enormous mahogany wardrobe with an excessive amount of carved embellishments and a mirrored centre panel.

"This is where I kip." Daisy had flung herself onto the bed beside the door. "You can 'ave that one if you want." And she nodded towards the one in the opposite corner. "Just shift Nora's stuff - untidy cow she is, dumps 'er finks everywhere."

Retrieving a bottle from under her pillow, she waggled it suggestively. "Wanna drink?"

"No, thank you."

"It's the real McCoy. None of yer 'omemade rubbish."

"It's not that," Thea replied politely, "it's just that I don't drink."

"Bleeding 'ell!" Daisy stared in astonishment. "Temperance, are yer? Never had one of them in 'ere, 'ave we Ezz. Well, Temperance or not, yer gunna 'ave to learn. 'Ow on earf are yer going to get yer customers paying for the stuff, if you don't drink it wiv 'em?"

"You will have to loosen up a bit." Having created a space for herself on the bed that had been offered to Thea, Esme was smoothing out the wrinkles in the coverlet as if nothing was amiss.

"You alright?" Daisy said, for Thea was gazing around in astonishment. Not so much at the oddments of furniture, but at the unmade beds and discarded clothing and the debris littering the top of every surface. Perfume bottles, cosmetics, bits and bobs of cheap jewellery, stubs of candles, advertisements torn from a woman's magazine, hairbrushes and pins, curling fluid, tins of talcum and tooth powder, crushed cigarette packets and even coins. She had never seen such a mess.

"I'm fine, thank you," and seeing as how Daisy was still holding up the bottle she continued, "well, perhaps a very small one."

While a spot of discretion might not go amiss, for she didn't want to alienate anyone, she was also wondering how long it would take for everyone to accept she had no intention of mixing with the bordello's customers, drinking or otherwise.

"That's me girl," Daisy said approvingly. "Fetch us them glasses."

She was pointing at a washstand set into a recess, and although more used to giving orders than receiving them, Thea went over and collected three of the five tumblers left upside down on the marble top.

"To yer 'ealth."

Having poured a generous amount into each glass, Daisy was holding hers up in time honoured tradition.

"Yes, indeed." After passing the third glass to Esme and carefully relocating a fur-collared coat onto the bed of its rightful owner, Thea screwed up her nose and took a tentative sip.

And shuddered.

She had never tasted anything so dreadful, not even from a medicinal cupboard; strangely Esme seemed quite oblivious to the flavour, as did Daisy.

Discreetly lowering her glass she looked around again, and then asked where everyone else slept.

"I'm next door. There are four of us in that room and the rest are opposite," Esme said.

"That sounds like a lot of women."

"It is, but not everyone lives in."

"Oh I see. So, some of them go home at night?"

"More like in the mornin'," Daisy replied with a wink.

"Oh." Thea felt herself colouring.

"Don't worry. No one expects you to know everything yet," Esme said gently.

"That's just as well." Thea returned her smile. "This is all so new to me."

"'Ave to say it shows. But don't worry, yer'll get used to it. Before yer know it yer'll be an expert."

"I can't see that happening."

"Course yer will."

Thea knew that for the time being her options were limited. She really did have nowhere else to go. Nor did she have the money she'd offered Kitty, as all her personal accounts and savings had been transferred into joint arrangements on her marriage and required Silas's signature to withdraw even the smallest amount

In fact all she had to call her own were the few shillings in her purse.

She had to remain calm. Try to find a way to stay in the background and out of Kitty's way, at least until she could work out what to do. But for that she needed a good understanding of how the place worked. Nuances and all. Besides, she wanted to ensure the conversation remain on innocuous topics, especially since both girls must be more than a little curious about her situation.

"So how does this place function?"

"Wotcha mean?"

"Well, where do the men come from, for one thing?"

Daisy opened her mouth as if to speak, but Esme got in first.

"They're just ordinary people. No one to be frightened of really."

"I see. If it's not impolite of me to say, you don't seem very old. How long have you been here?"

She hoped the question was not too indelicate.

"I'll be nineteen in a few months' and I've been here a little over a year."

Thea couldn't help gasping. That meant Esme had been only seventeen when she'd started at Kitty Malloy's, and as if guessing the direction of her thoughts, Esme was already shrugging off any notion of pity.

"Pa died," she said, matter-of-factly. "It was an accident. Plus he'd had a drink or two. Ma couldn't cope with the farm and all us kids, and on top of that we hadn't any money. As soon as I was old enough, I got out."

"Wasn't there anything else you could do?"

This time Daisy got in first. "Like wot? School-teacher? Bank clerk?"

Right away Thea knew she'd blundered and apologised profusely. But Esme's tutting and shaking of her head was reserved for her friend.

"Daisy you shouldn't." And reaching for Thea's fingers she gave them a reassuring squeeze. "It's alright."

"Yeah. Sorry," Daisy said, though with little contrition, "me mouth runs away wiv me sometimes. Get me in right trouble one day, won't it."

"It will," Esme agreed.

"So, you wanna know how it all works?"

Thea nodded and took another tiny sip at her drink, but it tasted no better the second time around.

"S'easy. Customer turns up, pays Kitty and gets a token."

"The tokens are stamped with a number," Esme put in.

"Yeah, and that's 'ow we know wot they've paid for."

"I'm sorry, I don't understand."

"The number 'as a meaning. Clever innit? You look at the number and know wot yer 'ave to do. Anyway, after they've paid for their token they get to choose one of us. We take the token off 'em; provide the service they've paid for, and then give the token back to Kitty afterwards. She keeps a tally and once a week we get our money. Less expenses o'course."

"Expenses?"

Not wanting to be seen as stuffy Thea made a third attempt at the foul tasting liquid in her glass.

"Doctors bills, that sort of stuff."

"This is a clean house," Esme advised. "No diseases. That's why the doctor comes round."

"The doctor? I'm sorry. I still don't understand. Why would a doctor come here?"

"To give us a checkup, an' 'and out certificates saying we ain't got no pox, or clap, or crabs, or anyfink else nasty. That's why."

"Oh I see." But Thea didn't, having no previous knowledge of such maladies. One look at the other girls faces told her they were things to be avoided at all cost.

And then realisation dawned. "And he examines you… down there?" She was shocked to the core.

"Course. Where else would he look?"

Daisy and Esme broke into howls of laughter, and then Thea too saw the funny side.

"So," Daisy swung her legs off the bed and stood up, "let's get down to business. Wot 'ave we got for you to put on tonight? I take it milady is joinin' us?" She was running a practiced eye over Thea's waist and hips.

But Thea was having none of it.

"No. I'm not going downstairs today."

"Er, I fink you are. Just to get acquainted, like. Cos we don't wanna do anyfing to upset Belle or Kitty, now do we?"

"She's right," Esme agreed.

Leaning into the cavernous wardrobe Daisy was sliding hangers aside. "Hmm, this might work."

"I don't think you heard me," Thea insisted.

"I did. But that's not 'ow it works 'ere. Unless that is, you fink you're too good for us?"

The scraping and colliding ceased abruptly.

"Of course not." Thea was horrified.

"That's settled then. 'Ere, try this."

"Wot about underneath." Esme came over and took the flimsy, kimono-style robe from Daisy's outstretched hand.

"Wotcha wearing now?"

Thea was appalled. How had it come to this?

"Look, your dress is lovely," Esme assured her, "but it's not right for here. Why don't you stand up and take it off? Daisy will hang it up for you."

It was simply too much.

"I can't do this. I just can't."

"It's alright, we all felt like that at first." Esme laid a consoling hand on Thea's arm.

Even Daisy relented.

"Let's 'ave another drink. Plenty of time yet." And she splashed more vermouth to each glass.

Knowing the girls would find as much fault with her underwear as Miss Kitty, Thea tried to delay the moment of stepping out of her dress. The bandeau top designed to flatten her bust rather than emphasis it was, it had to be said, completely unflattering, and her modest drawers were embarrassing. Especially when compared to those of Daisy and Esme. On the up side, her pearl-gray stockings were pure silk and as stated on the box, imported from Italy.

"Hmm." Daisy was sizing up a blushing Thea. "You'll need a corset like mine if we're going to make the most of you. Squeeze you in 'ere," and she pressed her fingers on either side of Thea's waist, "and bring you owt 'ere."

The realisation of exactly where Daisy intended to put her hands made Thea jerk back.

"Blimey, I was only gonna show yer 'ow we can improve yer."

Arms crossed protectively over her breasts, Thea was trembling. "I'm sorry. I am truly. I'm just not used to being touched."

"Can see that!"

"It's a bit overwhelming for her," Esme said gently.

"Well, yer gonna 'ave to get used to a bit o' physical attention, ain't yer?"

Thea took a deep breath.

"No I'm not. And anyway, what's wrong with the way I am? Who cares if I don't have curves? I certainly don't."

And then she hiccupped.

"Sorry," she said quickly, her cheeks on fire, "I'm not used to drinking."

"Yer've 'ardly touched it," Daisy remonstrated.

"I had another one earlier with Miss Kitty."

"Did yer now. Well ain't you the 'onoured one. Anyway, most men like a woman wiv a body like mine." She was running her hands proudly down her sides, from ribs to thigh. "Gives 'em something to grab 'old of."

"I'm sure they do," Thea'd had enough, "but these days it's far more in vogue to be slender. Emphasising a figure the way you're suggesting is so behind the times."

"Behind the times? Not 'alf as behind the times as your 'air."

It was Thea's turn to take umbrage. Of course the style was woefully outdated, but she didn't need reminding of it by this... this trollop!

Then she stopped. Right at that moment she needed friends not enemies.

"I know," she said in a more amenable tone, "I intend to cut it all off at the first opportunity."

"Do you?" Esme had been staring from one girl to the other with growing dismay. Reaching up she touched a finger to the tight roll at the nape of Thea's neck. "But it's beautiful."

Daisy closed her mouth, as if she too had thought better of what she'd intended to say, and after acknowledging Esme's compliment with a tight but appreciative smile, Thea took a deep breath and offered Daisy an olive branch.

"Even in a corset, I'd never have your lovely shape."

"You're probably right." Daisy gave a careless lift of her shoulders. "Anyways, someone wiv a bit o' class like you needs to be different. That way yer'll stand out.

And Esme's spot on, yer 'air is lovely. Mine would never grow like that. Gets down to me shoulders and then frizzes owt summit awful. Look," she continued with a shrug, "yer going to 'ave to come downstairs tonight, else there'll be 'ell to pay. And yer don't want to start out wrong, do yer? Why don't I lend you a brassiere and a pair of silk knickers?" She was already pulling open a drawer.

"Do you really have nothing of your own?" Esme asked her brows creased in a frown.

Thea shook her head. Even the stuff in the basement would be woefully out of place.

"Then we need to go shopping," she said, looking first at Thea and then to Daisy, who'd straightened from her rummaging.

"Now that ain't a bad idea."

"I'm afraid that might be a little difficult."

"Why?"

"Well, I'm not sure I have enough money at the moment."

"No money?" Daisy was clutching a froth of silk and lace.

"I'm afraid not."

"Oh, you don't need your own money," Esme said matter-of-factly, "Miss Kitty will lend you some."

"Esme, I can't ask her."

"Why not?"

Thea exhaled loudly. "I just can't. Heavens, I've never borrowed a penny in my life."

The other two looked at each other again.

"Of course you can. It's what she does. Lend money, that is. She won't mind."

"Oh, I'm sure she won't!"

"That settles it then. We'll go tomorrow. 'Ere, take these and put 'em on." Daisy pressed the delicate items on Thea.

Knowing she was beaten, Thea glanced around wondering where she was expected to change. Perhaps the dressing room was elsewhere? If not, there would be a screen at the very least. Wouldn't there?

She turned to Esme, but Daisy had already picked up on her dilemma.

"Don't mind us. I doubt you've got anyfink we ain't," she grinned. "Go on. Put 'em on. Then we can do the best bit."

"The best bit?"

There was a best bit to all this?

"Helena Rubinstein. All the way from New York."

Turning from the chest of drawers once more, Daisy was proudly holding up an enamel face-powder compact and a gold-coloured tube of lipstick.

8

Wishing to block out the salon's activities; the comings and goings, and the fug of aromatic tobacco overlaid with cheap perfume and warm bodies, Thea deliberately selected the farthest and darkest corner of the salon and curled up. Lowering her head she, concentrated on things that were less fearful. Her newly shaped and painted fingernails for example, or the tiny stitches on the silk kimono wrapped tightly around her - even the complex design of the Persian rug at her feet.

Daisy and Esme left her alone for the most part, though not without first trying to cajole her into joining in with the others. Only when she was certain no one was looking did she steal darting glances, and that's how she knew how busy both girls had been. Why, they must have attended to some two or three gentlemen apiece, and supporting what Esme had said earlier, thankfully each one seemed perfectly normal. What was amazing though, was the change that came over the place with the arrival of each new customer. A girl might have been languishing on a sofa and gossiping, or dealing hands of gin rummy, or even taking a sly doze, and suddenly she was posing and posturing and showing an indecent amount of leg. More astonishing was the touching and offering of breasts in a manner Thea would never have believed had she not seen it for herself. And the gentlemen - she thought indeed that most were of that class - preened and smirked in return and paid outlandish amounts of money for what she guessed would be mediocre liquor and supposedly fine cigars pressed upon them. And all without complaint.

It was, she thought, a circus. A view that was reinforced when she saw Esme romping on a young man's knee in a manner that could only be described as unbelievably forward - though one look at the customer's drooling expression told her he was loving every minute.

Not all the girls were as popular, not that there weren't enough men to go around, especially as the evening progressed, and when Daisy left the room yet again, this time with a decidedly upper-crust gentleman complete with monocle and cut-glass accent, and Esme came over in between customers to join her, Thea finally allowed her curiosity to get the better of her.

"Daisy seems to be rather, er…" struggling to find an appropriate word, she finished lamely with, "… popular?"

"She is. Gentlemen like her."

Esme was bending forward trying to adjust the back of her corset, the reddened furrow across her back evidence of her discomfort.

"I can see that," Thea replied carefully. "The one who has just gone upstairs with her?"

"What about him?"

"Well, he seems rather refined."

"He is. He's a toff, and a member of Parliament." Puffing and breathing hard, Esme continued tugging. "This isn't a place for riff-raff, you know."

"No, of course not," Thea said quickly.

"What about him then?"

"I'm just curious, that's all."

"Well, he's a regular," upright once more, Esme had turned her attention to the arrangement of the boning at the front, "and he always asks for Daisy."

"Why?"

"Why not?" and twisting a little, she sighed in relief. "Oh, that's so much better. You want to know Daisy's secret?" she added mischievously.

"Only if it's not too outrageous." Thea knew when she was being teased.

"She's a right little strumpet." Esme had mimicked Daisy's Cockney accent to perfection.

"Oh. I see."

"Do you?"

Thea shook her head. "No, actually I don't."

"Don't worry you soon will. Men? More like children most of them."

By midnight Thea was finding it impossible to stay awake. It had been a long, emotionally fraught day and she wasn't used to being up so late. Or it might have had something to do with the succession of cocktails she'd felt obliged to sample whenever a new batch was concocted, since refusing didn't seem quite the done thing. Funnily enough, despite her insistence that alcohol was not to her liking - the few times she'd ever tried it, it was either too intense, too bitter, or simply too sweet - with each exchange of empty glass for a full one, she had felt more and more chipper. Such approval did not extend to the jazz music though, and to which some of the girls were still dancing, for the gramophone had been playing non-stop all evening and while she'd enjoyed it at first, for the past half hour the exuberant rhythms had been hammering at the inside of her skull.

"Go to bed."

Dropping beside her, Daisy gave her a nudge. "I'll be up meself soon."

"Don't you have to stay here all night?" Thea was finding she had to pronounce her words carefully, and even more importantly, think hard to ensure the words came out in a sensible order, though it seemed even that effort was wasted when the entire speech came out in a slurring singsong fashion.

"No. The older girls do that, like Myrtle over there."

Daisy glanced in the direction of a woman with a world-weary look, and a pronounced hardness about her mouth.

"They start later than us and go on 'til morning," and laying her head on a cushion she closed her eyes. "Usually customers 'ave had more than a drink or two by then and that can make 'em difficult. Especially if they can't get it up. Then they can get abusive. Course it's different if we're 'aving a party. Then we all work on. But not tonight, thank you."

9

THEA HAD FALLEN ASLEEP THE moment her head hit the pillow. Now though she was staring up at a dark and unfamiliar ceiling with an unbearably dry mouth and a splitting headache. The slightest movement of her head sent the room spinning, and with that came the dreadful need to vomit. She'd never suffered such agony in all her life. There was a chamber pot under her bed - cream coloured with sprigs of flowers for decoration, though the glaze was quite crazed and the handle chipped - so she could make use of that if she had to rather than face the back stairs down to the lavatory.

If only someone else would fetch her a glass of water. Had she been at home she'd have summoned Ada who would have brought damp, cooling cloths for her forehead and a glass of cook's homemade remedy. But it was unlikely anyone here would go to such trouble for her.

She lay perfectly still listening to Nora snoring softly on the other side of the room. Daisy had stirred a few minutes earlier, as if somehow disturbed by Thea's unhappiness, but then she'd rolled over and settled once more.

What had she done to make Silas believe it was perfectly acceptable to leave her in such a place while he went off to enjoy the delights of Europe for four months? Had she ever rejected his night time advances? No. So why was he making her suffer? Just the thought of being forced to let other misguided creatures do *that* to her made her want to shrivel up and die. He must be mad if he thought she would ever forgive him. Instead she was going to bear a grudge for a very long time. Years even. She would make his life so miserable he would beg for forgiveness every day,

The room spun and suddenly Thea was hanging over the edge of the bed with one hand on the floor and the other trying to keep her hair out of the chamber pot as she brought up the foul smelling liquid that had been churning in her stomach.

Her head was still thumping when she went in search of Kitty later that morning. She wasn't looking forward to the confrontation since the bordello owner was patently a veteran at getting her own way.

But she had resolve on her side.

She'd found her in the hallway on her way out.

"I thought we'd discussed this," Kitty said, pulling on her gloves.

Thea took a determined pace forward.

"Discussed it? Hardly! If the truth were known, you bullied me."

"Bullied you, did I?"

"Indeed you did. Well, I'm here to tell you I won't stand for it."

"So," Kitty was flexing her leather-clad fingers, "and let me make sure I have the situation correctly. You are refusing to join the other girls in the salon."

"I am refusing to entertain men."

"There's a difference?" she made it sound as if it were something she'd never considered before.

"A minor one but yes, there's a difference. I am willing to show solidarity by joining everyone in the evenings, but that's as far as it goes."

"So you want preferential treatment?"

"If you wish to put it that way."

"And you think that would be acceptable in a place like this?" Turning away Kitty reached for her handbag. "You don't think the others would see it as you believing you're a cut above everyone else?"

Thea shifted her weight from one foot to the other for hadn't Daisy already accused her of that very thing?

"You haven't really thought this through, have you?"

"I won't do it," she repeated stubbornly.

"Well, I haven't time for this now, so is that all?"

"No. I would like the rest of my clothes and my books."

"I see no reason why you shouldn't have your books."

"And my clothes?"

"I'm sorry but they simply don't suit the style of my establishment."

"But what am I to wear?"

"I'll leave that up to you. But please, no more dresses like the one you're wearing. The colour is a touch drab. Even for you."

"Really?" Thea said scornfully, though she did glance down.

"I think so. Oh, and I'll have Frank get your books for you - when you bring me your first token."

It seemed the encounter was at an end.

"Now just a minute…" But Thea got no further.

"My rules and you will play by them. Now, if you don't mind, I'm busy."

"If you think I will be a willing participant in this farce you are very much mistaken."

"Really? Are you sure about that? Have you considered you might end up enjoying a little male attention? After all, not all men are inconsiderate to a woman's pleasure."

"And what is that supposed to mean?"

"I think you know exactly what it means."

Suddenly the pieces fell into place.

"Oh my God!" Thea's hand flew to her mouth. "He comes here?"

Kitty shrugged. "Occasionally. Men have needs. That's why I'm in business."

She turned to open the door but Thea had planted her hand firmly on the panel. She and Kitty were inches apart.

"I still won't do it."

"Oh but you will. All it will take is a dose of sedative. A drug that will have you as helpless as a baby," Kitty said. "Not enough to knock you out. Where would be the fun in that? But enough for you to know what is happening without being able to prevent it. The choice is yours."

Despite Thea's resistance, Kitty had managed to pull the door open. "Take control of your own fate. Or I will."

10

THEA SPENT MUCH OF THE afternoon lying on her bed, pleading a severe headache. So much so, that by late afternoon Daisy was concerned enough to suggest she try a mustard plaster on the back of her neck.

"Worked for me mum," she said, "and she were plagued wiv 'eadaches."

"Just leave me a while longer." Thea wished Daisy would hurry up and dress. "Perhaps once it's dark I'll feel better."

"But the curtains are already closed," Daisy argued. "Can 'ardly see to do me face." Then she straightened. "'Ere, you ain't trying to pull a fast one are yer?"

"A fast one?" Thea repeated weakly.

"Yeah. Y'know. Get out of going downstairs?"

"I don't think that's possible anymore."

"Wotcha mean?"

"Nothing."

"Yeah you do. You ain't like the rest of us, that's obvious. So wot's goin' on?"

"I've already told you."

"No, you ain't. You said yer old man 'ad left you. But that's not all there is to it, is it?"

"Yes it is."

Closing her eyes Thea groaned, hoping Daisy would take the hint.

"Fink I came down in the last shower? There's summit you ain't sayin'."

"No. You've got it all wrong."

"'Ave I?"

Daisy's expression left no doubt she wanted answers, and struggling upright Thea leaned her aching forehead on her knees.

"I went to see Miss Kitty today and asked if she would allow me to remain up here for a few days."

"Why on earf would you do that?" Daisy was clearly taken aback. "You ain't going to make any money that way."

"I don't want to make any money."

"I don't get it. Why would you be 'ere if it weren't to earn money."

"Please," Thea begged, "just allow me to rest a little longer. I'll come downstairs later."

Hands on hips Daisy stared hard.

"You'd better. If Miss Kitty knows yer up 'ere when you shouldn't be, she'll be up them stairs in a flash."

Thea knew she was right. Kitty would be furious at being disobeyed. She might even carry out her threat to drug her. Though surely not. It would be illegal for one thing. But who would care in this den of iniquity? On the other hand, if she were to be taken against her wishes and whilst incapacitated, it would exonerate her of all culpability once this was over, since she could hardly be expected to put up a fight if she couldn't move. And that would place Kitty Malloy in a very bad light, exposing her as the lowest of the low, a cruel and heartless she-devil trading the honour and innocence of her less fortunate sisters. Thea could already see the raised placards and hear the loud cries of repugnance from the well-dressed woman demonstrating their anger on the pavement outside. And when Kitty Malloy appeared, surrounded by burly policemen to be led away to the paddy wagon, those shouts would turn to jeers. Things would be thrown.

She sighed. It was all very cheering, but even she knew justice wouldn't happen tomorrow or the following day. Such wheels turned slowly.

She could see only one option. She would go along with Kitty's demands - at least on the surface - and then throw herself on the mercy of her customers, pleading her case that she was there under false pretences. If they were truly gentlemen and she refused to accept their tokens, they would be free to choose another girl. Someone a little more willing and practiced. It should work, at least for a while, and then she'd have to think up another scheme.

And in the meantime, all she had to do was to keep out of Miss Kitty's way.

Easing herself off the bed, she gathered her flannel and soap and went over to the washstand where a glance into the pitcher showed it contained just enough water to cover the bottom of the china basin. That meant she would have to go down to the scullery afterwards - a dreary, lean-to affair at the back of the house where the girls washed their smalls, and after putting them through the mangle a couple of times, hung them on long pine slats hoisted up to the ceiling - and fill the jug for the next girl.

Another house rule, according to Daisy, and something else Ada would have done for her at home. She was beginning to appreciate the housemaid more and more. Dipping the flannel into the inch or two of water and scouring the surface with the cake of lavender soap she was soon raging over the unfairness of her situation. And now there was another thing adding fuel to the fire. The knowledge of where Silas had been going on the nights she'd believed he was with friends or at his club.

Such depravity didn't bear thinking about.

Meanwhile if nothing else, last night had taught her a very important lesson. No longer would she accept every drink put in front of her. Even thinking about all those cocktails - and there had been plenty - made her queasy all over again. No, from now on she would keep her head and her wits about her.

But she couldn't do it alone. She needed the support of the other girls, so it wouldn't do to push her differences too much. Although when she'd remarked that morning, just how kind everyone in the salon had been, Esme had looked puzzled.

"Keeping the customers away," Thea had explained.

Esme had burst out laughing.

"They weren't doing it for your benefit, silly."

"No?" Thea's confusion must have been evident.

"They were protecting their income," the younger girl explained a little more kindly. "New girls are always popular, so you're wanting to stay out of the limelight is a blessing as far as they're concerned."

Now Thea understood. She could even see the funny side.

"Then I'm happy for them. And if it helps, I will stay out of the way for as long as they want."

11

THEA HAD A PLAN.

And she had two obstacles. Miss Kitty was one, but the more pressing need was for money. Nothing could be achieved without it, even if she did manage to slip past Frank and escape.

The solution was obvious.

She couldn't hide beneath Daisy's kimono indefinitely. It wasn't fair for one thing, and anyway wouldn't she want to be in something of her own choosing if she had to be in the salon?

The entire plan hinged on the unthinkable.

"Twice in as many days," Kitty said, as if they were old friends and the visit an unexpected delight.

"Indeed," having stepped into the front room Thea fixed her smile in place, "let me get straight to the point. I understand there are circumstances in which you might be called upon for temporary financial assistance."

Closing the journal in which she'd been writing, Kitty looked up thoughtfully.

"A loan do you mean?"

Thea winced. Did the woman have to be so direct?

"I do."

"It has been known. Although it does depend on the individual's situation. And," Kitty's eyes narrowed, "what the money is to be used for."

"I see."

Thea was left to flounder. No one had ever questioned her before, not even Silas, and the imposition rankled.

"You are aware of my situation of course?"

"Completely."

"And you recall advising me that my clothes are not appropriate for your establishment?"

"I do. And that is the purpose of your request? Suitable attire for your work here?"

Put so dreadfully Thea couldn't form any reply, for to do so would damn her as willing, if not eager, to fall in with Kitty's plans. On the other hand, surely the woman must realise she'd been wearing the same dress since she'd arrived.

The two women glared at each other, each waiting for the other to speak.

And then Kitty turned back to the desk and taking a key from the topmost drawer, opened another further down and withdrew a metal box.

"How much do you need?"

Thea found herself breathing again.

"Five pounds?"

"Expensive tastes." Kitty had raised an eyebrow.

"Isn't that what you intend to promote?"

She couldn't help craning her neck for a glimpse at what might be in the box. Of course it was a gross imposition, but Kitty hardly deserved her respect after all. And whilst most of the contents were shielded from view, she couldn't believe the quantity of personal cheques and bank notes she saw before the lid was snapped shut again.

Clearly it was a thriving business.

"An advance on future earnings." Having folded the note in half, Kitty was holding it out. "And when you go shopping, please take one of the other girls with you. I do want you to return with something suitable. Unlike the clothing in your suitcase. Wouldn't you agree?"

Thea stretched out a hand.

"I don't bite, you know." Kitty had retracted the note a little, forcing Thea to take a pace forward. "That's better. Aren't you going to thank me?"

"Of course. Thank you." Thea's response, as she tucked the bank note into her pocket, was insolent though it seemed Kitty neither noticed nor cared.

"Oh, and just one more thing."

Having reached the door Thea stopped and looked back over her shoulder.

Kitty was fixing her with a hard look.

"Yes?" Dear God, her heart was pounding.

"I do hope you're not considering trying to leave us?"

"Leave you? What a strange thing to say."

How she got the words out she had no idea, for her mouth was as dry as a bone.

"I'm so glad to hear it. Just remember your husband's good name."

Thea frowned.

"Your husband's position in the community," Kitty went on.

"And what of it?"

"I'm sure you wouldn't wish to damage his reputation by being indiscreet."

"Surely it is far too late for that." Straightening her shoulders she stepped back into the room. "How could anything be worse than what he has already done?"

"Let's put it this way. I will give you three hours in which to make your purchases. If you aren't back by, shall we say four o'clock, I will have no option but to call my friends at the police station and inform them you are missing."

The blood drained from Thea's cheeks.

"But that's not all. I will also tell them you have stolen a substantial amount of money from me. Far more than you have just put into your pocket. The newspapers will have a field day. You'll be famous. Or should I say, infamous. Either way your next home will be gaol, and it will be for a very, very long time."

"You're despicable," Thea said, her fists clenched at her sides.

But Kitty had already opened her journal again.

"Just make sure you buy something my customers will appreciate."

12

IF THAT MORNING'S EXPERIENCE HADN'T been torturous enough, shopping with Daisy and Esme that afternoon more than made up for it.

"Where shall we go first?"

Having jumped on the tram at the top of the road, they'd alighted a few stops further on in the midst of the department stores on bustling Karangahape Road, and with her arm linked in Thea's, Esme was looking up and down the street with barely contained excitement.

"Well, we need to find somewhere that sells ladies underwear I suppose."

"Wot's the rush?" Daisy wanted to know. "Ain't we got all afternoon?"

"I suppose we do."

If Thea had been despondent at the failure of her plan, now she felt a surge of exhilaration. Freedom! Normality! Even for just a few hours.

"Then, let's enjoy ourselves," Daisy was saying. "Now, on this side of the road we got Rendell's, Hannah's and Bon Marche," the stores were ticked off her fingers. "And Courts where we could 'ave tea later on as well, that's if yer want?"

"It sounds lovely," Thea eased the trio out of the path of two hurrying women weighed down with bags. "I've never been on a shopping trip like this before."

"Nah? Then 'ow'd yer buy yer stuff normally?"

Thea shrugged. "I would go straight to wherever we had an account."

"See Ezz," having taken Thea's other arm; Daisy leaned forward and spoke across her, "comes from a different world. Sad, innit!"

And she laughed gaily.

"It doesn't sound like a lot of fun," Esme agreed as they stepped off in the direction Daisy had indicated.

"Well, I don't suppose it was meant to be."

"You'll like today then."

The words were hardly out of Esme's mouth when both girls were tugged towards a large plate glass window.

"Oh look at that," Daisy cooed. "Ain't it just the business?"

Four mannequins, displayed in what was noted on the card as being the latest Paris fashions, had caught her eye, though it was one dress in particular, a v-necked shift in shimmering bluey-green shot through with gold thread, that seemed to hold her captive.

"Gawd, look at the price. And for 'ardly any material." Daisy was shaking her head. "How much shorter can them hemlines get?"

"Over the knee it seems," Esme said. "Ma would have a fit if she saw me flashing so much leg in public."

Laughing and squeezing Esme's arm Daisy retorted, "Well, since it ain't likely yer can afford to buy it, we don't 'ave to worry about 'er keeling over then do we."

"Daisy!" Thea didn't know whether to be shocked or amused.

"You'll get used to her," Esme was grinning.

The last to dress, Thea made her way down to the salon at six.

"Looks like you're settling in."

Having wandered over as if in greeting, Belle was casually fingering a detail on Thea's new kimono.

"I thought I should try. Not that I want to step on anyone's toes," she added quickly, for others' too were showing an interest in her appearance. "In fact, I intend to stay in the corner and read a magazine."

There were some nonchalant shrugs.

"And what about Miss Kitty," Belle was saying. "How does she feel about that?"

"Oh I'm sure she won't mind. At least for now."

But Belle was having none of it.

"Indeed? That's not quite how I understand it. A little bird told me we have only a few short months' to make the most of your charms. I gather your time with us is limited?"

One or two of the girls had looked up again.

"So, in that case," Belle continued, a hand on Thea's arm, "I would have thought you'd want to be busy."

"Please. I'd rather no one put themselves out for me. Truly, I'm more than happy to keep out of the way."

"Suit yourself."

Thea was not surprised that Daisy came over and planted herself in front of her the moment Belle left to rejoin the huddle around the gramophone.

"Wot does she mean?" She was looking in the other girl's direction.

"Nothing at all. When I arrived I told Miss Kitty I would be here only until my circumstances changed. And I'm hoping that will be sooner rather than later, that's all."

It was clear by the needle-sharp look Daisy wasn't wholly taken in by the explanation.

"So 'ow long do you fink you're going to be 'ere then?"

"Like Belle said, a few months. Just long enough to hope something better comes along. Now, why don't we sit down?" Thea pointed to the nearest sofa. "My feet are still killing me after all the walking we did today."

"No. Let's get a drink first."

Taking Thea's arm, Daisy ushered her towards the bar.

"Sounds like yer no different to anyone else," she said, reaching for a bottle, "except some will still be 'ere come judgment day."

"Not you, Daisy. One day someone will come along and sweep you off your feet."

Leaning on the black lacquer counter top Thea watched Daisy measuring quantities of alcohol into a silver shaker.

"Not in 'ere, 'e won't."

"Then you'll have to be prepared to go elsewhere and find him."

"'E'll need to be a geezer wiv a bit of money."

"Is it so important he's wealthy?"

"Course. Better a rich man's Sheba than a poor man's wife."

"Oh Daisy, you're so cynical," Thea laughed.

"No I'm not. I just don't see the point in sugar-coatin' everyfink."

"Alright," Thea said, when having shaken the mixture thoroughly, Daisy filled two glasses and pushed one towards her. "So what other attributes does this gentleman have to have?"

"Oh. Good looks. And a motorcar. A posh one, like a Bentley or a Roller. Either one'll do."

"A woman of refinement."

"Wot? You fink you're the only one?"

Thea grinned back, for she knew exactly what was being referred to. Earlier that afternoon Daisy had made a beeline for a particular sale item - *a real bargain* she'd announced, fingering the goods on display. But Thea had pushed on to the more exclusive areas of the store. Quality, not quantity, she'd retorted to the two following in her wake. Daisy had called her Miss Hoity-Toity and the episode had not only been embarrassing but had cost Thea scones and teacakes later!

"So, just to make sure we haven't forgotten any-thing," Thea said between tiny sips of her cocktail, "we're looking for a good-looking chap with a decent car. I'm sure we could manage that."

"Be nice if yer could."

Thea managed to stay out of the limelight for just one more evening. And then, as she followed Esme into the kitchen for breakfast, Belle pulled her aside.

"Miss Kitty isn't very happy with you."

"Oh really?" Thea tried to look unconcerned.

"And you know why," Belle continued.

"I'm afraid you've lost me."

Having turned away, Thea leaned over the table and began filling a bowl with porridge.

"You need to start work. Pay your way like every-one else."

"I see."

"Do you? Only Miss Kitty said to remind you of what will happen if you don't."

Thea stared. Suddenly she'd no appetite. Not for porridge nor the reheated baked goods left over from the previous night.

Back in their bedroom later, Daisy and Esme had been astonished when veering between anger and despair, Thea had finally revealed the full extent of her naivety around all matters of a private nature between a man and a woman. The former more so than the latter, but before she could say anything, Esme had taken Thea's hand.

"You'll be fine. We'll help, won't we Daisy? We'll teach you all the tricks you need to know."

"That's the problem," Thea's mouth was contorted in disgust, "I don't want to learn any tricks."

"Then what are you going to do?" Esme asked gently.

"Explain the situation and if he's any sort of gentleman he'll understand and choose someone else."

Daisy and Esme exchanged glances.

"You don't fink that will make 'im even more keen?"

"Why on earth should it?"

"Cos of where you are? 'E'll fink it's a game. That yer playing 'ard to get."

"Surely not." Thea was shocked.

"And if 'e did agree to choose someone else, don't you fink Miss Kitty would come to 'ear of it before 'e'd even made it up the stairs?"

"She would," Esme agreed.

"Yer ain't got a lot of choice really. Just 'ave to make the best of a bad job."

"But the mere thought of having to do *it* is more than I can bear."

"Do wot?" Now Daisy was looking perplexed, "d'yer mean sex?"

Thea sniffed.

"Wot about yer old man? Didn't yer do it regular wiv 'im then?"

Esme had noticed a handkerchief on Thea's chest of drawers.

"Come on," she said, handing her the fine linen square, "nothing can be that bad."

"Yes it can," and with her eyes welling up Thea sniffed again.

"Don't be daft," Daisy said. "Everyone does it. At least everyone in 'ere."

Thea managed a little gulp of laughter at that.

"There you are then," Esme said. "Look, why don't we all get comfortable and we can go through things, bit by bit."

"Lucky I've still got a bottle, innit?"

And once again the vermouth was retrieved from under Daisy's pillow.

13

WITH HER EYELASHES CURLED AND darkened, and her cheeks rouged, Thea made her way into the salon. If she was a little unsteady on her feet it was in part due to the effects of alcohol; two more tumblers of vermouth drunk in quick succession whilst getting dressed. *Dutch courage* Daisy had reassured her, and without it she would never have made it down the stairs, let alone found the confidence to entertain her first customer. Even so, it took a superhuman effort not to panic on realising she had caught the eye of a rather tall, and thankfully it must be said, pleasant looking gentleman.

Desperately she tried to remember the advice she'd been given.

First, she showed interest by asking him if he were expecting to be in town long. Then, after fetching him a brandy, she continued to converse politely whilst he sat back and enjoyed being the focus of her attention. Discounting the amorous advances he obviously thought perfectly acceptable, that part wasn't too onerous - though no man she knew would dare sit so close to a lady he'd only just met. Or expect to place a hand on her knee. Nor would he take a lock of her hair, or nuzzle the lobe of her ear. Or worse, touch his lips to her silk-clad shoulder. Of course, such things might be acceptable elsewhere. But Auckland was not New York, at least not the last time she'd looked, and it had been an effort to hide her distaste, and smile and laugh gaily.

The next part wasn't quite as straightforward though, for she had to judge the moment to invite him to spend time with her in one of the rooms upstairs.

Not too soon, Daisy had warned. *Don't forget, Miss Kitty likes 'em to splash out on the drink first. That, and cigars. It's 'ow she gets even more money out of 'em. But on the other 'and, it's your time that's being wasted so get 'em onto that next drink and then up to the next floor as quick as you can.*

But everything paled into insignificance with what came next, for once in the bedroom and before things went any further, she had to find out whether her customer wanted the protection of a 'Frenchie', or preferred his intercourse *au natural*. According to Daisy most men would rather forgo the use of a prophylactic, especially if they were older, since it spoilt the enjoyment - or so they said.

Thea had touched a wary fingertip to the rubber sheathe draped the length of Daisy's palm.

"Why would they want to wear such a thing anyway?"

Daisy had shrugged.

"Some of 'em fink we might be diseased even though we 'ave our certificates. Cheeky buggers. And if we were, just 'oo do they fink gave it to us?" she'd said, casually rolling up the condom and returning it to its box.

With only the little knowledge of sexually transmitted diseases she'd gleaned earlier, Thea was even less aware of the existence of protective devices.

"Came from the war it did." Daisy was clearly knowledgeable about such things. "Too many of our boys cutting loose wiv all them continental girls and catching fings they shouldn't. Knowing they couldn't stop the fun, the army gave out rubbers instead. Now blokes get 'em from the barber when they're 'avin' their 'air cut."

"Oh," was all Thea could say.

14

ALTHOUGH OF SIMILAR YEARS, Thea's customer had none of Silas's attributes. Whereas he was slight, her customer was a little more rounded. And whereas Silas's gray hair was already thinning, his was thick and sandy coloured. Like a lion, she thought, though it wasn't just the hair on his head that caused her to think so, but the equally bold curls peeking from the neckline of his underwear.

Sitting on the edge of the bed with his shirttails bunched on his thighs, he was overseeing her work.

He had declined the offer of a protective device, whether due to age or not Thea had no idea and so, after assisting him in removing some of his clothes, she had knelt down and carefully examined his private parts for any signs of disease or disfigurement. Never having looked closely at the male body before, let alone touched one so intimately, it was a fearful moment. But Daisy and Esme had talked her through what was expected and given a number of demonstrations, albeit with the handle of a hairbrush. Now she was gently washing his parts with a diluted solution of disinfectant.

"You have a nice touch."

Thea swallowed hard and lowered her eyes. Not because of the compliment, but just as Daisy had predicted, her customer was becoming noticeably aroused.

"I would like you to do something for me."

His hand was on her shoulder.

"I don't think it's too difficult," he said gently, having no doubt sensed her unease. "Would you take down your hair?"

Grateful for the respite, she moved to the dressing table and eased out the pins, and after lowering each section, ran her fingers through to the very ends until it all fell about her shoulders.

"My dear, you are so very desirable."

They lay on the sheets together, she in her chemise and he in his undergarments. His hand was resting on her belly, its warmth radiating through the delicate fabric and she was afraid he would feel her trembling and realise her lack of experience in these matters. Concentrating hard, she tried to remember what to do next.

It seemed though he had an inkling as to her dilemma.

"I am aware this is new to you," he whispered, leaning over and touching his lips to her neck.

Thea was unable to speak and instead kept deadly still as he eased the ribbons of her chemise from her shoulders and slipped a hand inside the loosened garment. Never having been handled in such a fashion she felt ill. His palm was smooth and his touch expert and when, after cupping her breast, the tip of a finger found her nipple, she couldn't help but start with shock. Nor could she prevent the mewling sounds escaping her throat as he deliberately flicked a nail back and forth over the engorged nub. It was all she could do to squeeze her eyes shut and pretend she was elsewhere. But it was hard to ignore the tingling coursing through her body and the strange throbbing between her legs.

He was holding her to him and without thinking she arched her back, pressing herself against his hand.

The sensations were divine, and oh my goodness, who could not want this? When he turned his attention to her other equally aching nipple, her head went back and her lips parted.

And then she came to her senses. Oh God! What was she doing? This was all wrong and she was acting no better than the lowest harlot. What would the others say if they discovered she'd enjoyed such behaviour? She had to keep her head. Think. What had she been told? Something about taking the lead, and how it was all for the customers benefit? Perhaps whilst he was touching her, she should be touching him? But where?

In desperation she placed her hand on his arm, on a spot a little above his elbow, and when he looked up and smiled, she understood she'd done the right thing. Then to her dismay, he took his hand from her breast and eased it up and under the lacy edge of her chemise, intimating with his knuckles that she should part her legs.

He must have taken her gesture for a sign that she was ready for him. Now she truly was breathing hard - with fright. This was the bit she hated. The dry, painful pushing, and afterwards the stinging soreness that went on forever.

But it seemed her client wasn't quite finished with her.

Teasing open the pearl buttons he pushed aside the silky fabric and turned his attention to the dark curls of her lower belly, stroking her mound in a most affectionate way, before gently parting her secret, fleshy outer lips and running the tip of a finger up and down the inner crease as if to expose the centre of a flower.

Thea gasped.

"Like that, do you?"

She could only nod.

Then he found another hidden treasure, and this time his manipulations caused her to moan deliriously. Her head rolled from side to side as if unable to countenance such delicious agony, and although she had no idea what he was doing to her, she knew she couldn't let him stop. Grabbing his wrist she held his hand firmly in place, wanting to reassure him that as shocking as it might be, it wasn't hurting a bit.

But it was already too late, and he was rolling on top of her.

Oh God!

She couldn't decide which was going to be worse. The physical pain or the moral. But she had little time to decide, as having positioned himself in the very same manner as Silas, in one brief moment the vow of fidelity she'd taken on the day of her marriage was no more.

15

AFTER SEEING HER CUSTOMER TO the top of the stairs Thea quickly returned to the room, and undoing the gusset of her camisole, douched and scrubbed with a preparation formulated by Kitty and strongly recommended by the girls as a means of preventing both infection and conception. It was knowledge of the latter that was already filling Thea with dread, even more so than any disease since that, at least, had a chance of being cured. And, as if to underline the fact, Daisy and Esme had both hinted at girls who had not been so lucky and who'd had to undergo all manner of unpleasant things to rid themselves of the evidence.

Suddenly it was all too much, and sitting on the edge of the unmade bed she stared at her reflection in the mirror. She looked different, but that was hardly surprising since she was no longer the same woman who had entered the room less than an hour before. The hollowness in her eyes was unnerving, and her mouth, no longer vivid with lipstick, looked far less inviting.

More telling was the hair hanging about her shoulders, tangled and matted from fingers other than her own.

She had little compassion for the woman staring back, and that was frightening. But she did know one thing for sure. No one could turn back the clock and undo what had been done.

Ignoring the surreptitious glances, Thea went straight to her corner and tucking herself into her armchair, pulled her legs up beneath her. In her absence two new customers had arrived to drink Kitty's cheap booze and laugh outrageously at some joke or other.

It was as if nothing momentous had happened. Nothing were untoward.

It didn't help that Daisy was nowhere to be seen, nor Esme. Even Belle was absent. Thea was unaware of Nancy settling bedside her until a honey-gold cocktail was placed into her hand.

"What is it?" she asked, picking at a cushion seam.

"It's called a Sidecar. A Yank taught me how to make it. Try it," Nancy encouraged, "it'll do you good."

"Do you know I'd never touched spirits before I came here. A glass of wine at Christmas was my limit." Thea's tone, like her spirit was flat.

"Don't be hard on yourself. It had to happen," Nancy was pragmatic. "I know it was tough for you, but at least you did it."

When Thea didn't respond she narrowed her eyes, "You did, didn't you?"

Thea nodded.

"Well then, let's face it, you can move on now."

"And that's supposed to cheer me up?"

"No," Nancy shrugged, "but it's the reality. So anyway, how was it? Are you alright?"

"I got through it."

"There you are, you see, simple and straightforward. They're the best ones. It could have been worse, you know," Nancy sipped on her own drink. "You should be grateful he didn't want anything too fancy. Especially since he would have known you were new to all this."

"How would he have known that?"

"What colour was the token?"

"Silver."

Nancy was nodding. "One of Kitty's specials. The rest are brass so he would have paid over the going rate for it."

Thea was horrified. "She would have told him?"

"Not her. Frank. He's the one behind all the transactions. Saves her from getting her hands dirty. Besides, they're more likely to spend up big when they're dealing with a man. It's like they have this dirty little understanding. Where is it?" she added, almost as an afterthought.

"What?"

'The token?"

"Heavens!" and Thea sat bolt upright, "I've left it on the dressing table."

The glass was quickly removed from her hand. "Well for God's sake, go and get it. If anyone else finds it, they'll hand it in as theirs."

"But it's silver!"

"As if they would care. And nor would Miss Kitty. You'll have to get better at looking out for yourself."

Thea was soon back, breathless but with the precious token safe in her hand.

"Good," Nancy said, waving her glass in the direction of the curtains. "Now go and give it to Kitty. And remember, in future always hand them in before coming back in here."

Kitty saw no reason to put her pen down or close the ledger in which she had been recording the day's takings since the rapping on the door meant simply another transaction and a further entry in the book. Or it was Frank coming in to tell her of a particularly important arrival. She was expecting a good night. Not because it was Thursday - always a good day for business - but because the port was busy with a number of recently arrived vessels, and two of them were Norwegian whalers reprovisioning before heading down to the Southern Ocean. As fearless and tough as their Viking ancestors, their crews would be in need of entertainment after their long voyage from the northern hemisphere, and she knew her girls would be more than happy to welcome the strapping blond Norsemen.

"Come in."

She wondered if something were amiss when Thea stepped into the room, but one look at the girls glowering expression told her everything she wanted to know. Well! She'd been wondering when she would finally see sense.

"I have a token."

The tone was a touch haughty.

"Do you now?"

So, Frank had done the business. Well, she would still be good for at least another three or four of that colour, and after that? If she came to her senses and played her cards right, it could be a winning arrangement for both of them, for she certainly had class; there was no mistaking that. Deportment lessons, elocution lessons, riding lessons, singing lessons; Kitty knew how the bourgeois raised their offspring. Hadn't she herself seen it back home in Dublin? The toffee-nosed nannies and their expensive perambulators, pushing their charges around St Stephen's Green while her kind were lucky if they had enough to eat.

She held out her hand. But the girl didn't move. Rather her back was rigid and her eyes seething with barely disguised contempt.

Did she expect praise, Kitty wondered? It was always hard to tell with the new ones. She'd had one girl who'd gone to pieces after her first time, and it had taken almost a quart of brandy to get her back into the salon. Mind you, the girl had been a virgin up until then. Now she was one of her better girls, so there was really no telling.

"I take it you pleased the gentleman? No histrionics or anything?"

"I believe he went away happy."

"Good. The token?" Choosing to ignore the cynicism Kitty held out her hand

When it was placed in her palm, she balanced it as if testing it for weight. "I've no doubt that over the coming weeks you'll be bringing me many more of these. Though which colour is up to you."

Thea remained silent leaving Kitty, for the first time, nonplussed.

"You are aware you earn more with these ones?" and she held it up. "I like to be fair to my girls."

Still Thea said nothing.

Kitty shrugged.

"Did you want something else?"

"No."

"Good. Then I suggest you go back and continue earning your way out of debt. By the way," about to return to her accounts, she stopped and pointed at Thea's robe and chemise with her pen, "very suitable."

In fact, Thea's outfit, what she could see of it under the midnight blue kimono, was quite divine. But there was no acknowledgement of the compliment, no polite 'thank you' - not that she had expected there would be.

And if the truth be known she would have been quite disappointed if there had.

No, this way was far more entertaining.

16

AWARE THAT HER SURVIVAL DEPENDED as much on the other girls as herself, Thea tried to find ways to play down her differences, and more importantly, reassure everyone she was no threat to their livelihood. Of course she still had to entertain Kitty's customers, but with her obvious lack of enthusiasm and preference to remain in the background, she was often the last to be selected. Such a solution did not please everyone however, and soon Kitty had to pull her aside, threatening that unless she saw her way to taking more men upstairs, it would be her duty to inform Silas of her less than cooperative attitude.

By now though, Thea had gained an understanding not only of the workings of the house, but of her own worth.

"I'm aware you charge more for my services, and so if you wish for me to become commonplace and join in the squabbling over men, then you must be prepared to lose that extra percentage. And as for my husband," she said, standing her ground, "I care as little for his opinion as I do your bullying."

Daisy too had noticed the change in her.

"Yer different now," she said one morning, when having worked through a particularly busy night, they were taking advantage of lying in until noon.

The discovery of a lending library only half a mile away had been Thea's saviour, and the only light in a very dark tunnel since she could now read openly and to her hearts content. Half under the coverlet, she was trying to work out the clues in her latest whodunnit.

"Am I?" she said without looking up.

"Yeah. More..." sitting up in bed Daisy was concentrating on painting the centre of her fingernails with dark red varnish whilst trying to avoid both the cuticles and tips, "... more sure of yerself."

"Then I've obviously been here too long."

"That clock still ticking is it?"

"Isn't it the same for everyone?"

"You never talk about yer old man, do yer?"

Daisy wiped the brush on the rim of the bottle. Of all of them, Nora was the one with a talent for clever manicures and other beauty treatments - wasn't she always telling them she was going to open her own beauty parlour one day once she'd saved enough money - and Thea knew Daisy preferred to leave the tricky stuff to her. But indisposed with her monthly visitor, Nora had gone home for a few days.

"That's because there's nothing to say."

"You must 'ave loved 'im once?"

"No. I don't think I ever did."

"So why d'yer marry 'im?"

The tip of a pink tongue appeared as a layer of polish was carefully applied to a thumbnail.

"It seemed a good idea at the time."

It had been after one too many cocktails that Thea had divulged certain details of her marriage, and in particular that her husband had deserted her, and why. She'd even gone so far as to admit he was in Europe, but not that in a few months he would be returning to claim her.

She'd had a profound regret over the lapse ever since.

"Don't it always?" Daisy was still concentrating hard. "Wot is it wiv us women? Bleeding stupid when it comes to blokes. All they 'as to do is click their fingers and we come runnin'. Look at the pair of us. Sittin' 'ere 'oping for Sir Galahad on 'is white 'orse."

"I don't think there's much chance of that." Thea sighed, inserting the front flap between the pages of her book. Leaning over she placed it on the bedside cabinet and drawing the coverlet up around her neck, snuggled further down the bed. Over the last weeks the weather had definitely turned for the worse, and they would soon need more wood for the stove if they were to have any chance of staying warm, for the draughts finding their way through the poorly fitting window frames were bone-chilling.

"So how did you really get here?" she asked.

Daisy didn't even look up.

"'Fort I'd found the right one, did'n I. Nice bloke, 'e was. We grew up on the same street. Went to the same school, though 'e was way ahead of me. When 'e came back from France 'e said 'e didn't want to go back to the way finks were before the war. Said he wanted a new life. Go somewhere there was air to breave and no one to tell 'im wot to do. When 'e said he was comin' 'ere I said right-oh, I'll come too. Nuffink to stay in London for. 'Specially seeing's how crowded it were in the 'ouse wiv me bruvvers back too. All joined up togevver they did. Anyways 'e got me a ticket and we pretended we wus married."

"What did your mother say?"

"Not a lot. Glad to see the back of me I reckon."

"And then what?"

"Well, when we arrived 'e got a job down the line. Tinkering wiv engines, it were. Tractors, motorbikes, that sort of fing. Picked it up in the army. But I ain't no country girl that's for sure. All them sheep and no people. Prefer a bit of life I do. So, one day I left. Came up 'ere to Auckland. Trouble was I didn't 'ave any money to get any further. So 'ere I am."

"And have you thought about what you'll do when you've saved up enough to move on?"

"No. All I know is yer a long time dead."

Thea nodded. Daisy was one of life's survivors.

"On a different subject," she said, choosing her words carefully, "there's no spy-hole in here, is there?"

"Spy 'ole? In our bedroom? Why would there be one of those?"

'Well, perhaps someone might want to watch us getting undressed. Secretly. Without us knowing."

"Gettin' undressed?" Looking up for the first time, Daisy pulled a face, "don't be daft. Who'd want to do that when all they 'ave to do is come downstairs and see us in all our glory."

"You're right. I'm being silly."

"Any 'ow, why'd yer ask?"

Unfortunately she now had Daisy's full attention.

"Frank," she said, trying to sound as if it were nothing. "I've caught him outside the door. And not just once either."

"Don't worry about 'im. 'E finks 'e's in charge, more fool 'im."

"He is a little frightening though. Do you know much about him and his wife?" Thea asked.

"Only that they're from up North. Same tribe, o' course. Not sure if they're actually married though. Huia's on the level."

Thea nodded, for one night unable to sleep, she'd made her way down the back stairs thinking to heat up a pan of milk on the recently installed electric stove, and had come face to face with the Maori woman scrubbing and rinsing pans even though it was the early hours of the morning. Without saying too much, Thea had been given to understand that when Frank was drinking, his wife was better off away from their rooms at the back of the house.

"Oh. Do they have any children?"

"Pretty sure they do," having given the last nail a final lick Daisy was waving her hand about to encourage the varnish to dry, "but they're farmed out to relatives."

"That's rather sad."

"Not really. It's quite common round 'ere if you 'ave to work. Sometimes they even give their kids away for keeps. And I mean forever. Especially if the other person don't 'ave any of their own."

"If I had children," Thea mused, "I would never leave them."

"Maybe not. But then you come from another way of life."

"Yes but don't forget, we're also the ones who send our children to boarding schools from an early age."

"Yeah, you do don'cha." It was Daisy's turn to look thoughtful. "You want kids then?"

Of course Thea wanted children - at least she had. Now she wasn't even sure she wanted to remain married, not that she had any real choice. Her time at Kitty Malloy's would see to that. And even if she did apply for a divorce it would be a lengthy undertaking requiring every detail of her case to be investigated and noted. How could she explain it all? She'd be shunned for the rest of her life. Vilified even. And then there would be those unanswerable questions such as why she'd accepted such a shocking arrangement in the first place? And wouldn't it have been a case of drastic situations requiring drastic measures?

Rolling onto her side, she peered over the coverlet at Daisy. ""What about you? Have you ever wanted children?"

"If I 'ad the right man. Yeah. I would."

"The man with the car?" Thea teased.

"Yeah. That's the one."

"You know, if you're ever to meet him, what we really need to do is broaden your horizons."

"Me 'orizons? We gonna go somewhere?" Daisy had raised a derisive eyebrow.

"Don't be silly. You know what I mean. We need to make more of you."

"Oh. Yer want me talkin' posh then?"

"No, even if we had all the time in the world, that would still be impossible," Thea grinned back. "We need to think up a plan."

"Oh, course. How about this one then?" No longer waving her hands about, Daisy was blowing on each nail individually. "I leave 'ere, go to America, become a famous movie star, and marry a rich toff."

"If that's what you want, why not? Anything's possible if you want it badly enough. Imagine it. A mansion in Hollywood and starring in movies with Rudolph Valentino and John Barrymore."

"They should be so lucky!"

Both girls sighed in unison, then Daisy said, "Well, it ain't gonna 'appen any time soon, is it?"

"Oh Daisy, who's to say what might be around the corner?"

"Knowing my luck, a dirty big 'ole for me to fall in. Tell you wot; talkin' of 'Ollywood, let's go to the pictures tomorrow. Any idea wot's on at the Tivoli?"

"No. We can check the newspaper when we go downstairs. And we'll splurge afterwards. Have tea somewhere."

But when Thea made her way down to the salon later that day she found Frank at the bottom of the stairs, leaning against the banisters with one foot planted firmly on the first tread. It was clear he had little intention of stepping aside.

Instead a burly arm shot out and trapped her.

"Good afternoon Frank," she said, coming to a halt.

"You're lovely, you are. And just what this place needs."

With one hand braced on the wall he was so close she could smell the hops on his breath and knew it would be all the worse if he'd been drinking the stuff he brewed himself, for that was known to turn him hostile rather than just cantankerous.

"Thank you. Now if you would just let me by…"

"In a hurry to get somewhere?"

She wasn't. It was still early, just after three and everyone knew trade was slow at that time.

His eyes were glinting dangerously and she stood perfectly still as his free hand slipped inside her robe.

"Knew you'd have no trouble settling in," he said, leaning in until his face was just inches from hers.

"Get off me," she said quietly.

She felt him tense, but he recovered quickly. "Or what?"

There was no *or what* and Thea knew it. What could she do? Scream?

His fondling was rough, and despite her determination to remain calm, she couldn't help shuddering.

"That's better," his lips and nose were hard against her cheek. "Tell Frank how much you like it."

"Why would I lie?"

"Cos you're a whore. Just like all the others," he said in a slurring, sing-song voice.

"And you're nothing more than a tart's glorified errand boy."

Summoning her strength, and with her hands flat against his chest, Thea shoved him away, though she couldn't help flinching when he took a staggering step backwards and clinging to the banister for support, raised his fist as if to strike her.

"Think you're too good for us, don't you? Well, you're not. Even your husband knew that when he dumped you here. Frigid, he said. That's what you were. Ice cold," he sneered, as she made her escape across the hallway. "Not any more though are you? Don't make an enemy of me. I can make or break you. Do you hear me?"

But Thea had already disappeared through the curtains.

17

MONDAY EVENING HAD STARTED OUT no different to any other day. Business was a little slow, not unusual for early in the week, and Thea was sifting through a new delivery of gramophone records. One or two girls were already talking about the possibility of an early night when suddenly there was an excited squeal.

"Oh my God! Darius!"

"Darling, you're back."

"Heavens! The prodigal son returns."

Looking first at the girls and then to the new arrival, Thea couldn't fail to notice that unlike most customers, whose preference was for a little more discretion, this man was brazenly surveying the room with an almost expectant air. More astonishing, his smoldering dark looks and impeccable attire might have been transported straight from the silver screen.

"Ladies," he grinned, his arms wide as if to encourage further adulation.

Thea couldn't believe her eyes. For Nora, Nancy and the others; girls known to be calculating in their advances, were simpering and flirting and offering their hands to be pressed to the newcomer's lips, and judging by their expressions it was all completely genuine.

So who was he? Granted he had strikingly good looks and he seemed to have an ego to match. It was the little things that were so effective; remembering a girl's name caused her to swoon, while gazing long and seductively into her eyes was even more effective.

Though she thought the entire performance a little over the top, he seemed to have his entire harem in the palm of his hand.

Or did he? Soo Ling, the bordello's only Oriental offering hadn't moved from the sofa. Rather she was shaking her head in disgust, while Nelly, sweet Nelly with her homespun features and soft, generous curves was staring pointedly at her feet. And when Darius was hustled to a seat, and the others then engaged in an outright nudging contest in order to gain prime position beside the demagog, Thea was left with the notion that the whole thing was rather distasteful, even for a bordello.

It obviously didn't bother Darius though. In fact he seemed to be reveling in the fuss, and coming to the conclusion this was one customer not to be taken seriously, Thea got up and went over to the bar thinking it was a shame Daisy and Esme were upstairs with clients for they were certainly missing all the fun.

"What are you making Thea?" someone called out.

Having tipped a shot of brandy into the shaker, she was reaching for the orange liqueur.

"A Sidecar," she shrugged. What did it matter to anyone else what she was drinking, and glancing up she skimmed over the group. The girls were flushed and giggling, and Darius…?

He was returning her gaze with one that was disturbingly perceptive and suddenly it was hard to breathe. How had she thought him shallow? His features were lean and angular and as implacable as if hewn out of a rock face, and if there was a flaw it was that his nose was perhaps a little too long, a little too Gallic. Even so, the imbalance made him all the more attractive.

The hairs on her arms stood erect.

It made little difference they had never met; she knew him as well as she knew herself. The taste and smell of his skin, the low notes of his sleeping murmurs, the warm sensation of his hand touching hers.

His eyes had crinkled at the corners, whether in amusement or intrigue she'd no idea.

And then he raised an eyebrow.

Just a fraction.

Well?

Her heart was pounding and she had to put down the cocktail shaker. She needed to get a hold of herself.

"Make one for me," someone called.

"Me too."

"Just make a batch, there's a doll."

Yet she saw only Darius.

And then he broke the mood by slipping an arm around Nancy's waist and announcing he too would have whatever everyone else was drinking.

"Totally spiffing."

"Music someone. Let's get this party going."

Grateful to be out of the spotlight, Thea added more spirits to the shaker. It was none of her business how the girls conducted themselves and even less how Darius did so. He was nothing to her after all, though she couldn't help the occasional glance in his direction. Given the lively chatter and hoots of laughter it was impossible to do otherwise. That was how she knew that when eventually he went upstairs it was not only with Nancy hanging off his arm, but Nora too.

18

TWO NIGHTS LATER DARIUS WAS back, and he wasted no time.

"You," he said, holding a token towards her.

He seemed unperturbed that the laughter and chatter had died away and tumblers lowered.

Thea on the other hand was mortified.

Closing her book and setting it aside in the most dignified fashion she could manage, she stood. She made no fuss. Offered no welcome or any other small talk. Instead she walked purposefully to the curtained-off staircase.

"Well," she said. Having found an empty room she was midway between the end of the bed and the heavily draped window. "Do you intend on coming in?"

Darius was leaning against the door frame.

"You're different from the others," he said, unfolding his arms and taking a pace forward.

"I doubt that."

"Oh, but you are." And closing the door, he reached into his jacket.

Thea couldn't help but stare as he casually flipped open the silver case, and after picking out a cigarette and tapping it once or twice on the lid, put it to his lips.

Then felt into another pocket for a lighter.

There was something disturbing in the way he lit and then drew on the tobacco, perhaps because his eyes never left hers the whole time.

"The token?" Her breathing was laboured when she held out her hand.

"All business," he said, dropping it into her hand, "I like that."

"I'm glad you approve."

He seemed amused, though whether by her or the situation she had no idea, and she did wonder if for some reason he was baiting her, although she couldn't think why he would. Or what she might have done to deserve such treatment.

"Do you need help removing your trousers?" she asked over her shoulder while adding a small amount of the harsh smelling disinfectant to the water in the china bowl. Next, she took a clean square of cloth from a drawer.

"That would be most agreeable."

Her heart sank at the challenging note in his voice. Worse, when she turned around, he was leaning against the beds curved footboard with an annoying grin plastered all over his face.

"On the other hand, I think you are you old enough to do that for yourself."

"And miss out on all the fun?"

"Hardly that. It is a simple matter of undressing. That's all."

"Then what is the problem?"

Damn him, she thought. Why had he chosen her? What was wrong with Nancy or Nora? They'd been full of themselves when they'd returned to the salon the other night, so surely one, if not both, would have been more than willing to entertain him again.

Having taken off his jacket and lodged his cigarette in the metal ashtray beside the bed Darius was slipping the knot of his tie. Thea held her breath until he'd folded it tidily and placed it on the cabinet.

"Would you care to do the rest?"

He was obviously finding her discomfort amusing. The smile playing on his lips told her that, and when she shook her head he shrugged as if it were of no matter and dropped the brightly coloured braces from his shoulders. Then he began releasing the buttons on his shirt. Slowly. One by one. Starting at the top and moving down.

Thea was rooted to the spot as he tugged the shirt from his trousers and carelessly discarded it over the footboard, and even more so when his singlet was dragged over his head.

Whatever he might do for a living she thought, staring first at the broad and powerful-looking chest, and then at his muscular, taut stomach, he did not spend his days in a factory or an office.

"Well?" Darius posed hands on hips.

Thea had to clear her throat. "Your trousers?"

"I thought you might manage those."

She knew her cheeks were pink with embarrassment. Never had it been so difficult. Not even with her very first customer, and Heaven knows that had been hard enough.

Deliberately keeping her eyes lowered, she undid the buttons and then knelt and eased the brown flannel trousers down over his legs. Her cheeks burned even more when her fingers grazed first his thighs and then the darkly matted hair on his shins.

"Shall I sit?"

Thea was furious. God, he was enjoying this.

"If you would."

Getting to her feet she turned once more towards the dressing table. But it was as if all her nerve endings were exploding, and dismayed at the throbbing between her legs, she leaned on the furniture for support.

"Would you prefer to use a Trojan?" She reached for the tin, hoping, praying.

"And miss out on your tender ministrations?"

Of course she wasn't going to be let off that easily.

Gathering up the bowl and cloth she returned and knelt between his legs.

"Are you going to tell me your name?" he asked, watching her dip the cloth into the milky liquid and squeeze out the surplus solution.

"Thea."

As she began her work he straightened his shoulders and with a lusty sigh gazed up at the ceiling.

"Thea," he repeated, as if trying the syllables out for size, "so Thea, why haven't I had the pleasure of your company before?"

"Perhaps because I haven't been here long."

"Ah. That explains it. I'd never forget you."

Head lowered and concentrating on her task, Thea raised an eyebrow in derision. If he thought flattery was going to work he was very much mistaken. She was thinking back to the other evening. He could have chosen her then if he was of a mind - or was the thrill of being attended by more than one girl too much to forgo?

"I have to say I'm enjoying your touch."

"Really? I'm only ensuring you're free of anything untoward."

"And have you detected anything I should be concerned about?"

She knew he was studying her hair, her shoulders, the curve of her neck.

"No."

"You sound surprised."

"Do I? Then I must apologise."

"So go ahead."

"What?"

"Apologise for the slur on my otherwise impeccable character."

Dropping the cloth back into the bowl Thea sat back on her heels.

"You are making this very hard for me."

"I would have said it was the other way around."

She glared at him, for this was not the time for childish humour.

"You know, you are completely insufferable."

"And you're incredibly desirable. Especially when you're angry."

"That's the most ridiculous thing I have ever heard."

"Is it? I would have said I was paying you a compliment."

"Then we have completely different ideas of the meaning of the word."

Getting to her feet she threw him the haughtiest look she could.

Darius obviously hadn't finished. "I seem to have struck a nerve. Are you this rude to all your customers?"

"Only those lacking any social graces."

"Ah! Then I suppose I do qualify."

"At last we agree on something."

Thea had dropped the bowl a little too forcefully and was hurriedly mopping up the spillage, for left unattended the solution would mark the dressing table's varnished surface.

"So you think I have a shortcoming or two?" he questioned easily. "And what about you? What are your shortcomings?"

"My shortcomings?" she turned around.

"So you do admit to having one or two? I wonder if I can guess at what they might be. Now let me see…"

Not only was she was regretting she'd let the conversation get this far, she was even sorry to be in the room with this boorish oaf.

"Look," she interrupted, "I really can't see the point of prolonging this any further. Shall we just get on with the reason you're here?"

"By all means."

Lifting his feet onto the bed and making himself comfortable, Darius patted the coverlet beside him. "I'm ready when you are."

But it was too late. All the fight had left her.

"I'm sorry," she said wearily, "I can't do this. Here," and she held out the token. "Take it back. Go downstairs and choose another girl."

"But that's not what I want," he said quietly.

"Well I'm afraid that's the only choice you have."

For the first time Darius seemed at a loss.

"This isn't quite going to plan, is it?" he said, sounding and looking regretful.

"No."

"Fair enough."

And swinging his legs off the bed he reached for his undershorts. But it also seemed as if he wanted to make amends, for once he'd put them on he went over to her, and taking for her hand he curled her fingers back over the token.

"Look. Can we start again? Keep this. Let's just sit here and talk for a bit. Then I'll go. Would that be acceptable to you?"

"Well…"

"I promise I'll behave."

Thea found herself wavering. There was still a mischievous glint in his eyes, but she'd no wish to draw attention to herself and taking a customer upstairs only to reappear minutes later would do just that. Especially when it was this particular customer.

"Perhaps for a few minutes," she relented.

Fishing in his jacket pocket for his cigarettes, Darius leapt back onto the bed only to offer a rueful grin when the brass finials of the headboard banged against the wall.

"See? If there's anyone next door they'll think we're at it like rabbits."

"Rabbits?"

"Well aren't they always procreating? There are enough of them around to be an ongoing complaint. Or so it seems."

Easing herself up beside him, Thea pulled her robe firmly over her knees. "So what would you like to talk about? And please don't tell me rabbits."

Darius grinned again. "You. I think I'd very much like to talk about you."

"I can't think why. It will be a rather boring conversation."

"I doubt that," and striking the flint wheel of his lighter he held the flame to the tip of his cigarette.

"Then you truly don't know me."

"Exactly. And that's why I'd like to find out more."

In no way did she wish to appear rude, but surely he could take a hint?

"I'd rather we talk about something else," she said. "What about you?"

"Fair enough. What would you like to know?"

Having inhaled a large draught of fragrant smoke, Darius slipped a little further down the bed and locked one arm behind his head.

Thea was flummoxed. Privacy was sacrosanct in places like Kitty's, and most clients had little desire to admit to anything. Men lied all the time and everyone knew it. She racked her brain. Asking him something personal wouldn't do, she needed something innocuous.

"You seem very worldly. Have you travelled at all?"

A slow and steady stream of smoke was aimed at the ceiling.

"Yes, quite a bit. Europe, of course. But America too. Have you?"

Thea shook her head.

"Would you like to?"

"Perhaps one day. Tell me about America."

Satisfied the topic could be made to stretch out for as long as necessary, she lay back on the pillow and clasped her hands over her stomach.

"What would you like to know?"

"Everything. Have you been to New York?"

"Once. I've also been to the West Coast. And a few places in between."

"The West Coast? California? Truly?"

"Yes."

"Now I think you are trying to impress me."

"And why would I want to do that?"

"I have no idea."

"And if that was my intention, has it worked?"

"No."

Thea couldn't help giggling when Darius placed his hand over his heart, professing hurt that she would doubt him and rolled over to remonstrate. Then stopped. A few more inches and they would be touching.

"It's alright," he said lightly, drawing on his cigarette once more.

Even so she edged away. "What were you doing in America?"

"Ever heard of barnstorming?"

"No. What is it?"

"Flying an airplane rather dangerously."

Once again Thea couldn't decide if he was teasing or not.

"After the war, a pal and I ended up drifting for a while. Ended up in the good ole US of A and managed to get our hands on a military bi-plane the government had no use for. Did a bit of delivering, mainly farm parts and stuff, and then joined a flying circus."

"You can fly an airplane?"

"Yes, ma'am," Darius replied. "We used to turn up in places in the middle of nowhere and stage air shows. In some places the entire town would turn up wanting to see the stunts."

"What kind of stunts?"

"Loop-the-loop, barrel rolls. Hell, we'd even dance on the wing if it was going to earn us a buck."

Thea was astonished.

"But where did you learn to fly?"

"England. During the war."

"You were in the Flying Corps? My father used to take me to see the newsreels at the cinema. It all looked incredibly dangerous. Weren't you ever afraid?"

She sensed a withdrawal and thought perhaps she'd overstepped the mark. But after tapping the ash from his cigarette he replied evenly, "No, not really. We were just kids having fun."

"Fun?"

"Sounds crazy doesn't it. But that's what it was all about. We knew the dangers. Of course we did," and he shrugged, "but we thought we were invincible. We were kids," he repeated.

"But it was war. People died."

"We knew that. And we also knew every time we went up, there was a good chance we'd not make it back. Who knows, perhaps that's why we did it."

"To challenge the Gods of fate?"

"Something like that."

"And you won."

"You could say. Yes, we won, unlike so many others. We saw them every time we flew in low to drop our bombs. Men on the ground and in the thick of it all. Hundreds, thousands of them, like ants."

Staring up at the ceiling Darius seemed in a world of his own.

"At least we got to go home once we were done. Clean up, have a pint in the mess. Those poor buggers weren't going anywhere. Not for weeks, maybe not even months."

Drawing on his cigarette, he exhaled thoughtfully. "I guess that's why when the war ended I didn't come home. I knew I'd never settle. And if I'm honest, I'm not sure I ever will."

Thea was uncomfortable. Of the two Darius's, she preferred the brash version. At least at that moment.

And he must have sensed it, for rolling towards her he propped himself up on his elbow.

"Okay, my turn to ask a question. Tell me about you," he said.

"My life is nowhere near as interesting as yours I'm afraid. Why don't we discuss something else?"

"A woman of secrets." The words were light enough.

"Not at all."

"You're making me all the more curious."

"Then please don't be."

Her fingers were pleating the loose cotton sheet.

"How can it be helped with someone as beautiful and as enticing as you?"

Darius had taken her other hand. His thumb was caressing the base of her ring finger and the indentation left by her wedding band.

"Widow?" he said, bringing her fingers to his lips.

"No."

"Wife, then."

Thea said nothing.

"You won't be the only one, you know."

No doubt he intended to convey a sympathetic understanding, but she also heard a tinge of disappointment and for some reason that riled her.

"You know nothing about these things," she said, jerking her hand away and swinging her legs over the edge of the bed. "Nothing at all. You swan in here, have all the girls fall at your feet and think you know all about us."

Hand on her mouth she stopped, horrified at her outburst.

"Forgive me. That was completely uncalled for. Look, perhaps we should go downstairs now. I imagine we've been up here long enough to allay any suspicions."

"I do have just one more question."

"What is it?" Thea's hands were shaking as she adjusted her robe and ensured her hair was tidy.

"Do you love him?"

She closed her eyes. Her throat hurt, and she felt like crying. What right had he to ask such a personal question? What right at all?

19

KITTY MALLOY WAS GAZING DOWN over the patch-work of shingled and corrugated iron roofs towards the harbour. It was a view she enjoyed, for while parts of the city were undeniably in need of clearance - and hadn't she already investigated a number of newly created building lots for sale -the shoreline opposite was destined to be a clean and pleasant place for families. Of course there was still the belching sugar works and the wharf at which ships were regularly docking and unloading the tons of cane that came from Fiji. But behind that, on land that only a few years earlier had been native bush, trees had been felled and scrub cleared to make way for roads and houses. Progress was happening before her very eyes, and if the wind was in the right direction she could even hear hammers banging nails and pegs into timber framing.

But there was a darker side to the panorama too, at least for her, and that was catching sight of a passenger liner nudging its way out between Devonport headland and Rangitoto, the island that was, in reality, the cone of a dormant volcano. Some of those on board would be going home, and there were times she would have given up everything to be doing just that herself. But for what? Her family was scattered. A brother in England, another in America. And her sisters, all four of them married and with lives of their own. She'd been the fiery one, the passionate one. And according to her ma, the one who'd die a sinner or a saint, for there'd be no in between for her.

Well, she wasn't bound for Heaven that was for sure!

And if she did go back? Return to the streets in which she'd been born. Then what? How could she explain her circumstances, her wealth? Father O'Carroll wouldn't be fooled for a minute.

"Mary Catherine Malloy," she could hear him now, his voice harsh and booming as if he were still in the pulpit. "D'ye take me for an eejit? D'yer not think I know what yer've been doing these past years? The devil's work. That's what!"

He'd have her on her knees for the rest of eternity, repenting her sins and begging forgiveness until she was blue in the face. And that would be on top of the substantial donations she'd have to make to the Sisters of the Poor and the missions.

No, she wouldn't give him the satisfaction. She'd made her bed and that was the end of it.

"Good. You're here," Kitty had turned at the sound of kitten heels tapping across the wooden verandah. "Now tell me what's been happening in the salon lately."

"There isn't anything, Miss Kitty. At least, nothing I know about."

Pulling her long cardigan about her as if to ward off a sudden chill, Kitty folded her arms.

"Really?" she deliberately kept her voice level. "Are you sure?"

The girl was nodding emphatically. "Yes Miss Kitty."

"No gossip from our gentlemen friends?" she prompted. "No scandals? No whispers of impropriety in high places?"

"Not that I've heard."

"No business dealings that might be of interest?"

'No Miss Kitty.'

"And you would hear, wouldn't you?"

"Of course."

"And Thea. Is she behaving?"

"Thea?"

The girl's expression betrayed her confusion.

"Yes, Thea. Would you say she's settled in?"

"I suppose so, Miss Kitty. Though she still keeps to herself most of the time."

"And she's made friends?"

The girl shrugged, as if not sure what was required of her.

"Well, I want you to keep an eye on her," Kitty said, "do you understand?"

The girl nodded.

"You come to me the moment she says or does anything I should know about."

Kitty paused to allow the words to sink in and then reached into the pocket of her cardigan.

"Think of it this way. Loyalty never goes unrewarded, as you very well know."

At the appearance of the folded paper packet the girl inhaled sharply and nodded.

"So what are you going to do for me?"

"What I always do. Keep an eye on things."

Leaning back on the wooden railing Kitty nodded, pleased.

The girl's eyes flicked from her employer back to the packet.

"Not now," Kitty said abruptly, "later. When you have something for me."

The girl's eyes were huge with yearning and Kitty decided to give her one last opportunity.

"Unless you have already thought of something?"
The packet was back in her hand, held out almost.
But it seemed the girl really did have nothing to give.

20

DARIUS WAS A ROGUE, at least according to Daisy.

"Why do you say that?" Thea asked.

It was a day or two after she'd taken the gentleman in question upstairs, and with a cold rain lashing down and filling gutters and downpipes with a torrent of water, they'd elected to take breakfast - tea and toast with a scraping of Huia's infamous feijoa jam - in the warmth of their beds.

"Because 'e is," Daisy said between mouthfuls.

"Has he done something to you?"

"Nope."

"Then why say he's a rogue?"

"Like I said. 'E is."

"Then why don't you like him?"

Thea had no idea why she was being so persistent, but Daisy's criticism had rankled.

"Didn't say that."

About to take another bite, Daisy put the square of toast back onto her plate instead. "This ain't about me though, is it? It's about you."

"Me? We're not talking about me. I was merely discussing one of our customers."

"Nah yer weren't. Yer've never done that. It's like they don't exist."

"That's not the case."

"Yes it is! You shut 'em out completely. Even when yer laughing and jokin' wiv 'em it's all an act. But it looks like someone might be different."

Dispensing with the remnants of her breakfast Thea concentrated on brushing a scattering of crumbs onto the floor. "I have no idea what you're talking about."

"You can't fool me. You like 'im, don'cha?"

Now it was Daisy who was not letting the matter drop.

"You're being ridiculous. We've only met the once."

"Met? That's a funny way to describe it."

"You know what I mean. But have you ever talked to him? I mean really talked?"

"I take it yer don't mean the chit-chat before 'and?"

"No. I mean talk. As in a meaningful conversation."

"And you 'ave?"

"Well, yes."

"And 'ow was the sex?"

"That's just it. We didn't do it."

Now she had Daisy's full attention. "Yer didn't do it? Wot on erf did yer do instead?"

"That's what's I'm telling you. We talked."

There was a profound silence, and then Daisy said in a more affable tone, "Look. We're friends, right?"

"Of course."

"Then take my advice and keep away from 'im."

"That's supposing he comes here again." Thea tried to sound as if she hardly cared either way.

"Oh 'e will. 'E's back in town a while. Then 'e'll be gone again before you know it. Not one for goodbyes is our Darius. You want my opinion? If 'e asks for yer again, tell him yer already booked."

But there was little need for Thea to worry, as it appeared Darius had vanished all over again. At least, it seemed that way for a week or two.

Thea was returning to the salon after spending half an hour with a gentleman who, although agreeable enough beforehand, found an urgent and pressing need to rush away afterwards. She couldn't have cared less. In fact, she wanted to get back to her novel which, two thirds of the way in, had conjured up an extraordinary number of suspects along with a confusing array of clues, and while she thought she had the identity of the murderer down to one of two individuals, she still couldn't work out how either could be seen in one location *and* guilty of the foul deed played out in another.

With her mind elsewhere she was just one tread from the bottom of the stairs when she heard the deep bass laughter. Had it not been for her hand on the banister she would have stumbled. Instead she froze.

Sure enough, there was another rumbling laugh, as if delighted by a response, and gathering her wits she tiptoed over to the velvet curtains and pulling one aside, peered into the salon.

Glass of whiskey in one hand, the other arm resting along the back of the sofa, Darius was completely engrossed with - of all people - Daisy.

Thea's jaw dropped, and clutching her kimono about herself she raced back upstairs only to lean breathlessly on the corridor wall.

"Wotcha doin' up 'ere?" Daisy said, joining her some three or four minutes later.

"Oh Heavens, Daisy. Did he see me?"

"'Ardly. More concerned wiv 'aving another drink. Yer did look a right dumb Dora spying round them curtains," Daisy grinned.

Thea was pacing from one side of the landing to the other.

"I can't come down," she said, glancing anxiously over the banister.

"Why not?" No longer amused, Daisy had an all too knowing look on her face.

"You know why not."

"Now 'ang on a minute, I thought yer didn't care two 'oots about 'im?"

"I don't."

"So, wotcha worried about?"

"I'm not worried."

"Really? 'Cos yer could 'ave fooled me. Look at yer. Stand still for 'eavens sake. Wearing the carpet out, yer are."

"Has he…?" Thea was wringing her hands.

"'As 'e wot? Asked where yer are?" Daisy finished. She was tutting and shaking her head as if in exasperation. "As a matter of fact, he 'as."

"And what did you tell him?"

"That yer were busy."

"And what did he say to that?"

"Bloody 'ell Thea. Wot am I, yer secretary? Why don't yer just go down and see 'im?"

Thea shook her head.

"Yer've really got it bad, ain't yer? Well, you can't 'ide up 'ere all night. Yer'll 'ave to make an appearance soon."

"Not if I'm unwell."

"Unwell? Yer unwell all right! Up 'ere." Daisy tapped the side of her head.

"You're not being very sympathetic."

"Wot do you expect?"

"A lot more from you. We're supposed to be friends." Thea had resumed her pacing. What if Darius came looking for Daisy? What if he came upstairs?

"We're friends. And yer right, I should be sympathetic, especially under the circumstances."

"What circumstances?"

"Yer 'aving a sheltered upbringin'."

"Oh for goodness sake, I didn't have a sheltered upbringing. It was perfectly normal."

"'Ow many boyfriends did yer 'ave before yer got married then?"

"You know how many, Daisy. None," Thea retorted.

"Exactly. See, if yer was more worldly yer wouldn't be making such a fuss. Yer'd be calm and collected and know 'ow to handle the situation. Like I would."

"You're not helping matters."

Daisy shrugged good-naturedly, and then sidled to the mirror over the walnut hall table. "Eivver way, yer just 'ave to go down," she said, peering critically at her reflection. "It'll be okay."

"You couldn't make an excuse for me?" Thea's voice rose hopefully.

"And wot yer gonna do next time? Or the time after?"

Thea knew Daisy was right, and sighed.

Then she straightened her shoulders.

"Good girl," Daisy's reflection nodded approvingly. "Take anovver couple of minutes. Sort yerself out. I told 'im you might be a while, but 'e said 'e was happy to wait." She adjusted a platinum blonde wave. "Look, fink about it this way. 'E's 'ere for one thing, and one thing only. Sex. Not you in particular but you'll do. Get it? You'll do. That's all it is. No romance, no 'earts and flowers. So just go down and get it over wiv."

Thea was beginning to feel extremely foolish.

"I have no idea what has gotten into me. What was it you said on my very first day? A bloke's a bloke, and a cock's a cock?"

"You got it," Daisy said approvingly. She was holding out her elbow. "Now, com'on milady, let's go and make an entrance."

21

THEA'S COMPOSURE WAS VERY NEARLY lost when she and Daisy entered the salon, for right at that very moment Darius looked up, and as his eyes widened in delight she would have almost believed he was pleased to see her. Appreciating Daisy's reassuring squeeze as she let go of her arm, she smiled and greeted him with all the grace she could muster.

"It's good to see you again."

Having risen from the sofa, Darius took her fingers and held them to his lips. But the gesture which seemed all too acceptable to the others, was a little too over the top for her, and she gently but firmly retrieved her hand.

"May I get you another drink?" she said, looking pointedly at his empty tumbler.

"Thank you. But I'm afraid you are a little late for that."

Following his gaze Thea glanced over her shoulder. Nelly was walking towards them with a fresh drink in her hand and realising the significance, she stepped back.

"Ah, I see. Then perhaps you will excuse me?"

"It's not like that Thea." Nelly did not look particularly happy as she handed over the whiskey. "He's waiting for you."

Given she might have been hoping to receive his token Thea wasn't surprised when the girl flounced off. She would have done exactly the same under the circumstances.

"You shouldn't tease people," she said quietly.

"You're right, and I'm sorry. Believe it or not, it wasn't intentional." He gestured to the sofa and waited for her to sit down. "We seem to have gotten off on the wrong foot again, haven't we?"

A crestfallen Nelly had found a spare seat on the other side of the room.

"I would have come back sooner but I had business in Australia," he said, crossing one leg over the other, "not that my being there made much difference in the end. But it did give me the opportunity to catch up on other things."

Thea nodded politely but her mind was elsewhere. That he had waited for her to finish with her customer meant this time he would expect more for his token than simple conversation. He would probably want the full works, and she wondered how long it would be before his hand was resting on her knee, or he'd lean back to caress her neck in the overly familiar manner she had come to expect. Hopefully not too long, as then she could suggest they went upstairs, and with luck the whole ordeal would be over in less than an hour.

"You have business interests over there?" she asked quickly, remembering her duty as a hostess.

"A large sheep station in Gippsland. Not that I have anything to do with the day-to-day running of it. Belongs to the pal I was in the States with. He's from Victoria and when he told me he wanted to come back and buy the station but was a little short of the asking price, I threw my share of the plane behind him."

"And is it a good investment?"

"Depends on how you look at it. Long term it will be."

"And your friend is happy?"

"Very. Got a wife and kiddy now."

"So what do you do to pass the time now you're no longer flying?"

"I have other interests," he smiled. "I haven't given up the dangerous stuff altogether. I can't. I think it's in my blood."

"Dangerous stuff?"

"I race cars when I can."

"Around a race track?"

"Yes."

As before, she tried hard not to be impressed. "A daredevil then."

Darius smiled.

"And do you own a race car?"

Pander to their egos, Daisy had advised early on. Works wonders. Most men love building themselves up, especially in front of a woman.

Darius would be no different.

"Not exactly. I drive someone else's."

"Where? Here in Auckland?"

"No. In England."

"Now I'm confused," she couldn't help herself. "If you have business interests in Australia and race cars in England, on which side of the world do you actually live?"

"You could say I'm a nomad. But I think your real question is why am I in Auckland?"

The blood rushed to her cheeks, but Darius didn't seem to notice.

"My family owns a large spread down in the Waikato, though my father died a couple of years ago.

By rights the property should have gone to my elder brother. But he was killed in the war."

The number of New Zealander's who'd gone to fight for the Empire was huge, over forty percent of men of military age. Even so, six years later there were still no social guidelines around such conversations.

"France?" she asked tentatively.

"No. Gallipoli. Towards the end of fifteen." He took a good slug of whiskey. "And that means there are certain things that fall to me now. Legal and financial issues mainly."

There was no enthusiasm in his voice as he leaned forward, cradling the glass in his hands.

"Do you have to come back often?"

"No, thank God."

"So what is it you don't like? New Zealand? Or coming home?"

"Both, I guess. This country is too small for me, and home? Well, it's no longer the same."

He was glancing around and Thea guessed their conversation had become a little too personal for comfort.

"Do you want to go upstairs?" she asked quietly.

"Why not," he said, relief etched on his features.

There was no resistance when she took his half-empty glass and after placing it on the dressing table, slipped her arms around his neck. The gesture was impulsive and surprised her as much as him. But then his arms were around her, and closing her eyes she lost herself in the pleasure of feeling safe and of being protected and treasured.

The fleeting touch of his lips brought her back to her senses.

"I'm sorry," she said, pulling away, "I shouldn't have done that."

"I disagree." Although he'd loosened his hold, Darius's arms remained firmly around her. "There is nothing wrong with two people sharing a moment of affection. In fact," and he drew her back so that her head rested once more on his chest, "I rather enjoyed it."

Thea was grateful he couldn't see her blushes.

"I have a thought," he mused, his head on hers, "and one that might make you feel more comfortable. Why don't we pretend none of this is real? Not you. Not me. Not this place."

She didn't need telling that he meant the garish furnishings and the erotic images hanging on the walls.

"Let's step away for a while and see what happens," he continued.

"It's a lovely idea."

'Then let's do it. Keep your eyes closed," he said.

As his arms tightened around her she lost herself in the rising and falling of his chest and in the sound of his breathing.

"I want to kiss you," he said quietly, "Properly."

It was an intimacy rarely allowed in the bordello and never, until that moment, by her.

"Perhaps just the once," she said shyly, tilting up her face.

His lips explored hers in a way that was knowing and yet hesitant until, with a soft groan, he took full ownership of her mouth. The sensation of breathing as one was new to her, and with her knees weakening she clung to him, wondering why in all her life she'd never experienced such delights before. She and Silas had never exchanged kisses, not once, not even on their wedding day and she'd thought nothing of it. Now she was pleased, for it would never have been like this, and caring little that Darius might be shocked by such forwardness, she lifted herself onto her toes and clasped her hands behind his neck.

But it seemed she had little to worry about, for his arms had tightened even more, and now his tongue was gently probing hers.

"I'm not sure…" she stumbled, having finally pulled away - not because she wanted to, but because she needed to catch her breath. "We shouldn't have done that."

"Why? Don't tell me you didn't enjoy it, because I know you did."

"That's not the point."

"Then what is it?"

"Please. You're confusing me."

He held up both hands as if in surrender. "You know, you don't have to do this if you don't want to."

And that was the problem. She did want to. Very much!

"If you'd rather," he was saying, "we could simply pick up where we finished last time, and just talk."

His expression was reassuringly earnest.

"But you're not here for that, are you?" she was searching his eyes.

"Truthfully? No. But if that's what you want, then it's fine by me."

This time he removed only his shoes, his jacket and his double-breasted waistcoat before climbing onto the bed. Thea lay beside him, though as before ensuring there was a small distance between them, and for a while both stared up at the ornate plaster rose in the middle of the ceiling.

She felt an unexpected urge to giggle.

"I have an idea. Call it radical if you will," he said at last, turning towards her, "but if you move a little closer I could put my arm around you. Nothing more, I promise."

"Under any other circumstances I would think you a bounder," her lips were twitching, "but I see no reason to doubt the word of a gentleman."

As she nestled on his chest, her hand found itself in close proximity to the buttons on his shirt. How tempting to let her fingers slip between them and discover the soft cotton of his singlet. He even smelled delicious; a combination of pine and maleness, and with her senses in overload she thought she could have stayed that way all night. Especially with him placing the very lightest of kisses on her hair. Perhaps that was why she had no misgivings about lifting herself over him and lowering her lips to his once more.

His response was immediate and enthusiastic, and while at first he seemed happy for her to continue her exploration of his mouth, she soon found herself flipped onto her back, and it was his turn to look down on her.

"Woman," he growled, "how can I keep my promise when you tempt me in such a way."

Then he was nibbling on the lobe of her ear.

"If you want me to stop you must say so."

His voice was low and urgent, and a tremor ran through her. She had no doubt he would do just that if she insisted. But what harm would there be in allowing such wonderful pleasures to continue a little longer.

His hand found her breast, his touch feather light. It was as if he needed her tacit approval, and she pulled his head down to her again.

"Touch me," she begged.

His breath quickened even more at her moan.

"Stop me if you must, but please, do it now. If you don't my promise will mean nothing."

"Then I relieve you of your promise."

"Oh God," he managed, since her fingers were already working the buttons of his shirt.

Untying the ribbons of her camisole his lips were playing at the hollow of her neck. Then having parted the fabric he lowered his mouth further. Now it was her turn to gasp as his tongue and his teeth toyed with her. She was on fire, burning up with fever, and taking his hand she placed it on her lower belly, knowing what she needed, but not knowing how to tell him. When his hand cupped her mound and his middle finger pressed onto that most sensitive of places, she moaned in relief.

"Slowly," he murmured, "let me guide you."

Her emotions were raw and she felt like crying. "I've never felt anything like this before."

"I know."

It was truly wondrous. And even more so when having helped her from her camisole, he covered her nakedness in kisses.

"Please," she begged, over and over.

And then he was lying over her and taking her into a world where nothing else mattered.

22

SHE TRULY WAS A FALLEN woman, and with her head on Darius's chest and her cheek against his sweat-dampened flesh, Thea considered the scandal, the disgrace. Yet when she tried on the cloak of shame for size, she found it wanting because somehow she couldn't summon up enough regret. How could something so wonderful be at the same time so terrible?

Darius was idly running his hand over her back.

"What are you thinking about?" he wanted to know. His voice was lazy. Sleepy even.

"Nothing."

He nodded, as if he too lacked the energy to disclose his thoughts.

"So what will you do now?"

She considered the words. Heard them, and analysed them one by one. Somehow she knew he wasn't referring to rest of the evening. But his use of the singular *you* had hit her. Shouldn't he have said *we*? Or was it his way of telling her he did not feel as she did; that something of immense importance had just occurred? From his question it appeared to be so. In fact, it implied he was already distancing himself from her, and she suddenly felt as if she was tumbling into a dark and frightening void.

She had to remain calm. Put things in to perspective. Perhaps it was true what the other girls said, that men considered the act as little more than servicing a physical need. And shouldn't they know, after all, weren't they the experts? But if that were the case, then how did women cope, since she couldn't be the only one who'd allowed her emotions to get the better of her? And God, did it hurt. It was as if her insides were being wrung dry.

But there was no need for him to know that. No need for her to say that she couldn't possibly return to the salon that evening. Nor to explain that once he'd gone and she'd tidied the room, she'd go in search of Belle and plead a headache. For all she wanted right at that moment was to be tucked up in her own bed where she could cry all night until she'd exhausted herself. Daisy was right. Darius was a womanising cad and she'd been stupid to think she might be in any way different from any of the other girls he bedded.

The rogue's arm tightened about her.

"That was amazing," he murmured.

Of course he would say that, she thought bitterly. It was probably his stock phrase and one of the many meaningless compliments he offered before bidding adieu and moving on to his next conquest. Well, she would show him she could be just as blasé about the whole thing.

"I'm glad you think so. We like to give value here," she said, trying to make it sound as if it were all in a day's work.

His hand had stopped moving.

"I see," he said quietly.

To her horror her throat constricted. She tried to swallow, tried to contain the sob, but the sound that emerged was a strangled choking.

"Thea, what is it?" He moved, rolled a little to one side and held her cheek, forcing her to look up at him. "What's wrong?"

"Nothing," her voice shook.

"Of course there is. Is it me? Did I hurt you when I...? Oh God, Thea, I'm so sorry. I should have taken it slower. Shouldn't have gotten so carried away. But I couldn't help it. It'll be better next time, I promise."

The words filtered through her pain.

Next time? There would be a next time? This wasn't to be a solitary occasion?

Relief soared through her.

"I'm sorry. I'm being stupid," she hiccuped, smearing away a tear. Her carefully applied mascara would be ruined and she must look a mess. "I'm not usually this emotional. I've no idea what triggered it."

"Well, I like it." Easing back he looked down on her and smiled. "In fact, I like it a lot."

"Then you'd be one of the few men who do. Most would run a mile."

"I'm not most men," he said softly, peeling a strand of hair from her cheek and tucking it behind her ear.

"No," and she snuggled back against him, glad to have his arms tight around her once more.

"Do we have time to stay here a little longer?" he asked softly.

She nodded.

"Then let's make the most of it. I'm going to hold you until you fall asleep."

"I don't think that would be a good idea," she said weakly.

"I do," he assured her.

"Meet me the day after tomorrow," he said, pulling her into his arms.

"Meet you?"

Having got up and dressed - wistfully on her part - they were on the point of leaving the room.

"Yes. Let me take you somewhere special."

He looked around as if thinking hard.

"I know. The Grand Hotel," he said, naming the most prestigious hotel in all of Auckland. "We'll take afternoon tea. Would you like that? And if it's not too cold we could stroll in the park beforehand."

"Oh."

She had never in all her life been on a date, and surely that's what he was suggesting. Her heart raced. Should she go? She was a married woman after all.

Though hadn't she been abandoned?

And besides, who'd know?

She took a minute to calm her excitement.

"That would be marvelous."

"Good. What time would you like me to pick you up?"

"Heavens don't do that! We'll have every tongue in the place wagging?" she laughed. "I'll get the tram."

"I'll be waiting."

And his lips descended on hers once more.

23

DARIUS HATED NEW ZEALAND. Hated its remoteness and small town mentality. It was a backwater awash with colonial pride and though he'd only been back a matter of weeks he was already yearning for the vitality of Los Angeles. Or the excitement of London. Or the glamour of Paris. Places where hedonism and opulence were the order of the day. Thank God it wouldn't be too much longer before he was flush again and back amongst his own kind.

Hands in his pockets and leaning against the neo-classical façade of the woollen company's offices on Princes Street, he was in high spirits, and not just because of the cash advance he'd successfully negotiated from the sale of a couple of decent blocks of grazing land he'd managed to persuade his mother to carve off.

It was Thea of course. He hadn't met a woman like her in a long time. And to find her in a place like Kitty Malloy's was even more astonishing. It had been obvious from the start she was different to the other girls, although if he were honest it was curiosity more than anything else that had led to his asking her out. Of course, he could be wrong, and if that was the case and she was no more or less than a whore, then he had lost nothing. But one thing puzzled him. She had admitted to being married, so where did her husband fit in? Surely he wouldn't agree to his wife meeting a customer for a stroll in the park, let alone afternoon tea in one of Auckland's finest hotels. Unless it was a set up? But why? It made no sense. And not only that, she didn't seem the type to be involved in anything underhand. But when had he ever run from such dealings anyway? He could handle himself, he'd done it before. Not that he went out looking for trouble. Well, not exactly. But it wouldn't be the first time he'd had to face up to an irate husband.

He glanced at his wristwatch - a gift of course, though it was a long while since he'd last seen that particular lady. He'd been watching the trams pulling up and disgorging passengers for some time and Thea was late. Not by much. Only some five minutes.

Perhaps she'd changed her mind and wasn't coming.

He felt a pang of disappointment but decided he would wait a little longer. Until a quarter past the hour. If she wasn't going to turn up…

And then he was pulling himself up and exhaling slowly.

He had the impression that she'd deliberately remained at a distance, as if challenging him to see her in a different light. She was beautiful. But more than that, she was elegance personified. Her cranberry red coat must have been made from the finest wool for it had a lustrous finish, as did the matching close fitting hat. Dashing across the road and weaving around a passing motorcar, he was thinking how he'd been playing out this very moment all morning, seeing himself taking her into his arms and sharing a kiss in full view of everyone.

Now he knew that wouldn't do at all, and if the truth be known he was a little uncertain.

"I'm glad you came," he said, arriving on the pavement in front of her.

"I'm not late, am I?"

"Not at all. Shall we walk?" he said, holding out his elbow.

He thought she looked a little different and put it down to the more sparing use of cosmetics. The lack of overdone powder and paint made her look younger somehow. Vulnerable even.

"The weather seems to have held for us," he said, guiding her over to the park entrance. "Are you warm enough?"

"Yes. I love days like this. It's as though nature is having one last fling before painting everything gray."

"Very poetical," he teased and was pleased when she gave his arm a playful tap.

"If this is what you are going to be like, it will be a very short afternoon."

"Point taken," he couldn't help grinning, "but I have to say that whilst there is something delightful about sitting in front of a roaring fire, I would far rather be in a warmer climate altogether."

"You don't like the cold?"

"Not particularly."

"Then we should not expect to see you for a while. Everyone will be disappointed."

"I doubt that."

"Oh, I'm not so sure. You caused quite a stir when you first turned up."

"You noticed?"

"How could I not? The place became one big party that night."

"It did rather. Yet you didn't join in."

"No. I could see you had more than enough on your plate already."

"Ahh."

They walked on. Fallen leaves, damp and decomposing, muffled the sound of their footsteps and it wasn't long before the bare and skeletal branches and the park's empty flowerbeds bought forth a sigh from Thea.

"Where will you go in your quest for the sun?" she asked.

"Back to England I expect."

"Ahh, an endless summer. Enjoy the first in the southern hemisphere and then journey north for the second. That has to be the perfect solution."

"You would think so, wouldn't you?"

"Although we could hibernate instead."

"Crawl into our dens and sleep through until spring?"

"Something like that. At least we'd be safe and warm."

There was something in her voice that hinted at more to her comment than met the eye.

"Don't forget, animals also burrow away from danger," he said carefully, wondering if he could draw out whatever was on her mind.

"They do don't they. They seem to know when trouble is around the corner."

"It's a very useful second sense."

"And unfortunately not one possessed by the majority of humans."

"Are you speaking from experience?" he queried gently.

Her shoulders slumped a little.

"No. I was just thinking aloud."

Commanding an exceptional view of the Waitamata Harbour and Hauraki Gulf, and with its vaulted ceilings and marble statuary, the Grand Hotel was fashionably popular, and seated at a table close enough to the ornate fireplace to enjoy its warmth, Thea removed her coat. Her crepe de chine dress, with its metal beading and braids of ribbon barely skimmed her knees, as was all the rage and had cost her a small fortune. In fact the entire get-up was an out-and-out act of rebellion, since it was hardly suitable for Kitty's, and while intended as a statement of her independence, it had unfortunately meant another loan.

But certain things couldn't be helped. Especially on occasions like this when she so desperately wanted to impress.

She glanced around at the other tables. Elderly ladies with erect backs and old-fashioned manners were conversing quietly, and a father was attempting to quell the excitement of his children by glaring sternly at his wife. Further over by a window a trio of women were chatting enthusiastically, the number of department store carrier bags at their feet indicating that perhaps they were from out of town otherwise their purchases would have been delivered.

This was not the first time she'd taken tea at this hotel.

"My father brought my mother and me here," she said, as if to explain her wandering thoughts. "He wanted us to celebrate the end of the war."

Darius had raised an inquiring eyebrow, so she hurriedly continued. "By then he was becoming uneasy with the toll it was taking on the country. Both in terms of human sacrifice and the financial cost."

"Do you see your parents often?"

"No. Sadly, they are both dead."

Darius had looked a little shocked at that.

"The 'flu' epidemic," she explained.

"Both of them? You must have been very young."

"Are you trying to flatter me?" she said with a smile.

"Not at all. But it must have been a traumatic time."

"It was."

"My parents brought us here too," he offered as the tea trolley arrived and a smartly clad waitress placed a silver teapot and jug in the middle of the table. "Not that we came up to Auckland often. But when we did my mother would insist on certain social niceties. High tea being one of them."

"Does she still visit?"

"No. She hasn't really left the farm in years."

"That's a shame. But then perhaps you do enough venturing for both of you," she said with a smile.

"You're probably right."

"What about your father?"

"He never really got over my brother's death."

It would seem they were equally burdened by the past.

Having poured tea for both of them and passed over the fine china cup and saucer, Thea was enjoying the unexpected intimacy when the young waitress returned, and with a polite *excuse me* began creating space on the table for their three tier cake stand. As she did so, Thea couldn't help noticing the surreptitious and somewhat admiring glances sent in Darius's direction.

"So why did you leave New Zealand?" Thea asked, when finally satisfied with the positioning of everything, and having given Darius what could only be construed as a very encouraging smile, the waitress left them alone once more.

"Well," he paused, as if he needed to arrange his answer into some sort of order, "it was something I wanted to do. Always did, even from an early age. I was seventeen when I worked my passage to Liverpool."

"Gosh! And what did you do in England?"

"A bit of everything really. Made my way down to London and ended up with a bunch of other colonials in Earls Court. We turned our hands to whatever needed doing. Working in restaurants, labouring on the new underground line. And then war broke out and everything stopped."

"And then what?"

"I signed up." He shrugged as if to say, what did you expect?

She nodded.

"And who cares for the farm if you're off roaming the world?"

"My brother-in-law. And he's very good at it too. Even my mother has to admit that. Thanks to him the place has gone from strength to strength."

"She must miss you though?"

'I've no doubt she does. But it would also be fair to say the death of my brother has left the biggest gap in her life."

Thea was about to protest.

"Don't get me wrong, I'm not after sympathy. He was her first born and he loved the farm. Knew every inch like the back of his hand. And he had plans for it. Wanted to expand."

Thea sensed Darius was talking as much for his own sake as hers.

"He even discussed buying the block next door and clearing the bush. Hundreds of acres of back breaking work, but you know what? He would have done it and not thought twice. Whereas me? Well, can you see me in a pair of gumboots?"

The mere thought had her lips twitching.

"I just don't want the same things," Darius finished. "But it's not only that. I want to move forward. Break new ground, so to speak. Try new things."

"But it sounds as if your brother-in-law is capable of looking after the place for you."

"He is. My sister is lucky."

"And do you have nieces and nephews?"

"Yes. Well, nephews at least. Three of them."

"Well, that's a blessing. And what of your brother? Was he married?"

"No. There was a girl. Someone he met on the troopship to Egypt. She was a nurse."

Thea wondered just how much his brother's untimely death had contributed to Darius's lifestyle.

"And you," she smiled playfully, "what about you? No wife on foreign shores?"

"No," he said firmly.

"Hmm. No fiancée pining for you anywhere?"

"No," he repeated.

"Just a bevy of girlfriends then."

"I wouldn't even say that."

"You surely don't expect me to believe you?"

"Of course. Why wouldn't you?"

His eyes, dark, velvety, and oh so seductive were drawing her in, and her stomach flipped.

"Are you fishing for compliments?" she managed, trying to restore a little equilibrium.

"Only if they are justified."

"In that case, you had better give me a minute to think of one."

"Are you saying nothing immediately comes to mind?"

He was wearing a comical expression of utter disbelief, and playing along Thea gave the impression she was thinking.

"Hmm. Sorry. Nothing at all."

"Now you disappoint me."

"I somehow thought it might."

She couldn't believe how much she was enjoying herself. But having tilted his head, Darius was unexpectedly frowning.

"Ah ha! I knew there was something different about you," he said triumphantly. "Turn your head."

She did.

"Your hair. You've cut it off."

"I'm surprised you can tell under this hat."

"I couldn't at first. What made you do it? I would have said your hair was your crowning glory."

Without thinking Thea lifted a hand to the back of her neck. It was taking a while to get used to the sense of weightlessness, but Maurice the stylist had been fulsome in his praise of her decision, exclaiming how fabulously the jaw length cut drew attention to her beautiful eyes.

"I thought it was time for a change," she said, a little overwhelmed by the attention.

"It suits you," Darius reassured her. "So," and he reached to the cake stand for a pastry, "tell me about your husband."

"There's nothing to tell."

"Really?"

"Perhaps I'd rather not talk about it."

"I do understand that, but you don't think I have a right to ask? After all I am having tea with his very beautiful wife."

Thea had straightened. Up until that moment, she'd been having such a lovely time.

"I don't want the details," he said casually, "just what you are able to tell me. And if you really can't tell me anything, then we'll forget all about it."

"He's in Europe," she said, her tone curt, "on business. London, Paris, Berlin…" and then she stopped, realising her words were fuelling his curiosity rather than satisfying it. "He'll be back in November."

Darius waited.

"Isn't that enough for you?" she said.

"He knows what you're doing?"

"Oh yes."

Around her, the genteel rattle of teacups continued unabated.

This should have been her life. This elegant ritual of taking tea with friends and engaging in social gossip and other pleasantries. And more. Of being involved with charitable events and the arts, and receiving elegant invitations in the post to view newly arrived fashions, or to request her attendance at soirees and other gatherings.

This was the future she'd expected when she'd married Silas. Instead, and by his doing, she was entertaining men in a bawdy house.

"I see," Darius was saying, "and when your husband returns, will you be leaving Kitty's?"

She was shocked he would think otherwise.

"Of course. Why wouldn't I?"

What else could she possibly do, she had nowhere else to go. But the words wouldn't come, and for a long moment they simply stared at each other. Then he reached over and gently laid his hand over hers.

"You do have other options."

Incensed he could think things were really that simple, she pulled away.

"Do I? Like what? I'm a married woman."

"But you're not a prisoner."

"What would you know?"

"Very little it would seem. But divorce doesn't carry quite the same stigma these days. Not if handled in a discreet and sensible manner."

She shook her head scornfully. "You really think it's as simple a matter as placing an announcement in the London Gazette?"

"No I don't think that."

Glancing around in the hope their exchange had not attracted any undue attention, Thea pressed her lips tightly together. "Let's not talk about it anymore."

"Whatever you want," and leaning an elbow onto the table he reached for her hand. "Will you come out with me again?"

She shook her head in exasperation. Didn't he realise that bringing Silas into their time together had spoilt everything.

"What would be the point?"

"There's every point. It would please me for one thing."

When she remained silent he tried again.

"Perhaps if you consider I'll be gone abroad soon. Would that make a difference?"

She shook her head again, as much in frustration at his insistence as anything else.

"What are you frightened of?"

"I'm being sensible."

"Then don't. It's a very overrated trait."

"I can see you would think that way."

But deep down she was wavering. Didn't she deserve a little happiness?

"Well, perhaps," she said hesitantly.

"Good girl. I'll take a *perhaps* over a *no* from you any day."

Despite everything, she found herself smiling. "Flatterer!"

"You can tell?"

"You're accomplished."

"And yet you've agreed to see me again? I can't be all bad then."

"I haven't agreed yet. But if I do, I don't want anyone else to know."

"Ouch!"

"It's not that I'm embarrassed or ashamed. I'd just rather it was between us," Thea tried to shrug it off but her expression was pleading. "You know how gossip can spread."

"I do. And I completely understand. We'll keep it quiet."

24

DRESSING FOR THE SALON THAT evening, Thea was all over the place. So much so that eventually Daisy threw the two garments she'd been deliberating over onto her bed and faced her.

"Wot's wrong wiv yer?" she wanted to know. "And where was yer this afternoon."

"I went out for a walk," Thea said irritably, pulling open a drawer and foraging amongst the cosmetics and other bits and pieces.

"Not like you."

"If you must know, I was feeling under the weather and thought some exercise would do me good."

"And did it?"

"Strangely enough it did. I'm actually feeling very restored."

There was no let up to the rummaging, nor did Thea look up from the task.

"Glad to 'ear it. And did'ya wear yer new dress and coat by any chance?"

Thankfully her fingertips touched on the missing tin of kohl.

"Why do you ask?" she said, trying to sound as if it were of little importance.

"'Cos it wasn't 'anging in the wardrobe earlier."

"Oh. Well, yes. Actually I did. All part of lifting my spirits." And leaning close to the mirror she carefully applied a thin black line close to her bottom eyelashes.

"That's okay then. I was worried someone might 'ave borrowed it wivout asking. Gotta look after yer finks around 'ere. Bunch of tea leaves 'alf of 'em."

Having made her decision on what to wear, Daisy was perched on the edge of her bed, rolling a stocking over her foot when she let out a profanity.

"Bugger. Got a bloody ladder. Do me a favour? Lend me a pair of yours."

Concentrating on creating a perfect outward sweep from the corner of each eye, it was a moment before Thea pulled open another drawer.

"Got a new girl starting tonight," Daisy offered, fingering and admiring the fineness of the silk she'd been tossed, "at least according to Nora."

"Oh? Live in or out?"

There were a handful of girls who came and went each day. Like Nancy, who according to gossip, was working to keep her husband out of prison. Apparently he'd been caught with his hand in the till.

"In. Got the sack from a big house over in Remue-ra, so Nora says. Probably puttin' out for the Big Cheese and the missus caught 'er."

"Daisy," Thea admonished, scrutinising her reflection in the mirror. "You know that might not be true."

"Either way, she's one of us now."

One of us.

Thea studied her pale complexion and rouged cheeks, her charcoal eyelids and the perfect arch of her heavily thinned eyebrows, and the fashionably bobbed hair and turquoise and enamel earrings hanging from her lobes. For one long moment she didn't recognise the woman staring back.

But Daisy was wrong. The new girl might be *one of us*, but *us* didn't include her. She was different, for in a little over two months she would be back at home and all this would be behind her. No more Miss Kitty, no more tokens. This wasn't her life, unlike those poor unfortunates who had no other options.

Or was she fooling herself? Was it truly possible to wipe away such an awful experience, or would it remain just beyond the periphery of her consciousness, waiting for the right moment to reassert itself? She certainly wasn't the same person who'd arrived back at the end of June that was for sure. And not just outwardly either. She'd changed inwardly too. But when had it happened? Was it when she'd had her first customer? Or the day she'd made a stand and cut off her hair?

Or was it when she realised how much she appreciated good friends like Daisy.

Settling in her usual corner in the salon she found she couldn't relax, and finding herself re-reading the same lines of her book for the third time, she decided to give up altogether and get herself a drink.

Violet, the new girl seemed ordinary enough. Not particularly pretty, in fact she was rather thin though her legs were quite splendid. Long and shapely, as if she once might have been a dancer. Mixing the ingredients for her cocktail Thea glanced over to where she was chatting with Nelly, thinking that if she kept up that condescending tone she would find it hard to make friends. As if Nelly needed any help with men. She might not be the bordello's star attraction but with her easy-going and accommodating nature she was highly popular. Perhaps Violet didn't know that appearances could be deceiving? But an hour or so later when the place had begun to liven up it seemed the girl was no longer content to merely offer advice to anyone willing to listen, she had practically taken over the floor, although looking around it was obvious the others were completely ignoring her. To Thea's shame even she was waiting for Belle to put in an appearance and cut the newcomer down to size.

Then in walked the very last person she expected to see and before anyone could react Violet had swanned over and daringly placed a finger on his tie. Her smile was dazzling.

"Well, hello honey!"

"Hello yourself," Darius offered his own hundred-watt grin.

Thea didn't know whether to be pleased or not at his arrival. Hadn't they agreed that if they were to have any chance at keeping their friendship secret he should perhaps stay away for a while?

Violet was pulling out all the stops.

"Welcome to Kitty's." Her voice was deliberately low and sultry and her hand had moved an inch or so to finger the narrow lapel of his jacket.

Everyone was staring and Thea was fuming. Didn't the girl know better than to act this way on her first night? There was after all, a hierarchy.

More to the point, why did it have to be Darius on the receiving end of her charms? Why couldn't it have been someone else?

"You're new here," he was saying, one hand casually in a trouser pocket.

The other girls listened with bated breath.

"Yes, I am. New and exciting."

Tilting her head Violet was gazing up at him with what Daisy would describe as a *come-hither* look, and which Thea would have said was so completely contrived that anyone with half a brain would have recognised it as such.

"It's very nice to meet you." And in the manner she had come to expect, he lifted Violet's fingers to his lips while she simpered and glanced around as if to say '*see, this is how it's done*'.

If Thea was cross before, now she was furious. Why was he playing up to her? She was hardly his type - if he had one, that is. Plainly, any girl would do.

And then, with a courteous nod, he edged around the girl - who was visibly taken aback - and turning to the room said, "Good evening ladies, is anyone going to offer me a drink?"

He didn't have to ask twice, and stealing a glancing in Thea's direction, he flashed his eyes wickedly.

She shook her head, as much with exasperation as anything else. If he carried on like that he'd ruin everything, though it seemed he was undeterred.

"Well now," he said, reaching for the proffered whisky and allowing Nancy to draw him towards a sofa, "isn't this nice."

Clearly unimpressed at being rejected, and so publicly at that, Violet came over and dropped beside Thea.

"Wow, he's really up himself. Who is he anyway?" she said.

"Darius. He's very popular here."

"So I see."

"You know," Thea said, watching Nancy and Darius from the corner of her eye, "I understand you want to get right into the swing of things, but you'd do better to start out by getting to know everyone first. Make friends, and settle in slowly."

"Settle in? You think I'm going to hang around? I'm only here to get a bit of money behind me and then I'm off."

"Then you're going to find it very hard."

With a withering look the girl got up. "We'll see."

"She all right?" Daisy said, taking the newly vacated seat - having just arrived in the salon she'd completely missed all the fun.

"She will be. Not sure about your theory she was in service though. I think she's done this sort of thing before. Anyway," leaning on the arm of her chair she asked, "where have you been?"

"Kitty wanted to see me."

"Oh? What about?"

"Nuffink much. I see golden boy is back."

Thea found herself blushing. "And your claws are showing."

"Well, look at 'im. Like a fox in an 'en 'ouse, 'e is."

"He is rather."

"'E won't change, y'know."

"You can never be sure Daisy, you can never be sure."

"Oh Lawd, you 'ave got it bad. Reckon yer gonna be the one to put 'im on the straight and narrow, do yer? 'Ave 'im settle down? Kiddies and all that?" Daisy was shaking her head. "Well, don't say I didn't warn yer."

25

"MAY I DISTURB YOU?"

Darius was gesturing with his glass at the empty place beside her, and with a polite smile Thea closed her book for the second time that evening.

"Of course," she replied evenly. "You've just missed Daisy."

"I know. I thought I'd wait until you were alone."

"It's always nice to see you here," she said, conscious of others within earshot.

"And I enjoy being here."

"Perhaps because the girls spoil you."

"That does have its attractions I must admit."

"I thought," she continued quietly, intending the words for him alone, "we agreed you would not be coming here for a few days."

"We did. But I found myself having a quiet drink in the city and wondering what you were up to."

"As if I would be getting up to anything."

"Well, you might. Heaven knows what goes on here when I'm not around."

"Let me tell you, when you're not here, the place is a darn sight quieter."

"Good," he looked around once more, and then leaned in, "I miss you. Let's go upstairs."

"How could you miss me," she whispered back. "We only left each other a few hours ago."

"Exactly. And even that's far too long for a red-blooded man like me."

Thea lowered her head to hide a smile. For some reason, his words had caused a little thrill of pleasure.

"You're lucky I'm not already otherwise engaged," she said coyly.

"It did cross my mind you might be."

"And then what would you have done?"

Darius tilted his head thoughtfully.

"I guess I'd have picked another girl."

She took a sharp breath, but one look at his face told her he was ribbing her - and enjoying doing so.

"You're incorrigible."

"Is that your way of saying I'm irresistible?"

"Not at all."

But she blushed nonetheless.

"This is sheer madness."

They'd hardly made it to the room before she was in his arms and pressed up against the door. Now she was coming up for air after a kiss that seemed to go on forever.

"Isn't it?" Darius breathed, nibbling little kisses onto her neck.

He was easing the delicate ribbons of her chemise from her shoulders and after working open the front, slipped his hand over her breast. "Oh my God, you're so lovely. I can't believe what you're doing to me."

Drowning in a deliciously heady passion Thea could do nothing other than groan.

"Do you want me to stop?" he murmured, though it was hardly a question and she was already shaking her head.

"No."

Held in place by his weight it was all she could do to get the word out. Her fingers were tangled in his hair. She wanted his mouth, his lips, his tongue. She wanted his hands on her body, claiming it for himself, roughly and without care as to her feelings. She wanted him to demand things of her. Things that would shame her.

She had to be punished for feeling as she did. For she was on fire. Every nerve ending was alive. Her head went back and she closed her eyes, yearning for the sheer pleasure of it all.

"Oh yes," she breathed. "Oh yes."

And then his mouth was on hers again. Hard and demanding and she was moaning like the wanton creature she was.

She couldn't think, couldn't make sense of anything anymore. Her body was making its own demands and she was losing her mind, her sanity. Nothing else mattered, only her unrelenting need, and taking his hand she forced it down so that his fingers were splayed over her mound.

"Please," she begged.

His breathing was ragged, his tongue meshing with hers.

Then his mouth was hot against her ear.

"Tell me what you want."

"You. I want you."

She was beyond caring.

"Tell me more," he demanded roughly.

"You. I want you... doing this to me... touching me... taking me... always... only you..."

Her knees were weak. It was almost impossible to hold herself upright, and when he found her most sensitive of places she clung to him as if she would fall. Deep down she recognised his skill. Knew she was by no means the first to be handled in such a way. But the pressure was building up and threatening to overcome her.

"Ohhhhh."

Her legs were buckling, and colours began to form behind her eyelids. Ruby and gold. She gasped for air, her mouth open but his kiss was sucking the very air from her lungs. She couldn't protest, couldn't do anything other than jerk and shudder against him. Wanting. Needing.

And then it happened. Shock after shock of intense pleasure, strong enough to have her legs give way completely. Every part of her was on fire. Every part alive with an intensity she would never have believed. She wanted to laugh or cry, she had no idea which, as a powerful energy surged through her, jolting her over and over again.

"Oh! Oh!"

He was holding her up, one strong arm around her waist. His cheek was against hers.

"Don't let me go," she giggled deliriously, clinging to him for all she was worth, for if he did she would collapse to the ground.

"I won't," and then he was laughing too, murmuring sweet nothings in her ear and calling her his darling.

26

"YER REALLY SURE YER know wot yer doin'?" Daisy asked.

Having pulled on her hat, Thea was checking out her appearance in the mirror.

"Of course I am." Tilting her head a little to the right she peered closer to the glass and frowned. Her lipstick was a little smudged in one corner, and folding her handkerchief she dabbed carefully. "It's not as if we're hurting anyone."

"*You* might not be," Daisy replied, her emphasis fully on the first word.

Thea sighed. "Look, I know you're worried. But don't be. All we're doing is having a little fun."

Leaning back onto her bed Daisy was rolling her eyes.

"Please, I don't want us to fall out over this." Thea was feeling more than a touch of exasperation. She hadn't known what to expect when, full of excitement and unable to help herself any longer, she'd let Daisy in on the secret that she and Darius were meeting each other away from Kitty's. But it certainly hadn't been for a lecture every time she snuck out for a rendezvous.

"We won't. But I still fink yer askin' for trouble wiv that one."

"You don't know him."

"Maybe not as well as you, but I do know 'is kind. 'E ain't for you, Thea. Truly."

"But then neither am I for him." Thea shrugged a little sadly.

"So wot yer gonna do when yer old man gets back?"

"Return home and be a dutiful wife I suppose."

Even thinking about such a thing lowered Thea's spirits.

"Not long now though, is it?"

"No. Two months."

And that was another secret Daisy was keeping. Even Esme was in the dark as far as Silas's intentions.

"Maybe yer right," Daisy relented. "Maybe you should 'ave a bit o' fun while yer can. So where's 'e takin' yer this time?"

"The cinema. We're going to see *Beau Brummell* and then we're going for tea. You could come with us if you like?"

"And be a gooseberry? No thanks!"

"Just don't say you weren't asked," Thea retorted, slipping on her gloves and pirouetting. "How do I look?"

"Smashing. And far too good for 'im."

Thea gave her friend a warning glare.

"All right. I won't say any more. Wot time will yer be back?"

"About six."

"Okay. I'll cover for yer if anyone asks. Say you're at the library. Again."

"You're a real sport." And going over she planted a grateful kiss on Daisy's cheek.

27

MANY OF THE GIRLS HAD regular customers which Thea had, at first, thought strange. As far as she was concerned, entertaining the same man over and over again bordered on an unacceptable level of intimacy. But Darius wasn't the only one to search her out repeatedly. Though not in great numbers, there were others too, and while it could never be said her heart lifted at the sight of a returning customer, she usually managed to sum up enough warmth to assure them that they meant as much to her as she appeared to do to them.

But there was one who hadn't made it easy for her. One she'd had to work hard at being pleasant to.

His first visit had been as the guest of a regular and it was clear from the outset he was ill at ease. The friend was popular with the girls, and so both men had been welcomed and treated to the usual overly familiar ways of the place, but whilst one had taken it all in his stride, indeed giving back as good as he got, the other had kept himself very much on the outside. Thea was glad not to be involved, since it appeared this particular customer was finding the whole business rather distasteful, and if that was the case she couldn't help wondering why he was there in the first place.

But worse was to come.

"I'll take you," he said, pointing at her when it was clear the party was about to move upstairs.

Thea's hackles rose at such rudeness and at his casual dismissal of those who were on the point of claiming his token.

"You sure, mate?" Having already had a little too much to drink, his friend, minus his tie and with the top buttons of his shirt already undone, was bemusedly waving his glass around.

"I'm sure."

"Ha! Then in that case I'll keep both these beauties for myself." And somewhat unsteadily he lunged towards Daisy and Nora and threw an arm around each.

Gritting her teeth, Thea determined she'd allow this customer twenty minutes of her time and not a moment longer. She could have refused altogether for it was an unwritten rule that no one was forced to entertain a customer giving them cause for unease. It meant unpleasant situations could be diffused early on, and if that failed? Well, they could always call upon Frank should a little muscle be required to get the point home.

But plain obnoxiousness hardly called for something as drastic as that.

Allowing the others time to navigate the stairs, and judging by the number of times they lost their footing whilst trying to maintain their hold on each other it was an effort fraught with difficulty, Thea and her customer brought up the rear. His soberness was in marked contrast to the gaiety and laughter of the others.

"Am I allowed to know your name?' she asked politely, after the revellers had found their way into one room and she had led him a little further along the corridor to the smallest of the bedrooms.

"Gerald."

Aware of his discomfort she knew that if this visit were to be successful then one of them would have to make a superhuman effort, and since he was the one paying, it would fall to her to find the means to do so.

"I'm Thea," she said encouragingly.

He made no reply. Simply stood beside the brass bed looking down at the coverlet until it become abundantly clear he would rather be anywhere but in that room.

"Would you like help with your jacket?"

"I'm quite capable of taking it off, thank you."

"Of course."

Stung by his discourtesy, she went over to the dressing table and gathered the cloth and bowl in readiness but when she turned back he still hadn't moved. She found herself wondering what she could do or say to move the proceedings along.

"Go ahead and gawk. There's no charge." His tone was cold.

She thought him probably no more than twenty-nine or thirty but he was aged, and in truth she was trying to look anywhere but at the scars on his face. The skin in parts had whitened. Other areas, notably his right cheek and jawbone, were a patchwork of raised and shiny ridges, while the eyelid on that side too, was afflicted and slightly pulled down.

"Might I ask how it happened?"

"Does it matter?"

The injury was fearful and would seem not only external.

"Not to me," she said mildly.

"Then shall we get on with it?" and with a practiced awkwardness he removed his jacket and slipped off his braces.

He continued undressing whilst she prepared the solution, though when she faced him again it was all she could do to smother a gasp. For it wasn't only his face that that was horribly affected. The same scars were also apparent from shoulder to elbow, as well as on that side of his chest.

"If I revolt you, then we need take this no further."

Thea had never seen anything like it before.

"No, you don't revolt me," she managed, and stepping towards him gently touched the tip of a finger to the damaged surface.

"And I don't need your pity," he growled, moving back and flinching as if the contact had caused him pain.

"Then I won't waste it on you."

Satisfied they had reached an understanding, she held out her hand for his token.

28

ONE OF FRANK'S RESPONSIBILITIES WAS to keep the fires piled high and blazing, and as winter continued he would often be seen skulking around corners with his arms full of split logs, waiting to get into rooms. By late September the warm Pacific breezes were a memory. Instead the weather blew hard from the south bringing chilling winds to whip around corners and rattle loose timbers, the mere sound sending goose bumps running over the skin. On the worst of those nights, few customers had any desire to leave home, and the girls would huddle together in the salon, drinking honey-laced whiskey heated by a red-hot poker.

These were the nights when Belle might be persuaded to demonstrate her other calling.

"Go on, Belle. Read my cards. Please," someone would wheedle, and if she were in the mood, which of course she had to be if the reading were to be successful, she would bring out an old pack of playing cards and hand them over for shuffling.

Thea didn't hold much faith in such doings. But some were always keen to have a glimpse at what might be.

Nine of Hearts, Belle might say having turned over that card, and there would be a collective sigh for everyone knew this meant dreams would come true. The King of Clubs drew even more appreciation, being the sign of a generous and affectionate man. And if the two fell together, then a successful and loving marriage was in store. Not that it was really that simple, for there were always other cards to be considered, and Belle would play out the drama with plenty of *Ohh's* and *Ahh's* and nods of sudden understanding as each one was turned face up. But it was when her finger hovered over one in particular, and her brow creased into a frown that hearts beat faster, for disaster was of course as much a thrill as romance.

If Belle was unwilling for whatever reason, then the girls might put on a gramophone record and attempt the latest jazz steps. This was Daisy's forte; she loved to dance and was always pulling the others to their feet.

"You know, you're very good," Thea told her one evening, "you should be on the stage."

Daisy had been practicing a routine involving a fast kicking step.

"Maybe I will one day. Com'on. Get up 'ere and do it wiv me."

But Thea had no desire to make a fool of herself. She knew that when it came to dancing she had two left feet and even made mistakes during the slower tunes when there were strong male arms to guide her.

When the girls weren't dancing or having their fortunes told, they were fashioning friendships. No longer the new girl thanks to the arrival of Violet, Thea often found herself sought out to resolve an argument or to offer an opinion, as if her very background lent itself to that purpose. But there was little she could do about the teasing when it became clear she was Darius's favourite.

"Where is he tonight, Thea?" someone might ask.

"How should I know?" she'd retort.

"But aren't you two close?"

"No closer than anyone else."

"That's not how it looks to us."

"Loves young dream," someone else might add.

"Don't be silly."

"Oh. Have we hit a nerve?"

"I won't even lower myself to answer that."

"But he's been in Auckland a while now. Will he ever be leaving again? Or have you got him firmly in your pocket now?"

"Come on, let us in on the gossip."

"There isn't any. At least none I'm aware of."

"Is he going to take you away from all this?"

"Is it true, Thea? Will you be leaving us and running away with him?"

"Don't get your heart broken."

"There's no reason my heart should be broken. And I don't know why you're all carrying on like this."

"We're not blind, sweetie."

"We can see he likes you. After all, he hasn't been with any of us for a long time."

"I can tell you for a fact, he's nothing more to me than any other customer."

"Thea! How can you say that?"

"It *is* written all over your face."

"And look! She's certainly blushing!"

"So, do you have anything for me?" Having discarded her magazine Kitty had gotten up from her armchair by the fire.

"I'm not sure, Miss Kitty."

"Well, you either do or you don't. Let me be the judge of that. What is it?"

The girl took a step forward. "You asked about Thea, Miss Kitty."

"Go on."

"It's probably nothing."

Kitty's patience was becoming strained.

"Yes?"

But having drawn herself up, the girl had tightened her lips. "I need some stuff. Just a little. I'm not feeling too good."

"I know. And I have just what you need here."

Going over to her desk and opening a drawer Kitty held up a paper packet.

"Well," she insisted.

"I think she's having a fling with Darius."

"Darius? The fly-boy? Indeed? And why would you think that?"

"It's the way they act together. As if everything is normal when it clearly isn't."

"I see."

Kitty was quiet for a moment, considering the possibility of such an unforeseen circumstance. Perhaps it was something she should have allowed for, after all, being married to a much older man would hardly be a picnic for anyone, let alone a girl of Thea's age. And if she hadn't the chance to spread her wings beforehand maybe it was inevitable she'd be a sucker for the first decent bit of male attention.

The situation would have to be watched carefully.

"And does he still see other girls?"

"No. At least he hasn't for a while."

Holding out the packet Kitty ensured it remained tantalisingly out of reach. "How long has it been going on?"

"I'm not sure. A few weeks."

"And why didn't you tell me sooner?"

The girl was eyeing her reward hungrily and no doubt wondering if it would disappear if she said the wrong thing.

"I wanted to be sure, Miss Kitty."

"Take it…"

The girl's hand shot out, but Kitty was faster and the elusive packet remained just out of reach.

"… and let me know everything that happens. Every detail, whether you think it's important or not. And not when you think the time is right. In future, I want to know the moment something occurs. Do you understand?"

"Yes, Miss Kitty."

The packet exchanged hands and the girl scuttled out the door.

29

KITTY HAD MIXED FEELINGS ABOUT her girls. There were times when she thought of them as family. And then there were the times when their demands and petty rivalries became all too much. That was when she told them to take a good look around. The place in which they worked was clean and decent, and there was food on the table. Furthermore, and whilst some of them might not fully appreciate it, she offered considerable protection from the worst elements of the business.

It hadn't been like that when she'd started out in the trade, and even now she wondered how her life might have turned out had she not come across Sean O'Riorden that night. She'd been working the bottom end of Queen Street - and trying to avoid the rozzers who seemed to have little better to do than arrest the likes of her - when he'd stepped out of the Queens Ferry Hotel for a breath of air. She'd known immediately he was a fellow countryman, though going on his appearance he was doing better than most. In fact he looked almost a gent. Almost, but not quite, and when he pulled out his pocket watch as if wondering whether he'd time for one more drink, she'd made her move.

"From Dublin, are yus?"

"And what in the name of God has that to with a strumpet like you?"

"A strumpet?" With her indignity knowing no bounds, she'd pulled herself up to her full height. "Is that any way to talk to yer own kind?"

"My own kind?"

"Look at yus. All dressed up with yer fancy waist-coat. Think yer too good for the likes of me, do yer? Well, let me tell you, yer not."

He had looked at her then.

He had taken her to a hotel, and that in itself made a pleasant change since the business was more often done in a dingy back room - and that was if she were lucky, for sometimes it took place in the dank and narrow passages between buildings or in the foul-smelling, rubbish-strewn yards at the back.

Afterwards, as they lay in the big brass bed, he'd reached for his tin and makings and had rolled her a cigarette. Then he'd made one for himself.

It turned out he was a patriot from south of the Liffey, only leaving the city to take his chance elsewhere after the failure of the Uprising in Sixteen.

"Sure, and I've no great desire to be murdered by the Brits for wanting our own governance."

She nodded, for she knew what had happened to those in Kilmainham jail.

"Yus could have joined up. Gone over to France and fought. Others did."

"And why the hell would I want to fight England's war?" he turned on her.

"And so yus did what? Yer came here instead, to her domain?"

"I did."

"Why not Australia?"

It was well known that there were more opportunities over there, even if the place was a land of convicts.

"Well now, the thought did cross my mind. But I had a friend here, if yus get my drift."

He might have been hinting at anything, but more likely his contact would have been political rather than criminal since many of the foot soldiers who'd fought for the Irish Free State were now abroad.

"And let me guess Sean O'Riorden, yer out to make yer fortune. Or have yer done that already?"

He had laughed. "Dear God woman! Are yus after knowing all about me?"

"I am."

And that had been how it started.

With a heavy sigh, Kitty stubbed out her cheroot. What was the point of dwelling on the past? Sean had been dead these past four years, beaten to death by a couple of thugs - no doubt paid to do so by one of his enemies, since he'd as many of that colour as friends. She'd been left to face up to those who would have taken over his business. And she'd done it with a threat here and a bribe there, until she'd gained enough respect to be left alone. Now all that remained of the man she had loved beyond any other was the house and the one item of furniture he'd contributed.

"Sean, will yus come and see this," she'd called when it was delivered on the back of the tallyman's truck. She'd come out onto the top step leaving the heavy black door wide open behind her.

"Ahh, tis here then."

"And do yer know about this?"

"Sure and it'll bring a bit of class to the place," he'd replied, slipping his strong arms around her waist.

'That?" she had been incredulous.

"You're looking at quality there, me darlin'."

"I'm looking at something me granny would have cast out had she the chance."

"Will yer not be showing a bit of gratitude?"

"For that old-fashioned thing? And where d'yer get it?"

"From a bigger place than you or I will ever own."

"Since when did you move into furnishings?"

"'Tis a one-off woman. The bugger had no cash."

She'd shaken her head, partly in amusement, partly in pride. The supply of eejits willing to gamble their hard earned cash was never ending. Horse races, dogfights, even bare-knuckle brawls, Sean ran a book on them all.

"Sure," he'd nuzzled against her neck and squeezed her waist even tighter, "and it's a sad world when even the gentry are on their knees."

But he'd done well for himself in buying the house. And not just this one for there'd been others, though not for them to live in. Bricks and mortar, he'd said. That's the place for your money. But she'd been the one to see another opportunity. A brothel on the fringe of a respectable area with a dozen or so classy whores and a reputation for discretion.

Getting up she went over to the large bay window and looked out at the young plane trees on either side of the street. It was Sean's birthday - may he rest with the angels - and she was throwing a party. But not just any party. It was to be one of her famous *extravaganzas,* and a spectacular affair of costumes, dancing and drinking. The gold foil announcement had been on the easel in the foyer for the past few weeks and ticket sales were good. Very good, in fact. She'd have to ensure there was enough food and liquor to carry them through until at least noon the next day. Maybe even longer. She'd better tell Frank to get down to the bottle shop and order more supplies.

After much of to-ing and fro-ing she'd settled on an Oriental Harem theme. Not that there was anything wrong with her other idea, a Roman orgy, but she felt the mysterious east had a more decadent feel to it. Brass lanterns, heavy perfumes and incenses, and of course belly dancers and hookah pipes. It wouldn't take a great deal of effort to transform the salon into a sultan's palace, especially with the enthusiastic assistance of the girls.

And they were excited. Kitty's theatricals happened three or four times a year, and when they did there was an indecent amount of money to be made. Especially for those who made the effort. Some were even going so far as to run up their own costumes, though most had raided the trunks in the loft looking for props and other bits and pieces leftover from the last event.

"Bloody 'ell, you can see me bush good and proper though this!" Daisy said, smoothing the opaque fabric across her hips and looking down.

Thea had laughed, though she was feeling far from elated, for now she and Darius were an item she was even more determined not to share her favours. The one trick she'd been using to great effect, especially when the salon was busy, was to station herself behind the black lacquered bar and busy herself concocting drinks for everyone. The girls were happy since it meant more tokens for them, but somehow she doubted she'd be so lucky that night for she'd heard Miss Kitty hired staff for such duties.

And on top of that, wearing little more than a jewel-encrusted brassiere and veil meant she would hardly blend in with the wallpaper.

"Anyfink wrong?" Daisy asked suddenly.

"No. Everything's tickety-boo," Thea said, finding an immediate need to examine the clasp of her necklace.

"Yer miles away. Finking about Darius?"

"Partly."

"Is 'e coming tonight?"

"I think so. He's paid for a ticket anyway."

"So, wot yer worried about?"

Thea hadn't time to reply for the door had swung open and with one hand still on the brass knob and the other circling in the air in an imitation of a harem dance move, Esme was standing on the threshold.

"Oh my gawd, Ezz," Daisy's jaw had dropped in admiration of her sheer pantaloons and the glass jewel in her navel, "you're a real stunner. Go on, give us a twirl."

Stepping fully into the bedroom, Esme obligingly did so.

"Very Sheik of Araby. Where'd ya get the tom?"

"It's only paste."

"Tom?" Thea looked from one to the other.

"She means tomfoolery. Jewellery."

Thea was as impressed as Daisy with the outfit. "Gosh Esme, you do look lovely. Is this all for anyone in particular?"

Over the past few weeks Esme had been regularly entertaining a mysterious middle-aged gentleman and Thea wondered if he too would be there tomorrow.

"Maybe," she said mysteriously, holding her veil just below her eyes and fluttering her eyelashes.

"Good for you," Daisy said approvingly. "You make the most of it and get wot you can out of 'im."

"Daisy!"

"No, she's right," Esme was herself again. "Why else are we here? You have to face it, there's no other way forward. Not for any of us. It doesn't really matter who you are," and looking at Thea she smiled gently, "so, if I want a half decent future, I have to make the most of things now."

Esme had once confided that the last few years had changed her attitude towards men and marriage.

"When I was growing up," she'd said one night when the salon was quiet, "I had this rosy picture of how my life would look. A good-looking fellow, a little house, kids tugging at my apron strings. The works. But I knew it was all a dream really. You only have to see where I came from to know that. Even the best of them can turn nasty when there's no money to spare, and suddenly you're old before your time."

"So what are your plans?" Thea had asked.

"I'm going to get myself a job."

"Really?"

"Yes. I want to go to night school and better my-self."

"That's marvellous, but you can still get married too."

"Not for a long while. I've had enough of men and their demands."

"That's a little sad," Thea was thinking of Darius and how well they suited each other.

"Not really. Haven't they already had the best of me? And anyway, there are so many chances for a woman to get on these days. Not like before the war. Now things are different and we're thinking for ourselves. We don't need to be second class citizens anymore."

"Heaven's Esme, you're sounding almost politi-cal."

"And why not?"

Having had no idea how deep Esme's thoughts ran, Thea had been amazed.

30

DOWN IN THE SALON KITTY was ensuring that everything was in place. The jazz band - one of Auckland's finest - was setting up in the annex, and she was checking items off on her fingers. The bar was stocked to bursting, the hookah pipes were filled and ready, and waiting to be brought up from the kitchen pantry were the nibbles and delicious hors d'oeuvres Huia had arrayed on platters.

"It should be a good night," Belle said, coming up and standing at Kitty's shoulder.

"It should if the number of tickets we've sold is anything to go by."

"Are we expecting anyone special?"

"There's a member of the English aristocracy in town." Kitty was moving about the room, her eyes sharp, looking for anything out of place. "A Duke. Second or third cousin. God knows, there's enough of them about and living on Easy Street. Frank," she said suddenly, "move that sofa against the wall. Let's have a little more room for dancing."

Frank immediately set to the task, though not without a certain amount of huffing and grunting.

"A real Lord," Belle continued, "that'll impress everyone."

"More to the point, let's hope they impress him," Kitty said before turning her attention back to the layout of the room, "and that table. Put it over there." She pointed to its new location.

"I'm sure they will," Belle replied.

Kitty fixed her with a shrewd look. "We need to ensure he and his friends are aware of the full range of services we offer."

"Consider it done."

"Good. We both know the sort of thing his type goes for, so you should be busy. And if I'm wrong, push Daisy his way."

"Of course."

"How many girls do we have on tonight?"

"Sixteen, counting those coming in later."

"Excellent. Keep a close eye on things. I don't want anyone getting too drunk. The punters, yes, but not the girls. They need to have their wits about them if they're to last all the way through."

"I'll make sure."

"And watch out for the dope. I want to know who brings it in. I want names. And you can tell them for the right price, I've got plenty more they can have. And better. Tonight we cater for every whim. Get that? Every whim."

"Yes, Miss Kitty."

By ten o'clock the evening was in full swing, and in her daring silver and gold gown and turban, and punctuating her conversation by the judicious use of an extremely long cigarette holder, Kitty was floating from customer to customer bestowing flattering compliments, or raising delighted eyebrows with salaciously witty remarks. This was her forte and she was in her element. She was also stone cold sober unlike everyone else present, but that was by choice for these days she preferred to maintain a certain glamorous aloofness at such functions. Even a touch of mystery. More importantly though, there was enough high jinx and rowdy laughter filling the place to keep all the girls busy, and no sooner had one returned from upstairs than another was on her way up. Thankfully two of Huia's younger sisters had arrived in Auckland that morning, and after spending all day in the kitchen chopping and slicing and tending to pans on the stove, all three were now on the second floor ensuring the rooms were constantly in a state of readiness. Kitty dreaded the laundry bill. Still, it was a necessary expense if the evening were to be an all-round success.

Standing by the curtains she cast a discreet eye about the room.

In one corner, Nora and Esme were giving their version of a Moorish belly dance to a gathering of admirers, whilst Nancy was leaning over the back of a sofa and whispering in a gentleman's ear. Kitty could tell from his reddening complexion that whatever she was saying, it was completely outrageous. And judging by the way Violet was draped over a young man in a tuxedo and holding a glass to his lips it seemed she had found her feet quickly enough. Soo Ling of course, was as unflappable as ever and showing absolutely no emotion as two gentlemen fingered the beads draping down her otherwise naked back. Other than that, the band was raucous and most girls were on their feet dancing.

All it needed now was for the Duke and his party to arrive and everything would be peachy.

And then Kitty narrowed her eyes.

"Not entertaining anyone, Thea?" she asked, making her way over to the bar.

"You could say I'm looking after your profits."

The girl was holding up the shallow, bowl-shaped champagne glass she'd been about to fill and it was all Kitty could do to contain her irritation. God she was a trial. All pride and self-control - just like others of her class. She wouldn't have minded quite so much if Thea was turning a profit, but even though she'd gone out of her way to promote her - *quality gentleman, and only for the discerning* - and placed a premium on her services, the novelty appeared to have worn off fairly quickly. Well, her price would be reduced after tonight.

"We have staff for that," Kitty advised coldly, looking in the direction of the bare-chested young man in a red waistcoat and fez at the other end of the counter. "You are worth more to me out there."

She was waving her ivory cigarette holder in the direction of the makeshift dance floor where the music was loud and the gyrations of half-naked girls were generating equally exuberant responses from their inebriated and heavily perspiring partners.

Thankfully the girl was in no doubt that the gesture was anything other than an order, since she pushed aside the empty glass, and gathering her veil and lifting her chin - a little too condescendingly Kitty noted and for which a reprimand would be given in the morning - obediently made her way out onto the crowded floor.

31

HE STOOD JUST INSIDE THE curtains, craning his neck to see over the mass of bodies whooping it up on the dance floor, wondering whether she was in the thick of it. Or perhaps she was upstairs with someone else. He grimaced. Strange how certain things had started to bother him. Not that he could do anything about it and besides, he had to remember she was someone else's wife.

"Darius, darling."

Nancy had draped her arms around his neck.

"Looking for Thea?" she shouted mischievously, her hips pressed against his as she jiggled to the blare of a trumpet.

"Is it so obvious?" he grinned.

"I'm sorry to say it is. Won't anyone else do? I've no idea where she is right now." Tightening her grip she looked invitingly into his eyes.

"Sorry babe."

"You're not sorry at all," she pouted, "in fact, you've been a complete drag lately."

"You don't mean that."

"I do. Well, if you ever need a change…?" and she fluttered her eyelashes.

"I'll find you," he said.

"Promise?" The eyelashes were fluttering again, though she'd removed his hand from where he'd placed it on the small of her back. And then she was gone. A trumpet had screeched an incredibly high note and as if it were a signal she sashayed back onto the dance floor.

He couldn't help watching as she gave herself up to the music, raising her braceleted arms and wiggling her pert bottom temptingly. Nor could he help the sigh that escaped. It really wouldn't do though and when Nancy, as if sensing his interest, turned and gave him a knowing smile, he grinned back and made a salute of acknowledgement.

He found Thea on the other side of the room, conversing with a rather pompous looking gentleman whose side-whiskers would have done the Kaiser proud. Catching her eye he motioned her over.

"I can't take my eyes off you," he said, holding her just far enough away to fully take her outfit in. "You look good enough to eat."

He meant it. The diaphanous trousers showed off her legs to perfection, while the jewelled brassiere was thrusting her breasts upward into two very delectable globes.

"It's just this stupid costume."

"Well I like it."

And he leaned in for a kiss.

"Darius! Not here. People will see."

"Honey," he grinned, partly in delight, partly in frustration, "take a look around you. Everyone's doing something they shouldn't."

It was true. The flirting and touching in full view of all would have been outrageous at any other time and in any other place. Girls were laughing and pressing themselves against men who in turn were just as eagerly fondling soft rounded breasts, or cupping scantily clad buttocks.

"Let's go upstairs," he suggested.

"We can't. At least, not yet. Its pandemonium up there. Even if there was a room available we couldn't keep it long. Frank is prowling the corridors and hustling everyone."

"Then we'll have to make the most of it down here," and reaching down he squeezed the deliciously firm flesh of her bottom.

"For goodness sake! You're just as bad as everyone else," she tried to remonstrate.

"Only with you. You bring out the worst in me."

"Somehow I don't think that's entirely true."

He grinned and looked around again. Everyone seemed to be having a good time.

"The party's going well. Kitty will be counting her takings all night."

"So will the girls. Some of them already have more than one token."

"And what about you," he leaned in, knowing full well it was a question he had no right to ask.

"Sadly I haven't had my dance card marked yet."

"In that case," buoyed by a feeling of relief he reached into his pocket, "perhaps I can change that for you."

"Three?" she was smiling at the tokens he was holding up. "You are spending up large. Though perhaps they're not all for me?"

"And who else would they be for?"

"Well, you might be planning on spreading your charms around tonight"

He nodded thoughtfully. "That's not a bad idea. Maybe I should decide later. See how my luck goes."

Thea's eyebrow had arched. "Really?"

"As if anyone could hold a candle to you," he laughed. But before he could pull her back into his arms she'd nudged him in the direction of the bar.

"Let's get a drink."

"You know," he said, as they skirted the edge of the dancers, "you don't have to be worried that someone will see us and put two and two together. Not tonight."

"Well, let's just say I'd rather not take the risk. Especially with Kitty around somewhere. Champagne?"

She was reaching over the bar for an already opened bottle and two glasses.

"Why not."

In the mood for something more exciting than his usual tipple he didn't bother glancing at the label since he knew like everything else Kitty served it would be slightly less than top shelf stuff. But before he could reach for his glass he had to catch and steady Thea who'd been jolted forward.

"Sorry." Nora's dance moves were a little wild, as were that of her partner, a rather portly and red faced gentleman whose wife would no doubt be speechless to see him carrying on in such a way.

"Isn't this all terribly spiffing?" she called back over her shoulder.

"Some party," Darius agreed.

"According to Daisy the night hasn't even started yet," Having untangled herself from his embrace Thea was sliding his champagne along the bar towards him, and concerned she might be bumped into again he nodded towards a sofa.

"Let's sit down."

"Heavens! Good idea!"

"I would have said this is all a little too risqué for this place," he retorted as they squeezed their way through the dancers.

"The band's good though, aren't they?"

"Sure are. Do you want to dance?"

"No. I'm more than happy to leave that to the others," she said dropping down and snuggling against him

Closing his eyes he breathed in her perfume. Married women were good fun, especially those whose husbands were prepared to turn a blind eye - and wasn't that what Thea's had done after all? But somehow she'd gotten under his skin. He wasn't sure how, but it was a worry all the same, especially given his carefully cultivated reputation as a *love 'em and leave 'em* type. Why, he'd once been called a cad to his face, and still found the memory of the lady in question and her outrage at his flirtation with her younger sister amusing.

So, was he was getting a little too involved?

For the first time in his life he sensed he might be.

Finally managing to bag a room, Thea wasted no time on preliminaries. Instead, tearing off her costume with vulgar haste, she pulled back the covers and jumped straight into bed.

"Warm me up," she begged, as Darius slipped in beside her.

"Good God woman! If you think this is cold how are you going to cope when winter really sets in?"

"It has."

"This isn't winter," he laughed, taking her into his arms and holding her tightly. "Not even close. You should see what it's like in the Rocky Mountains. Snow, ice, blizzards. That's real cold."

"Then I don't want to go there."

"Shall I remove it from the itinerary?"

It was a game they played. An imaginary Thomas Cook tour of all the places they would visit one day, had she not been married and things were different.

"I think so. Perhaps Morocco instead?"

"Ahh. The romantic desert sheiks. You know, you really have been watching too many movies."

She was playing with the light sprinkling of hair on his chest. "You'd look very impressive in one of those head-dresses."

"I think you mean a keffiyeh."

"Do I?"

And then raising her head, she searched his eyes.

"Why hasn't anyone already snaffled you up?"

Darius barely hesitated. "Perhaps I haven't found the right woman."

"A stock answer, and one I don't believe."

"Then you judge me too highly."

"I think," she said, dropping back down and resting her chin on her forearm, "that you simply avoid the responsibility."

"Perhaps. But then what sort of woman would want a man like me. Hardly in one place long enough to put down roots."

"I think that is just another excuse."

"Then give me your opinion, oh wise woman."

Hearing the smile in his voice she couldn't help doing the same.

"I think that despite everything, you are a coward when it comes to the fairer sex."

"Oh, that is too cruel."

"But potentially true."

"And yet I'm here with you."

"Ah. But I hardly count."

"And why is that?"

"Because it takes no effort to be with me."

There was the slightest moment of hesitation before he replied, "And that's what's required when two people become one and profess their undying love for each other? An effort? What about cupid and his arrows?"

"Overrated," she said firmly.

"I see. Then tell me more. What else is needed to complete this perfect union of yours?"

"Manners, graciousness."

"Anything else?"

"Companionship. Trust."

"And this?"

Rolling her onto her back, Darius lowered his lips to hers.

"Oh yes. Definitely that," she breathed.

"So," he said, nuzzling at her bare shoulder, "you have already decided I lack effort. Are you also suggesting I also lack everything else you've mentioned?"

Although she had no intention of losing the argument she was finding it hard to concentrate.

"No. You might pass muster on the first two. But what use are they without commitment."

"Ah, now we come down to it. A commitment."

"Isn't that what every woman wants."

"And are you the same as every other woman? Would you demand a commitment from me?"

Given he was caressing her breast and the sensations were exquisite Thea had little thought as to what might lie behind the question.

"Yes," she breathed, "that you never stop doing this to me."

She didn't hear the tiny sigh of relief.

"In that case…"

32

IT WAS DURING THEIR NEXT clandestine meeting that Darius told her he was returning to Australia for a short while. She'd pushed aside the buttered scone that up until then, she'd been enjoying.

"When do you sail?" she asked, unable to look at him. Instead she was gazing out of the teashop window.

"The day after tomorrow."

"As soon as that?"

He took her hand.

"I'll be back in a little under a fortnight"

"Will you be going to Gippsland?"

"There and Melbourne."

Two weeks. Regardless how few days in reality, it would seem like forever.

"Thea," he said earnestly, "I've been thinking. About us."

"Really?" she replied lightly.

Her heart was in her mouth. Was this the moment he told her he was he moving on? That he was tired of her. Tired of their friendship and the limitation of seeing only one woman. She could hardly bear it, though worse than that was the thought of seeing him at Kitty's and watching him give his token to someone else. That would hurt beyond belief.

"We're two of a kind you and I," he was tracing his thumb over the back of her hand. "We're meant for better things. It doesn't make it right, but have you ever considered getting away from all this?"

Thea had thought of nothing else, but the reality was that Silas was coming home, and then… well, she would just be exchanging one prison to for another.

"I don't understand."

"Getting out. Not dreaming of seeing the world, but really doing it?"

"How can I?"

"What's stopping you?" he countered.

"Everything. You know my circumstances."

"I want you to know when I get back, I won't be staying here," he continued, curling his fingers tightly around hers. "I'm leaving New Zealand and this time, I've no plans to come back. It could be years even."

"I see. But where will you go?"

"England. But not right away. I thought I'd take the long route back."

It was as if she couldn't breathe. Why did it have to be so soon? Couldn't he wait a couple of months? Surely he could manage that? Of course, she had no right to demand anything of him, but did he really have no idea how much she enjoyed his company?

"Come with me. What do you have to lose after all?"

Thea blinked. Now the world truly had stopped turning.

While she had no idea what to say, her mind was racing. There was Silas, of course. And then there were her parents and the shame her running away would bring to their good name. But they were dead, and anyway, wouldn't they be more upset at her true situation? How it must be hurting them.

She looked at Darius. Felt the warmth of his palm and the strength of his grip.

He hardly knew her yet he was offering her a new beginning and freedom from everything that had taken place these past years. Wasn't that worth having? Being with him every day would be a wonderful bonus. Waking up beside him. Sharing his days, his adventures.

Being his wife.

It was a heady moment.

"Look, I know it's a big decision, so don't say anything yet. Wait until I get back from Melbourne."

But she was shaking her head. It was all too incredible.

"Do you really mean it?"

She had to be sure.

"Of course, silly. It'll be fun."

"But how will we do it? How will I get away? Miss Kitty has eyes and ears everywhere. It won't be easy."

He was chuckling, as if pleased by her reaction. "Leave all those how's to me. I'll think of a way."

"But if we're going abroad won't I need a passport or some other form of documentation."

"You will. I hadn't thought of that. Don't you have one?"

'No. I suppose I must have had papers as a child. But I've never, ever seen them."

"In that case, you'd better apply to the Passport Office as soon as possible."

"And what if people find out?"

"Like who? I doubt your husband will since he's in Europe. And as for Miss Kitty, well she won't find out either. Unless you want to broadcast it to all and sundry and give the game away before we've even started."

Thea's eyes were wide with excitement. Could it really be that simple?

"I'll get a list of all the passenger ships leaving Auckland over the next four weeks, and then all that remains is to pick the one we want to sail on."

He was squeezing her hand again. "What do you say?"

"But you hardly know me," she said, trying to temper her elation.

"I know enough that we'd be a good fit together. Say you'll do it."

"I'll do it. I'll do it! Yes, I'll do it. Oh my God, Darius, are we crazy?"

"Of course we are. But it'll be a hoot."

And then, to the consternation of the manageress, who in keeping a sharp eye out for any improprieties in her establishment had already had marked out their table as one that might require her attention, he lifted Thea's hand to his lips and tenderly kissed each finger one by one.

33

BARELY ABLE TO CONTAIN HER excitement, Thea was torn between wanting to share her news with Daisy, and Darius's call for discretion. As he so rightly said, if she were to have any success in slipping out of the place it had to remain their secret, at least for the time being. And so, doing her best not to arouse suspicion she passed the time the only way she could, immersed in a book, although she was no longer limiting herself to murder mysteries. Instead, and on the very same day he'd left for Australia, she'd visited a different section of the public library in search of a stronger style of modern literature, as recommended by the friendly librarian. Being the perfect wife meant opening herself to new experiences, new interests. With Darius already well travelled and no doubt having many friends, she would need to be knowledgeable and able to hold her own if she were to successfully mix in such a society.

And it didn't stop there, for while devouring the works of Fitzgerald, Faulkner and even Hemingway she also tried a gentle quizzing of the house's more educated customers, hoping to get a better understanding of politics and affairs as well as the influences and impacts of the wider world. Not that she got very far. Having chosen to visit a bordello it was hardly what the gentlemen had in mind as a prelude to the main event.

What was becoming more and more apparent though was her lack of enthusiasm to entertain - even by her standards. Interested glances were met by scowls and if that failed - which on occasion it did - she would rush through the whole thing with sullen haste, as if it were the gentleman's fault for having the poor judgment to select her.

With the exception of Belle, who had taken her aside and threatened her with a visit to Missy Kitty, only Gerald was forthright enough to remark upon her appalling rudeness.

"What's the matter with you? Where's your spirit, your spark?" he wanted to know one afternoon.

Adjusting and rebuttoning her chemise, Thea chose not to respond. Nor did she look at him, though not out of squeamishness since his injuries had long ceased to affect her. Even witnessing the struggle to force a limb with restricted movement into the sleeve of his shirt had become as ordinary as watching a full bodied man button up his trousers or tie his shoelaces.

Nor did his surliness bother her anymore, perhaps in part because over time he'd opened up to her and allowed her a glimpse of the cause of his contempt. And that was a world that turned away from the true devastation of modern warfare.

"It's not sabres and glory," he'd said one day. "It's dirt and pain and fear. It's the screams of men trapped on wire and the crying of the maimed and limbless for their mothers."

Another time he had told her of the uncanny silence before the whistles blew, and they scaled the ladders and went over the top of the trenches.

"You didn't dare look into the faces of your men."

"Why not?" she'd asked.

"Because you were as afraid as they were."

One day, when she felt she knew him well enough, she'd dared to ask what had caused his injuries.

"Flame throwing devices," he'd replied impassively. "Very effective at immobilizing the troops."

So that wasn't the reason she refused to answer his question.

No, it was far simpler than that. For as far as she was concerned, her attitude - and what was behind it - was no one's business but her own.

"What's up Thea? No Darius to cheer you up?"

Having made space on the sofa beside her, Nora was kicking off her shoes.

"For Heaven's sake, why does everyone think that something must be wrong?"

"Well, look at you. Moping around as if you'd lost half a crown and found sixpence," and lifting her stockinged feet she placed them onto the nearby ottoman.

"I'm sure I'm not that bad."

"You are, take it from me. And that means you're not a good advertisement for this place. Has Belle said anything yet?"

"Yes, she has."

"I'm not surprised. You're hardly the life and soul of the party. Not that you ever were," she added carelessly, "but now it shows. It'll be even worse when Miss Kitty gets to hear. Then you'll know it."

"I don't really care."

"You will if she docks your money."

Thea closed her book with a snap. "Even that doesn't bother me."

"Prepared to give it away are you then? Look, if you want my advice, its chin up and smile for the customers. Here, have a cigarette."

Leaning over she offered her the pack.

"No thanks."

"Suit yourself. Where is Mister Wonderful anyway? Australia again?"

Thea started.

"Golly, don't look so frightened," Nora put a Chesterfield to her lips, "it was just an educated guess. He's been over there before. Business interests if I remember," and lighting the cigarette she inhaled gratefully.

"I have no idea where he is, and for all I know he may be gone forever. It's nothing to do with me, so why would anyone think it mattered?"

"One look at your face tells me it does."

"Rubbish."

"Don't take it badly. We all need a little spice in our lives. A little fun. A little romance. Just because we work here, it doesn't make us any different from anyone else."

When Thea didn't answer Nora shrugged.

"You should let me do your nails," and she studied her own long, slender fingers. "There's a lovely new colour from Max Factor I'm just dying to try."

"Perhaps some other time."

"Oh dear. You do have it bad."

Daisy had fewer qualms in telling Thea exactly what she thought, and roped Esme in as support.

"Get over it. It's wot you 'ave to do. Ain't that right Ezz?"

"You do seem to have fallen rather badly."

"Look, he's just a customer. That's all. I admit I like him." Looking from one to the other Thea was desperate to appear convincing. "He's fun."

"'E's a rogue. Told you that at the beginning."

"He's not a rogue, Daisy," Thea stated flatly. She was becoming tired of the same judgment over and over again.

"Of course not."

With a comforting arm around Thea's shoulders, Esme frowned a warning at Daisy.

"Only telling the truth."

This time both girls glared at Daisy who merely shrugged.

"He'll be back soon. Do you know where he's gone?" Esme asked gently.

"Melbourne." Thea saw no harm in confirming she actually did know where he was, especially now it seemed everyone in the bordello had already guessed.

"There you are then," she said cheerfully, "it could have been worse. He might have gone to England, mightn't he? Then you really would have something to be upset about."

"I'm not upset."

Esme and Daisy exchanged glances.

"Yeah? Well you could 'ave fooled me. 'Ow long's 'e been gone?"

"Eleven days."

"Eleven days? Give the bloke a chance. It takes four days to get there and then another four back. Yer'll see him in a day or two."

"Of course you will," Esme said, "and I'm sure he's missing you just as much as you're missing him."

"If 'e ain't 'aving fun wiv another -"

"*Daisy!*"

"Alright, alright. Keep yer 'air on. She's right Thea. 'E'll be back soon. Mark my words."

34

THEA APPLIED HER MAKE UP sparingly. Not too much rouge and not too dark a lipstick, for she wanted to be even more discreet that evening. She was desperately hoping Darius had made the right sailing. Otherwise he'd be returning tomorrow. Or the day after at the very latest.

Finding it hard to contain her excitement she opened the oblong box, and peeling aside the layer of tissue paper, lifted out the powder blue French knickers and matching brassiere. She'd kept them specifically for such an occasion, and when she slipped them on and the cool silk lay smooth and fragrant on her skin, she closed her eyes and breathed deeply, imagining his reaction on seeing such delights. How he'd hold her, leaning back to feast on the vision. And then, after that, how he'd run an appreciative finger down over her taut stomach and then further, over the ribboned seam and around her hip, until the palm of his hand was cupping her lightly clad bottom.

Goose bumps rose on her arms and she shook herself for being silly.

Thank goodness everyone was down in the salon, for if they could see her now she would come in for even more ribbing. Oh how wonderful it was to feel this way! So exciting and alive. It was as if she were a child again and it was Christmas morning. It was all his doing of course. He was the one who understood her. The one who knew exactly what she was thinking even before she did. Goodness, how strange life had turned out, and unable to help herself, she rose up onto her toes with her arms outstretched, twirling around before blushing at her exuberance and reaching for her kimono. Unlike Daisy's, hers far more in keeping with the Japanese styling in that it had wide sleeves and a colourful dragon embroidered across the back, and after slipping it on and dabbing a few precious drops of Shalimar on her wrists and behind her ears, she made her way downstairs.

Tucked in her usual corner she tried not to notice the minutes ticking by. Quarter hours became half hours, and then another hour had gone. That she'd been waiting since late afternoon didn't help, but perhaps the ship was late docking. Or he'd been held up in Australia and missed the sailing altogether. No matter, there was always tomorrow. But her disappointment was growing until hearing her name and looking up, she saw Nelly frantically nodding towards the curtains.

Had it been in her nature she would have jumped to her feet and run to him, regardless that it would have been the subject of gossip for days. Instead, overcome by an inexplicable shyness, she simply stood up and waited for him to come to her.

"Do you want a drink, Thea? Darius?" Violet was heading towards the bar.

"No." It was as much as Thea could manage. Unable to tear her eyes from him, she was also having difficulty in containing a beaming smile. "That is… unless…?"

His grin was just as wide. "Not for me either."

Neither of them noticed Violet rolling her eyes.

"Must be love."

And someone laughed and agreed.

"It would seem you have missed me," Darius said softly.

"Actually," she said, clasping her hands for want of something to do and looking at him from under her lashes, "I have only just realised you've been away."

He bent his head so that only she would hear his next words.

"Heartless woman."

Smothering a giggle she murmured back, "Surely you were already aware of that?"

"No. The Thea I know is passionate. Outrageous even. It would seem I have my work cut out for me if she has forgotten me during my absence."

"Let's go upstairs and find out," she said. She could hardly breathe for wanting him all to herself.

"Now?" he dared to tease.

"Now."

Their lovemaking was wild and spontaneous, and at one point, and in a show of mock anger for leaving her even for just two weeks, she sat astride him and held his wrists above his head as if in manacles.

"Did you miss me?" she demanded, leaning down to offer him her lips.

"You have no idea."

"Good."

"On the other hand," he countered, his eyes full of devilment, "if this is what I can expect on my return, then perhaps I should go away more often."

"Are you sure you really want to do that?"

She had tightened her grip on his wrists and he laughed in delight.

Afterwards they lay in each other's arms, content and happy and making wild plans for the future. Argentina, Cairo, Istanbul. Places for writers and artists and lovers of romance. They would visit them all. Make love in them all. And not only that he said, his lips nibbling on the roundness of her shoulder, they would mix with interesting people. People who cared less about money and more about throwing fabulous parties and soirees and grand balls in country houses.

Closing her eyes she allowed her imagination to soar. Him in a white tie and waistcoat, her in Lanvin or Patou. And as they made their way around the dance floor - her steps faultless of course - others would step back in admiration and in discreet whispers wonder about the glamorous couple.

But Darius wasn't finished.

They would attend gala nights at the theatre and invitations to sporting events, and in the private boxes of the sublimely rich she would be feted and toasted and drink champagne and nibble on the most divine hors d'ouvres.

Oysters.

His lips were moving towards her breast.

Caviar.

Closer still.

They would be part of the *in crowd*, going to Le Touquet for Easter before returning to Cowes for the yachting, and when they were tired of England they would go to America and spend time at luxurious holiday homes on Newport and Rhode Island.

His breath was warm, and unable to help herself, Thea arched her back.

Bermuda. The Bahamas.

In desperation she took his hand and placed it on her lower belly.

"Please," she begged. "Again. Love me again."

"My God, you are insatiable," he murmured happily.

"Now," he said once they'd fallen back onto the bed in a state of complete exhaustion, "where were we?"

Reaching for his lighter he lit up a cigarette.

"You were about to tell me about your trip to Australia."

Her head was on his chest, and so he settled his free arm around her.

"I was, wasn't I? Well, it went better than I thought."

"And?"

He took his time, knowing it would drive her crazy.

"Darius!"

"Okay. I'll tell you." He couldn't help grinning. "I knew the station was doing well and starting to turn over a profit, so I put it to Bill that I wanted my investment back. Well, we are going to need a little capital, aren't we darling? As I'd thought, it wasn't too hard for him to raise a mortgage."

When her head jerked up he could see her eyes were sparkling. "Oh! Is that why you went? That's marvellous."

Then, as if a little unsure such enthusiasm was appropriate, she'd added uncertainly. "It is, isn't it?"

"Yes it is," he reassured her, still thinking of Bill. Of how happy he'd been to have outright control of his future. Though it had come at the cost of a very large debt to the bank. Even at the time he'd shuddered at the burden his friend was to shoulder. Not that he had anything against borrowing. Heavens no! Didn't everybody owe something to someone? But that was different. In his world financial favours were often returned in other ways. An introduction here, a word in the right ear there. It was how the world turned. But the banking institutions didn't quite see it in the same light, and when push came to shove they were quite happy to squeeze a fellow dry. And that was why such places were a last resort for chaps such as him.

He glanced down at Thea. She was so beautiful. Or perhaps it was that she was still glowing from their lovemaking. No, he decided, taking in the softness of her skin and the perfect shape of her mouth, she was beautiful.

"I'm glad," she murmured.

"You should be, for now we have enough to make a go of our plans."

"Mmm. Well I have news too."

She had propped herself up on her elbow.

"What is it?"

"I am the proud owner of a passport."

Her face had lit up as if this was the most important achievement of her life.

"Well done! Did it take long to get?"

"No. I just went down to the passport office and filled out a form."

"My darling, you are a star."

"I'm glad you think so. So where to from here?"

He inhaled thoughtfully on his cigarette.

"Well, we need that shipping timetable. And we need to plan how to get you out of here without raising suspicions."

"That might not be so easy."

"No," he agreed. "But how do you do it now?"

"For shopping or the pictures do you mean? I go with one of the others. Daisy or Esme, more often than not."

"And they're the ones that cover for you when you meet me?"

"Yes. I tell everyone else I'm going to the library. They all know I read, and anyway, who'd want to wait around while I choose my books."

"Well that's not going to work if you've a suitcase in your hand."

"No, I've already realised that." She fell back onto his chest.

"We just need to plan carefully."

As if in agreement, there was a squeal of raucous laughter from another room.

"Will we really be able to get away with it?" she asked quietly, her fingertips light on his skin.

"Of course we will. At worst, you might have to leave your things behind. But that's the least of our worries. We can buy you an entire wardrobe once we're at sea. In the meantime though," and glancing towards the door he lowered his voice as if someone might be listening, "like I said, we just need the right plan."

35

DARIUS'S IDEA OF CAUTION WAS to suggest he cut back his visits to Kitty's in order for it to appear that his and Thea's relationship was nowhere near as strong as in reality. Thea hated that she wouldn't be able to see him as often as she wanted but she saw the sense in his proposal.

"It'll give me the opportunity to get down to the farm and tie up any loose ends," he said, reaching for his trousers.

Already in her kimono Thea was leaning against the dressing table.

"Your mother will be pleased to see you."

"I know."

"Will you tell her you're going back to England?"

"I'll have to." His voice was flat.

The next time he visited the weather was gray and miserable, and damp seemed to permeate every corner of the bedroom.

"I can't wait to get away from all this." he said, puffing on his cigarette and staring at the rain streaming down the window.

"Not long now," having sensed his mood Thea tried to cheer him up by snuggling closer and giving him a quick squeeze. "Tell me about the sailings you've found."

"There's two, both in the middle of next month."

"But isn't that cutting it fine?"

"It is. But we need to be at sea when he is. That way, even if Kitty manages to alert him, what can he do? He can hardly demand his captain circles around and chases after us, can he? And don't forget, if he has no idea of the route we've taken, he'll have no idea where we're disembarking either."

"Ships that pass in the night," she said quietly.

"Exactly. If we make our move before he leaves England he could contact Scotland Yard, who would in turn be onto the police here. Then all hell would break loose. Of course, we might be wrong about this my darling. He might prefer a little more discretion."

She nodded. The truth was she had no idea what Silas would do when he discovered she'd gone.

"Either way we have to plan for the worst and hope for the best. But let's not dwell on that right now."

Dragging himself upright Darius reached onto the bedside cabinet for the newspaper he'd brought with him, and after shaking open the pages and folding them into a manageable size, he indicated the list of sailings.

"You can choose. This one goes via New York and then up to Boston, whilst this one," and his finger moved a little lower and tapped, "goes around the Cape and stops off at Tenerife."

"New York," she said emphatically.

"Then that is the one we'll take," and at last he grinned. Clearly his mood had lifted. "You will adore travelling first class."

"Gracious! Won't that cost a fortune?"

The newspaper dropped onto the bed.

"What's money for if not for spending? You can't take it to the grave after all." When she didn't reply he continued, "Not only that, you never know who you will meet on these trips. Why, I once shared a voyage with an Italian count and his wife. Charming man. Had an enormous villa overlooking the Tiber and was completely obsessed with motorcars which is probably why we all got on so well."

Of course, it wasn't necessary for Thea to know he'd spent far more time in the countess's private stateroom rather than in his own decidedly less comfortable quarters.

"And on another occasion," he added, rolling over and slipping a hand beneath the coverlet, "I had the pleasure of meeting a rather splendid Argentinean gentleman. A first class polo player by all accounts. So you see it's really the only way to travel. Especially," having caressed her stomach he was edging down towards her thigh, "since I want to show you off."

Regardless of the distraction, Thea wasn't convinced. Shouldn't they be a little more circumspect? Perhaps travel second class and save the rest of his money for somewhere to stay in London? No doubt rent in the capital was astronomical, and while she had little idea of the extent of Darius's financial position, there was no likelihood of her being able to access any of her own funds and thus help out.

"Everything is going to be wonderful," Darius was saying, "and you my darling, are going to be a big hit back home. Though I'm beginning to realise I'll have to watch my step when the other fellows see you."

"Do you think so," she said, thawing a little and giggling. She was being silly. For Heaven's sake, he would hardly have suggested they run away together if he didn't already have everything mapped out.

But just as they had when he'd gone to Australia, once he'd left for the Waikato the days dragged, and even the thought that within a matter of weeks she'd have both the man she loved and the freedom she'd dreamed of did little to lift her spirits.

"Gawd Thea! Yer've got a face like the arse-end of a donkey," Daisy told her. "You need to get a grip you do, pining away like this. 'Ave you eaten today? No," she said without waiting for an answer, "I thought not. Get yer nose outta that book and get downstairs and make yerself a sandwich or summit. And if yer feelin' generous, yer can make me one, an' all."

Gerald was a little more circumspect.

"You're distant again," he told her, sitting beside her in the salon one evening, "just like last week. What's the matter with you? One minute you're fine and the next you're away with the fairies."

"Really?" Thea tried to contain her annoyance.

"Yes. What is it with you?"

"Good gracious, why should anything be wrong?"

"Please don't treat me as though I'm stupid," he said quietly. "It's clear something is not quite right," then his mouth tightened. "Unless I am mistaken and the problem is one of reluctance to attend to me?"

"Not at all." That at least was honest, and to her surprise Thea saw his expression relax a little.

"Then I would guess it is a man," he said in a more friendly tone altogether. "Am I close?"

"Why don't I get you another drink," and almost tearing the glass from his hand Thea marched up to the bar.

"That man can be insufferable at times," she said to Nelly in an undertone.

Struggling with a bottle of brandy and a stubborn cork, Nelly glanced over to where Gerald was forming pyramids with his fingertips.

"Really?" she questioned. "What's he done? Is it something Miss Kitty should know about?"

Thea didn't want to cause a fuss, especially not under the circumstances. "No. It's probably me. Maybe I'm being a little too sensitive."

"You don't have to entertain him, you know. Call one of the others." Nelly was shrugging as if the solution was obvious. "Mind you, I wouldn't like to be him with those scars. How did he get them? Do you know?"

"He was burnt in the war."

Nelly nodded. "Well, it's certainly ruined his chances with the ladies," and she took another peek in his direction. "Shame really, as he must have been quite a looker once. And I've noticed he carries himself well. Like I said, it's a shame."

Thea too looked over. She'd never considered Gerald as anything other than the way he looked now, but Nelly was right. His life would have been so different under any other circumstances. If nothing else, she doubted he'd have any need to visit a bordello. Why, he'd probably be married. There might even be children.

No wonder he was so hostile.

"Or," Nelly was leaning on the bar, her expression suggesting she was about to impart something confidential, "maybe he's already got a wife and that's why he comes here. She won't let him in her bed anymore."

"Nelly, you're shocking!"

36

"YOU WANTED TO SEE me?"

Having taken the usual couple of steps inside her employer's domain, Thea was rattled. Frank had been sent to fetch her and she was wondering why. Was it her obvious reluctance to entertain customers? Or was it something else? What had Kitty found out? Not that there was much to uncover since she hadn't told a soul of her grand plan. Not even Daisy. And anyway, the final details weren't ironed out yet so there should be little to worry about.

At least that's what she told herself.

"Ah yes." Kitty was taking coffee, and gesturing that Thea should take a seat on the chaise longue opposite, she reached for the geometrically shaped pot and poured a second cup.

"We need to discuss your husband's return," she said. "Milk? Sugar?"

Accepting the first, Thea shook her head at the second.

"Why don't we get straight to the point?" Kitty settled back, saucer in one hand, cup in the other. "As you know, I have been reporting on your time here and your progress."

Thea said nothing. Of course she was aware. Wasn't it part of the grubby little arrangement?

"In fact," Kitty said between sips, "you will be pleased to know we both feel your time here has been a success. You have made progress. Considerable progress," she emphasised. "So much so that he has also given me to understand that now that you have a better understanding of the duties of a wife, he is looking forward to the resumption of your marriage."

"I see."

"Of course I haven't acquainted him with every detail of these past months. I think we can both agree there are certain things he needn't know, don't you? Such as your little affair with a certain customer perhaps?"

Thea said nothing.

"These things happen. Darius is exciting, I admit that and I can see the attraction. But would it have served any advantage to inform your husband of your…" Kitty deliberately paused, "… affair of the heart? I think not. Men can be so unpredictable, don't you think? Revengeful even."

"What exactly is it you want," Thea said quietly.

"So suspicious Thea, and with no reason. Drink your coffee while it's hot." Kitty gestured to the cooling brew. "You know, just thinking aloud, it might be better not to go into too much detail when discussing your time here = if indeed you do. Play down the full extent of your involvement in the salon. At least that's my advice."

"And why would I do that?"

"Well, you don't want him thinking you are over qualified now, do you?"

"Over qualified?"

"I'm sure you know what I mean. Think of his sensibilities."

Thea's eyebrows lifted in response.

"Do you know when he is expected to arrive?"

Holding the other woman's gaze levelly, she hoped her voice sounded more confident that she felt.

"I do. He is leaving Southampton this week. And on a particularly grand ship by all accounts."

Thea couldn't have cared if he was travelling by canoe.

"And exactly when will it dock in Auckland?"

"The third of November. In plenty of time for Christmas," Kitty remarked. "Nothing to say? You do surprise me."

"Oh, I have plenty to say."

"Then feel free to do so." Kitty put down her cup and saucer.

"This has been a cruel and horrendous experience and at the first opportunity I intend to have this place closed down and you thrown in jail."

Thea had decided to fight fire with fire, if only to convince Kitty her one desire was to return home.

"You wouldn't do that."

"Wouldn't I? When my husband learns the full extent of the degradation you have heaped upon me - and the other girls too - I will convince him to go to the police."

Kitty was shaking her head.

"You haven't thought it through have you? How could he go to the police without informing them of his part in your being here? And not only that, as a valued customer I doubt he would want us closed down at all. Oh wait, I see," it was as if a new thought had just occurred, "you think that with you in his bed, and thanks to the knowledge and skill you have acquired here, he will have no requirement for our services? Well, you might be right. But somehow I doubt it. I admire your gall though. I always have, if I'm honest."

Continuing the fictitious argument, Thea lifted her chin and glared.

"We shall see."

"We shall indeed. And now I have something for you."

Turning to the table beside her chair Kitty retrieved an envelope.

"He enclosed it with his most recent communication," she said, passing it over. Written on the front, and in Silas's hand, was Thea's name. "I expect you'd like to read it in private but there's no need to rush off. Have some more coffee and you can tell me what you're reading these days. I am quite fascinated to know. I'm told you even read in the salon. Nothing too salacious I hope!"

The moment Thea had gone, the rear door leading to the small draughty vestibule at the back of the house opened and Frank slipped in. Without waiting to be asked he made straight for the fireplace and leaning down, held his hands to the warmth of the flames and rubbed them briskly.

"Well?" Kitty had joined him. "You heard her. What do you think?"

"I wouldn't like to say," he said slowly. "She sounds genuine. But she's a clever one. She and that Darius were definitely talking about her leaving before Crawford gets back. Like I said, I heard them when I was taking wood up to the rooms. Not that I was able to hang around long, what with all the comings and goings."

Kitty had always encouraged Frank's habit of listening at doors.

"Hmm. I'm inclined to believe it, since it fits in with her attitude in the salon." She was thoughtful for a moment. "But if she does intend to make a run for it, well, that could prove awkward. I want you to watch her. I want to know every move she makes. And her friends? Do you think any of the other girls might be in on her little scheme?"

"Couldn't say."

"Worst case, we lock her in her room."

"For six weeks?" Frank sounded aghast, and though she was staring at him, she wasn't seeing him. Instead she was thinking hard.

"As I said, that would be the worst case. But you're right. We'll take it one step at a time. Let her think we have no idea what's going on."

"I'll keep an eye on her."

"Good. When Silas Crawford gets back, she has to be here waiting and pleased to see him. For all our sakes."

It didn't hurt to remind Frank of his comfortable existence every now and then. His and Huia's quarters came with the job, as did the food and booze given so freely to him. Then there was the cash he made on the side from the homemade grog-shop he'd recently set up in the outhouse. Oh yes, she knew all about that little enterprise.

"You know you can rely on me," he said, somewhat aggressively.

"I know that Frank. Even though you drink too much and like to paw the merchandise, I know I can always rely on you."

37

REMAINING BEHIND AFTER THE OTHERS had gone downstairs that afternoon, Thea went over to Nora's bed by the window and read her letter. It wasn't a long correspondence, taking up just a single sheet.

My dearest Theodora, he began.

I trust this letter finds you in good health and that the past weeks have not been too onerous for you, nor in any way detrimental to your health.

Thea frowned at that. Was he inferring her mental well-being? Or her physical? Regardless, such concern was surely too late.

My business here in Europe is almost at an end and soon I will be sailing for New Zealand, arriving in Auckland during the first week of November. I have no doubt this will be pleasing news to you and expect that after such absence you are of a mind to demonstrate a willingness to resume your place in my household. I have been given to understand the treatment you have undergone has been beneficial...

Treatment, she wanted to scream? Had he any idea what she'd endured? Men, dozens of them, all waving tokens and wanting a piece of her?

... and for this I am as certain of your gratitude as my own, though I must now confess to a certain reservation that perhaps I had erred in my judgment and confidence of such a solution. I am pleased to learn that is not the case. However, and regardless of this, I must insist that on my return this period of marital

separation is to be considered at an end and never referred to again. I trust you will be in accord.

Furthermore, and immediately on my return, you may be pleased to know it is my intention to remove our household to the capital. Once again, I trust in your concurrence on this.

I remain your devoted husband.

Screwing up the letter in disgust Thea shoved it into her pocket. So, he wanted to sweep everything under the carpet and move her to Wellington as if the past months never happened - and she was to be grateful? Well he was in for a shock. She didn't know which pleased her more; Kitty's rage on discovering she had escaped her clutches, or the idea of Silas alone in a mausoleum of a house for the rest of his miserable life.

Of course, he'd no idea how much she'd changed. The old Thea would never have challenged her husband's wishes. Why, she wouldn't even demand the right to read whatever book took her fancy.

Nor would the old Thea have owned beautiful underwear or known how to make cocktails. Or experienced the joy of falling in love and the highs and lows of sharing her heart.

And not only her heart, but also something even more fragile, her dreams.

Perhaps after all, she did owe Silas and Kitty a debt of gratitude.

38

STROLLING ALONG THE PROMENADE, Thea slipped her arm into Darius's and leaned closer.

"Cold?" he smiled, drawing her closer.

Out in the bay the wind was buffeting the waves into foaming white caps, after which it tore up the beach and whipped at their coats and snapped at Darius's flannel trousers. Thea grabbed at her hat only seconds before it was snatched off.

"No," she laughed.

"Then why is the tip of your nose red?"

Pulling herself upright she made an attempt at scolding him. "It's not considered polite to remark on the colour of a lady's nose."

"But there's not a lady in sight."

"I'm not sure I want to run away with you if you are going to tease me like this," she said, confronting him with her best glare.

"Then I'd better watch my step."

"You should indeed."

"Oh Thea," he said, stopping suddenly and gazing around. Ungainly seaplanes were rolling and tipping at anchor, while closer to shore even the larger boats were straining at their moorings. "Not much longer and we'll be away from all this and on the other side of the world."

"It seems unreal."

"It does, doesn't it?"

"I can hardly image what our lives will be like."

"Wonderful. That's what they'll be like. You're not having any regrets are you?" he asked suddenly.

"Don't be silly. Why would I have regrets?"

"Well, you are leaving the only country you've ever known."

"There's no one here for me. Not anymore. So what's to stay for?"

And with the seagulls screeching and wheeling overhead they strolled on.

"Tell me about your mother," she said. "Was she upset when you told her you were leaving again?"

"She actually took it surprisingly well."

Thea thought he sounded relieved.

"At least as well as any mother would," he continued, turning away from the bracing wind.

"And did you tell her about me?"

She'd intended her words to be flippant, but even to her ears they'd sounded all too presumptuous.

"Of course."

Yet he didn't elaborate. Didn't add that his mother was happy for him or - and her heart sank at the very idea - that she was disappointed in his choice of companion. But then surely he wouldn't have divulged too much since he could hardly admit to where they'd met or God forbid that she was already married.

More unsettling was the notion he hadn't mentioned her at all.

"You were saying before that Kitty had summoned you? Is everything all right?" he asked.

"Yes," she nodded, thankful for the change of subject. "I was a bit worried at first, as you never know in that place. But all she wanted to do was to talk about Silas."

"Did she say when he'll be back?"

"The third."

"Well, that's given us something to go on. Either of the sailings we talked about will work since both will have us halfway across the globe when he docks. And even if he could establish the route we'd taken he'd have no idea where we disembarked. And that, my darling, is exactly what we are going to do."

"What?" Thea had stopped in confusion.

"Disembark en route," he explained.

"Oh. Do you mean we'll leave the ship in America?"

"I do. I still have friends there. Friends who will help us lie low for a while."

"Oh my goodness! That'll be amazing. And so different from living here. I've read the skyscraper buildings are a wonder in themselves."

'They are. You'll be amazed. Wait until you see the Woolworth Tower. It's so tall you won't believe your eyes!"

"Will we see the Statue of Liberty too?"

"We'll see everything," Darius laughed. "The Brooklyn Bridge, Times Square. I'll take you to them all."

"Oh Darius it's all so unbelievable. I can't wait. How long will we stay in America?"

"I have no idea," he said, tucking her arm back in his and stepping out again. "Weeks, months, maybe even longer. We'll just have to see."

But Thea was troubled.

"It all sounds perfectly marvellous, but how will we live? How will you earn a living?"

Removing his arm from hers Darius placed it around her shoulders instead.

"I don't want you to worry about that. Just leave everything to me."

Nestled into his coat Thea nodded. Clearly he had it all under control. She just had to learn to trust him.

"In the meantime," he was saying, "we must remain careful."

"I know. And that's rather hard when everyone thinks we're an item."

Darius was looking out across the bay again. "There's only one thing to do."

"And what's that?"

"Well, as much as I hate the idea, perhaps I should stop visiting you altogether."

Thea was horrified. "Is that really the only solution?"

"Remember it's only for another three weeks or so."

"But can we still meet like this?"

"Of course we can, silly goose." And he swept her into his arms. "Do you really think I could go that long without seeing you?"

"It won't be easy to get out as much as I'd like though."

"I realise that. But I'm sure you could manage two afternoons a week. Say Mondays and Thursdays?"

Thea smiled. "Between the library and shopping, I could."

"Well, there you are then."

"I just don't know how I'm going to cope without you on the other days."

His cheek was against hers.

"I hate being at Kitty's," she murmured.

"I hate that you are there too darling. But like I said, it won't be for much longer."

"I suppose you're right."

"Attagirl! You're a trouper."

She was shaking her head. "You make it sound so simple."

"It is," he replied. "It's simplicity itself. Look, there's a café over there. Why don't we get out of this wind and warm ourselves up with some tea."

39

GERALD WAS UNBUTTONING THE CUFFS of his shirt.

"I have to say, you're looking far happier than of late," he said, sitting on the edge of the bed. "I take it things are on the up for you?"

Glancing over Thea smiled. "I shouldn't really say anything but they are."

"And was I right? Is it a man?"

"It is."

"I see." He was yanking his shirt tails from his trousers. "And would I be right in thinking this man is important to you."

Although the heat had risen in her cheeks, she saw no reason not to answer. "You would."

There was another moment of silence, and busy with the disinfection solution Thea had no idea whether to be grateful or disappointed he didn't want to know more. Not that she had expected congratulations. Or even approval.

But it seemed his interest wasn't in Darius, but her.

"So why are your moods constantly up and down?"

"I think that's a little intrusive," she said gently.

Whilst it would be an exaggeration to say they had become friends, thanks to his opening up a little she understood, and even accepted, his gruff manner. In fact she'd even fought his corner one evening in the salon when Violet had called him an *invalid,* adding a little snidely that he had the hots for Thea.

"Don't call him that," she'd rounded on her in a fury.

"Why not?" Violet wanted to know.

"Because he's no more an invalid than you or I. He was hurt in the war, that's all."

"Well it's just as well he only wants to see you. I'd hate to have to look up at that face hovering over me."

"How dare you. You don't even know him."

"And I don't want to."

"Well he wouldn't want to know you either."

"Best pals are you? Looking after his interests? What exactly do you do for him Thea?"

"You evil cow!"

Someone gasped.

"Ohhhh. Hit a sore spot have I?" Violet taunted.

"Enough!" Belle stepped in just as Thea was about to launch herself at the other girl.

"It's your loss," Thea threw over Belle's shoulder, "because you will never know how gentle and respectful he really is."

"Respectful? In here?" Violet shot back.

"Yes. Surprise you does it?"

"He's not respectful, he's just grateful to anyone desperate enough to lower their drawers for him."

Thea made another lunge but Belle was too quick for her.

"*I said enough!*" and spinning Thea around she gave her a push in the opposite direction. Violet wasn't so lucky for she received a resounding slap.

"Ow! What was that for?" she shrieked.

"Maybe because I just felt like it," Belle retorted.

Now the gentleman in question had edged a little towards the foot of the bed and was patting the coverlet.

"Come and talk to me," he said, "tell me what's bothering you."

"Honestly, you're mistaken. Nothing's bothering me."

"It would seem that's not quite true." His tone was surprisingly gentle.

"Look... I..." Thea had no intentions of being rude.

"Please," he was patting the coverlet again.

"Well, if you must know..." she said, taking her place where he'd indicated. Would it really hurt to tell someone? It wasn't as if he were on first name terms with the other girls, so he'd hardly blab to them. Nor had he ever given any indication he knew Kitty.

"Go on."

"He wants to take me away from here." The words spilled out.

"And is that what you want?"

"Of course!"

She was incredulous that anyone would think otherwise. "I hate it here," she blurted out, only to realise how dreadful that must sound. "Oh look, I'm sorry. I didn't mean it to come out quite that way."

But Gerald didn't seem offended at all.

"If that's the case, why do you stay?"

"It's a long story."

"So tell me."

"I don't think that would be a good idea."

"Why not?"

Now she was really uncomfortable.

"I can't."

Hands in her lap, she was studying her fingernails.

Gerald too was quiet, as if he were thinking the matter over. Then he shrugged.

"So tell me about him. Your saviour."

"Well, I shouldn't really be saying anything."

"I won't tell anyone, if that's what you are thinking."

"Oh I didn't think that," and she smiled.

He too was smiling, and suddenly she realised how attractive his eyes were. Bluey-gray like the ocean in winter. And surprisingly gentle.

"So, you're going away?" he prompted.

She nodded. "To America. At least that's where we're going first."

"You're leaving New Zealand? What of your family? Won't they mind?"

Thea looked down at her hands again. "I have no family. Well," and she coloured at the half-truth, "none to speak of."

"No parents?"

"No. They died a few years back. The 'flu' epidemic," she said by way of explanation. "We came out from England when I was a child and I have no other relatives. Well, none that I know of, anyway."

"Ahh. So that's how you ended up here?"

"In a manner of speaking."

He nodded slowly. "Was there no other alternative?"

Thea's mouth tightened. "Unfortunately not."

"Money then," he said.

"Goodness, isn't that why most women end up in places like this?"

"There must have been someone you could have turned to."

Suddenly Thea was furious. Was he implying it was her fault that she was in such a place? That she'd considered it an easy option?

"If you must know, that's exactly what I did. I found someone I thought I could trust and got married," she said coldly, casting aside all need for discretion. "It was my husband who placed me here."

Gerald's face registered complete shock, but Thea wasn't finished.

"Yes. I'm a married woman. And I wasn't sent here for the money, as you put it," she ploughed on regardless, "I was sent here to be educated."

"Educated? But in what way?"

"In all the ways to please a man," she sneered. "How else was I to learn?"

Gerald was staring in disbelief.

"My God! Your husband did this to you?"

"He did."

"And that's why you're running away with another man?"

"It is."

He was nodding, as if at last everything was falling into place. "This man you are running away with. He knows all this?"

"Of course."

"I see. It's beginning to make sense. And do you love him? This man I mean."

"Yes." Thea lifted her chin. "Yes I do."

It felt strange to say the words aloud. She hadn't even told Darius after all.

"And he makes you happy?"

"Yes he does."

"Then I'm pleased for you."

But he'd looked away.

"So, where did you meet him?" he asked casually.

"Here."

"Oh."

"You disapprove?" Thea had caught the hint of censure. "What did you expect? That I attended a tea dance and he requested a waltz?"

"Put like that it does seem a little silly."

"It does. So what did you want to say about it?"

"It's not important."

"I think it is," she pressed, her voice steely.

"Well, if you insist. I was just wondering…"

"Wondering what?"

"Well, forgive me for being indelicate, but wouldn't you agree most men visit places like this for one reason only?"

"Go on."

"Well, some have little option. Men such as me for example. Others do have choices though. Perhaps they are waiting for the right daughter to be presented to them. Or they're already spoken for and are looking for a little extra on the side."

Thea was on her feet.

"Are you suggesting that my friend is married? Because if you are you couldn't be more wrong."

"Well, you seem sure enough."

"I am," she glared.

"I'm sorry. Truly. Please accept my apologies for any offense I've caused. I'm sure you know what you are doing." Having risen from the bed he had started to re-button his shirt. "Look would you mind very much if we didn't continue today? I think the mood has rather soured."

"Not at all," she said coldly.

Given he was some six or seven inches taller than her, she was forced to look up to give him the full blast of her indignation - and that riled her too. "I'm afraid you won't get your token back. We've been up here too long for that."

"That's fine. Keep it. Perhaps I will come back next week."

"Well if you do, I suggest that rather than indulge in conversation it would be better to keep to our purpose."

40

IT HAD BEEN TEN DAYS since Darius's last visit to Kitty's - a very long time as far as Thea was concerned - and while they'd kept to their schedule of Mondays and Thursdays, the empty days in between gave her plenty of time to dwell on where he went and what he did when they were not together.

Though she now knew where he was living.

"He's a decent chap. Let's me doss here whenever I'm in Auckland," he'd said when at his suggestion they'd gone back to his friends place in Herne Bay. And with nothing personal of Darius's on show, she'd had to contend with a superficial inspection of the newly built apartment.

They were in the front bedroom, relaxing in the after-glow of their lovemaking and though she knew the timing wasn't quite right, she brought up her recent conversation with Gerald.

"Don't let it get to you," he said after she'd gone into some detail.

"It doesn't," she shrugged, though it did.

"Another week or so and we'll be on the high seas."

Striking his lighter he was holding the flame to his cigarette.

"Can I ask you something?" she said hesitantly.

"Of course."

"Well, this may seem a strange question, but do you make a habit of visiting places like Kitty's when you're in town?"

"I'd have thought you'd have known the answer to that already."

"Me? How would I know?"

"Didn't you realise I was only there because I was hoping to find the perfect woman? And I did!"

There was amusement in his voice.

"Be serious."

"I was."

"Tell me. I want to know."

"What's wrong with using bordellos?" The light-hearted banter was gone. "They're places of fun after all. And the girls are clearly out for a good time. What more could anyone ask?"

"There must be more to it than that."

"Like what? What is it you want me to say? It's simple Thea, don't over-complicate things. Places like Kitty's exist to give chaps like me what we want, when we want it. And all without the worry of over-protective mothers and trigger-happy fathers. That's all it boils down to."

"Well, you won't have need of them anymore because as far as I'm concerned it's you and me. And no one else."

"Do you mean I have to give up all my other girl-friends?" he asked in mock horror.

Thea's head shot up. "Darius!"

"I love it when you're jealous," his eyes were twinkling again, "I take it as a compliment."

"You can take it whichever way you want," she huffed, laying her head back down. "But you do want to settle down one day? Get married? Have a family?"

She held her breath. What if he said *no*? Where did that leave things between them?

"Sure. Just not right now," he said easily. "Look," his fingers were playing on her arm, "life's too short to worry about the future. God knows, the war put paid to that sort of attitude. Live for the day and have fun while you're doing it. That's what we all have to do from now on."

"But you do want children one day?" she insisted.

"Sure."

"A son," she said dreamily, rolling onto her back. "A boy for you and a girl for me."

"You really are thinking ahead."

"Of course. Wouldn't you like something to show for your time here?"

"I certainly don't need to create the next generation for that. You're all I need."

"And you're all I need."

"Well then. If we have each other then surely that's enough."

Thea acknowledged his words with a smile.

"Good," he said, lowering his mouth to hers, "for a moment I thought we might be having our first disagreement."

41

LYING ON HER BED DAISY was flicking through the latest edition of the Ladies' Mirror.

"Fancy the pictures?" she asked, dipping into a tin of toffees and wedging a sticky lump into her cheek.

"When?"

"Tomorrow?"

"You know I'd love too, but I can't."

"Yer said that yesterday," she replied.

"No I didn't."

"The day before then."

"I don't think I said it then either."

"So wot are yer up to?" Daisy threw down her magazine. "And don't tell me nuffink, 'cos I know you. You're meeting 'im on the sly, ain't'cha?"

"Who?"

Keeping her head down Thea continued separating her laundry.

"'Is lordship, Darius. 'Oo d'yer fink I mean?"

"Really Daisy, why on earth would you think that?"

"I'm right, ain't I?" Daisy said triumphantly. "So where is 'e? Obviously still around or you wouldn't be sneaking out to meet him."

"I'm hardly *sneaking out*, as you put it. He's just too busy to come here, that's all."

"Been busy a lot then lately, ain't 'e? After all, 'e ain't been 'ere for a while."

"Heavens, Daisy, what does it matter if he comes here or not?" Holding up a pair of silk stockings she looked at them thoughtfully. "I thought I'd lost these," she said to no one in particular.

But Daisy wasn't giving up.

"So wot yer doin'? Going to his place and givin' 'im a freebie?"

Thea was shocked. "That's disgusting."

"So I'm right."

The two women faced each other.

"Whatever we're doing has nothing to do with you."

"It does if we're mates."

Thea sat down heavily on her bed. The truth was, she and Darius hadn't visited a teashop or enjoyed a stroll since the afternoon in Mission Bay. Why waste precious time he'd said, walking her in the direction of the apartment the first time.

So, in a way, Daisy was right.

But she was also wrong, for she and Darius loved each other and planned to be together for the rest of their lives. So she was hardly giving anything away, as her friend put it.

"Look, just leave things alone," she finally said.

"Fine by me."

Rolling off her bed Daisy went over to the wardrobe where she stuck her head inside as if looking for something to wear.

"Daisy, let's not fight," Thea said wearily.

But there was no end to the rattling of coat hangers, and unable to bear the thought of falling out with the only other person she cared about, Thea decided to tell her the truth.

"If I let you in on a secret, can I trust you?"

"Secret? Wot secret?" Daisy's head had reappeared.

"You must promise not to tell anyone."

"I won't," she sounded almost affronted.

"No one. Not even Esme," Thea insisted.

"I hear you. So wot's the secret?" she said, closing the overly ornate mahogany door and leaning against it.

"Darius is taking me away from here."

Daisy's mouth fell open. "Wot d'yer mean?"

"We're leaving. Running away if you like."

"Yer never!"

"I am."

"But yer can't."

"Well we are. I've had enough of this place and more than enough of Miss Kitty. And that's why he's lying low. Too many people were talking about us."

"Oh Lawd! 'Ave yer any idea wot yer saying?"

"Of course I do. But I need you to keep it quiet."

"So when are yer going?"

"In a week."

It was obvious the news had flabbergasted Daisy, for she'd dropped back onto her bed.

"Well! Yer could knock me down wiv a fevver! So, are yer an item? Does 'e really love yer?"

Thea shrugged helplessly. "I think so. Anyway," and tossing her head she continued, "that doesn't matter. He makes me happy."

"And yer reckon that's enough?"

"I do. Please," and coming and perching beside her, Thea took her hands, "this is my only chance."

"But do yer know wot yer doin'? 'As 'e made yer any promises?" Daisy said weakly.

"No. But nothing can be as bad as staying here."

"But yer married. Wot about yer 'usband?"

"By the time he gets back it'll be too late. We'll be gone."

"Miss Kitty is gonna kill you."

"Not if she can't find me."

But Daisy was shaking her head.

"Daisy, please be happy for me."

"Course I am," she said, giving Thea an exuberant hug. "Bugger me! Darius. Well, I dunno wot to say."

"Don't say anything other than I can count on you."

"Yer know yer can."

"Friends?" Thea searched Daisy's eyes.

"Always."

And they hugged again.

"So 'ow are you gonna get away?" Daisy wanted to know.

"We haven't worked that out yet."

"Wot! You ain't got any idea at all?"

"Not exactly."

"Oh for Gawd's sake! 'Ow d'yer expect to succeed if you ain't got a plan? Okay, we need to think this though. Exactly when are yer goin'?"

"Next Monday. There's a ship leaving for America."

"Blimey," Daisy said. "America! That's a bit ritzy, ain't it?"

Thea was grinning. "It is, isn't it?"

"So wot time do you 'ave to be at the docks?"

"Around five in the afternoon."

"Hmm. That's a bit late. Shame it wasn't earlier, 'cos if you ain't in the salon someone's gonna go looking for yer. And 'ow do you intend to get down there? Is 'is lordship coming for you?"

Thea shrugged a little self-consciously. She and Darius had planned to work out the finer details during their next meeting.

"Well you can't walk out the front door wiv a case in each 'and, now can yer?"

"That would give the game away," Thea acknowledged with a smile. "But I don't need to take anything with me. Darius says we can buy everything we need on the ship."

Now Daisy was grinning. "This really is excitin', innit?"

"It is going to be an adventure," Thea agreed, her expression equally as gleeful. "You know, I could say I had an overdue book, one I'd forgotten, and had to get it back to the library before it closed. If anyone asked, would you back me up?"

"Course I would."

"You might get in trouble."

"Not really. 'Ow was I to know you were doin' a runner? After all, yer ain't gonna be carryin' any luggage are yer?"

Thea stepped it out in her head. There was absolutely no reason why it wouldn't work. In fact it was probably the least suspicious option and the most simple.

"Oh Daisy, I'm going to miss you. I wish you could come too."

"As if you love-birds would want me wiv yer! But I'm gonna miss yer an' all. I've never met anyone like you before."

"Me neither. You will come and visit when we're settled?"

"Maybe."

Daisy's expression was wistful.

"I do mean it. I don't want this to be the end of us. I'll write to you the first chance I get. Tell you where we are."

"Fair enough." And having plumped up her pillow, Daisy swung her legs onto the bed and leaned back.

"Looks like one of us might end up in 'Ollywood after all."

"Wouldn't it be amazing if that were true? Oh Daisy, imagine that!" Thea gushed and then stopped. "You know, you'll get out of here too one day."

"Yeah, I know." But she didn't sound convinced.

"You will. I promise."

"Ain't I told yer before? Yer shouldn't make promises you can't keep."

Daisy's mood had gone from jubilant to despondent.

"Just tell me where I can send the letter," Thea said, reaching for her hand.

"It'll 'ave to be the post office. Can't 'ave it arrive 'ere or Miss Kitty will know we were in cahoots. And I can live wivout that grief."

"Consider it done. I'll write the moment we're on the ship and it will be sent from the first port we call at. I promise. I'm so glad I told you," she said, squeezing Daisy's hand once again, "I wanted to right from the start but I just didn't know how. Especially knowing how you felt about him."

"Anyway," and she looked in the direction of her own bed and the armful of washing awaiting her attention, "I need to get cracking if any of this is going to be dry by tomorrow."

42

FRANK WAS WAITING OUTSIDE KITTY'S front room.

"You wanted to see me?" she said, taking a key from her cardigan pocket and unlocking the door.

"Reckon you might want to hear what I have to say."

Pulling himself upright he followed her inside. "It's about Thea."

Kitty stopped.

"You'd better close the door."

"You remember wondering if she was planning on leaving us?" he said. He had come to stand directly in front of her.

"Yes."

"Well, she is."

"What makes you so sure?"

"Something I overheard."

"Indeed? And what was that?"

"I don't know everything yet because she and Daisy were already talking when I got there. But there's a trip to America on the cards. And soon."

"And Darius?"

"His name was mentioned."

"Damnation!"

Kitty was tapping the door key on the palm of her hand. So, the plan was going ahead. The girl had to be insane. Did she really think it was going to work out? That the flyboy loved her enough to give up his comfortable lifestyle and settle down? He would never knuckle down to regular work, and that's what it would take. No, give it a month or two and he'd be back flirting with every wealthy heiress in sight and looking for the easy option. And then what? Was Thea prepared to sit alone at nights wondering where he was? And worse, who he was with? She doubted it. Men like Darius never change. He would carry on flitting from one woman to the next, and leave nothing but a trail of broken hearts in his wake. Hers included. Of course deep down she must believe he'd change. That she was the one who truly understood him and could make a difference in his life.

Kitty shook her head in disgust. How many times had she heard that?

While Thea's future was nothing to do with her, the girl's life would be ruined, for the day would come when she would be cast aside - that is if she hadn't already had enough of his infidelities. And then what? She could hardly come home.

The trouble was, even if she tried to reason with her, the girl wouldn't listen.

"I'll keep a close watch on her," Frank was saying.

The tapping ceased as Kitty's fingers closed around the key. "Yes. Do that. Don't let her out of your sight."

He gave a nod.

"How often does she go out?"

"By herself?" Frank pondered for a moment, "maybe twice a week?"

"And where does she go?"

"Shopping I suppose. Oh, and the library for those books."

"Ah yes. The library."

"Should I follow her?"

"Yes. Better still, if she wants to go out, make sure from now on one of the girls goes with her."

"Anyone other than Daisy, right?"

Kitty nodded. "And I'm going to have a few choice words with her too. And with Darius. Let me know when he's here next. I'm going to put a stop to these shenanigans once and for all. Now, get me Belle."

With a dismissive nod Kitty went over to her desk and sat down.

It didn't bear thinking about. On top of everything else she'd be a laughing stock if the escapade were allowed to succeed. And then there was the reception she could expect from Silas Crawford when he discovered that far from becoming the willing bedmate he'd hoped, his wife had had the audacity to fall in love with a customer and run away. And a week before he returned!

All she wanted now was to hand the girl back and wash her hands of the whole debacle.

She was still in a foul mood when Belle tentatively put her head around the door

"Did you know about this?" she demanded before she'd even set foot in the room.

Belle took a couple of hesitant steps and then stopped, her expression one of bewilderment.

"About what?"

"Thea. And that playboy Darius."

"I'm not sure what you are talking about."

"Really? I thought you were the one I told to keep an eye on her. Fine job you've done." Kitty was scathing. "She intends to run away with him."

Belle had turned pale.

"And you knew nothing about it?" Kitty's voice had risen.

"No. Absolutely not." Belle shook her head. "I knew she was sweet on him but he hasn't visited for a while."

"Of course he hasn't. That's because they're meeting somewhere else."

Belle looked even more surprised, and that too annoyed Kitty.

"I thought I could count on you. Well? Aren't you supposed to be in charge out there? Know what everyone's up to? Dear God, do I have to learn everything from Frank?"

"I'm sorry. I really had no idea."

"Then you are of little use to me."

Turning, she opened the topmost drawer of her desk, "And if that's the case, would you care to tell me why I waste my time supplying you with this if I get nothing in return?"

Belle's eyes had widened with longing.

"Please," she wheedled, taking a step closer. "I'll watch her like a hawk from now on."

"That's what you were supposed to be doing all along."

"Please. Give me another chance."

"Why should I?"

Dropping the packet back into the drawer Kitty slammed it shut. It was amazing how just the sight of the folded paper square could bring about such a change in the girl, though it wasn't the packaging that did it, but the knowledge of what was inside. The fine white powder that helped cloud the memory of what an abusive father was capable of doing to his daughter, and of a violent drunkard of a brother only too eager to carry on the family trait.

No wonder she was so good in the treatment room. It was probably how she got her own back on the world.

"Please," the girl was begging softly.

"That's your trouble. You think because I give you a little authority you can run roughshod over me. Well, let this be a lesson to you."

"It won't happen again."

"See that it doesn't. Now get out."

43

THEA TRIED TO SET ASIDE her worries.

Deep breaths, she told herself mentally, dressing for the salon. *All you have to do is get through the next three days and all this will be over.*

But it wasn't that easy.

Twice lately she'd caught a fleeting shadow disappearing around the corner as she left a room on the second floor. At least she thought she had. The first occasion she'd dismissed as her imagination. But when it happened again she'd felt more than a little uneasy.

And that wasn't all.

Last Monday, the day she'd been due to meet Darius, she'd pulled on her hat and announced to everyone within earshot that she was going to the public library, and of all things Belle said she would go with her. Thea had been astonished since no one at Kitty's had ever shown the slightest interest in reading. In fact she wondered if some of the girls had ever learned how to do so. She'd had to nip back upstairs and collect her books - including one she'd not had time to finish - and then, when she'd handed in one set of books and begun checking out the long shelves for replacements, Belle had simply taken a seat at a desk and waited.

"Wasn't there anything you wanted to borrow?" she'd asked, as they made their way back to Kitty's.

"No. I changed my mind when I got there," had been Belle's reply.

And because she hadn't been able to get away, she hadn't seen Darius. Nor had she been able to get a message to him. She had tried to get out of the house again yesterday, only this time bumped into Kitty herself.

"Surely you're not venturing out in this weather?"

While it was true the rain was pouring down, it was nothing more than the usual Auckland weather. Give it half an hour and the sun would be out again. Four seasons in one day was how the locals summed it up.

"I'm sure it will brighten soon," Thea said, forcing a breezy note into her voice and waving her umbrella.

"I disagree." Having positioned herself between Thea and the door Kitty was standing her ground. "In fact, for your own sake I'm going to insist you stay inside. I don't want you catching a chill. Good Heavens! You might pass it on to the others and that certainly wouldn't do at all."

Thea was left with little choice but to retreat back upstairs.

Even then she couldn't decide if she was making a mountain out of a molehill. Was she being totally paranoid thinking Miss Kitty had ordered people to spy on her? In the cold light of day such a thing was absurd. Not only that, she and Darius had been so careful these last weeks, surely no one could have guessed.

Or had Daisy said something? Perhaps without thinking?

Smoothing out the lace mat on top of her chest of drawers - somehow she never did seem to accumulate the amount of clutter the others did - Thea tried to think things through. Daisy wouldn't give the game away, not even accidentally. She was a rock. Hadn't she taken to calming her down when the tension got too much these last few days, reassuring her over and over that everything would be hunky-dory?

But how could it, if she couldn't reach Darius and warn him something might have gone wrong? And where was he anyway? Why hadn't he turned up when she hadn't kept to their last two appointments? Wasn't he worried something might have happened to her? All she wanted was to be his arms and for him to tell her everything was fine. Was it really too much to ask?

Just then Nelly popped her head around the bedroom door.

"Hey Thea, are you coming down? Only you have a customer waiting for you."

Thank God!

"Is it anyone I know?" she asked lightly, reaching for the small, round box of rouge. And while she wanted to jump for joy it wouldn't do to let down appearances at this late hour.

"Yes. The guy with the scarred face. Shall I tell him you're on your way down?"

Thankfully Nelly didn't catch Thea's groan of disappointment nor, when suddenly the room swam and needing to steady herself, did she see her lean on the chest of drawers, scrunching and digging her fingers into the lace doily.

"I hope I'm not putting you out?" Gerald had risen from his chair. "Only I had a cancelled appointment in town and thought I'd make the most of it."

"No, not at all," Thea replied. "We're always glad to see you here. It's just that I've been a little caught up this afternoon."

"So I'm not intruding? Good."

There was a slight awkwardness when forgetting her manners, Thea failed to indicate whether Gerald should resume his seat, or if indeed they would break with the usual niceties and go upstairs immediately.

He waited politely.

"I'm sorry," she said, shaking her head as if to gather her thoughts, "may I get you a drink?"

"Thank you. Just a whiskey."

She was acutely aware that having glanced up from their card game, Belle and Nancy were watching her with open curiosity. Perhaps that was why her hand shook as she reached for the bottle and poured a large measure into a glass.

"I wasn't sure you would still be here," Gerald said pleasantly when she returned with his drink.

The blood drained from her cheeks and she sat down quickly.

"Gosh," she said, hoping against hope that neither girl had heard the damning words, "now why on earth would you ever think that?"

Gerald looked at her for a long moment.

"My apologies. My mistake."

Thea attempted another smile. "Are you finding the weather a little cold at the moment? I have to say I cannot wait until spring. The arrival of the sun and the longer days that come with it are so uplifting. And of course everything comes into bloom as well. Quite a joyous time really."

She stopped, for Gerald's expression was one of confusion.

"I'm sorry," she said again, "am I talking too much?"

"Not at all."

"Then shall we go upstairs?"

It was far too soon. What must he think? She'd only just given him his first drink but her nerves were frayed. And if he accidentally mentioned anything else...

"If I might..."

He was indicating his glass, implying he'd rather take a moment or two to finish the contents.

"Of course."

She looked about. Belle and Nancy had returned to their game, though not without another glance in her direction, whilst sitting beside the fire Soo Ling was reading what appeared to be a letter. From where she sat Thea could make out the strange hieroglyphics on the single sheet. Nelly was humming softly to herself.

Everything was as usual when the curtains parted and another customer arrived.

Thea didn't stop to think.

Didn't for one moment consider what would be made of her behaviour as she jumped to her feet.

And yet Darius barely gave her a second look. Instead he made his way directly over to a delighted Nancy, and taking her hand, bent down to whisper in her ear. Nancy responded with peals of laughter.

"Darius," she admonished with another giggle, "you are just too wicked!"

Crimson with embarrassment, Thea sat back down.

He was of course continuing to play the part and should be applauded for that, since her reaction to his appearance; impetuous as it had been, could so easily have endangered them. But she still seethed when after another tinkling laugh, Nancy slipped her hand around his neck and drew his head closer to hers.

Conscious of Gerald beside her Thea turned to him.

"Heavens, what must you think?" she said gaily.

But with a somewhat cynical expression he was focused on the others, and when she too turned back she saw that Darius had taken a chair at the card game.

One facing her.

His complicit wink said it all, and with a surge of relief she let go of the breath she'd been holding.

"Gosh!" she said turning once more to Gerald, "this is going to sound perfectly rude, and I do apologise, but I'm afraid I won't be able to see you right now."

He was nodding. "I thought somehow that might be the case."

"I'm sorry," she repeated, "will you let me find you another girl?"

'That won't be necessary." His tone was clipped. "From your reaction to his arrival I take it that is the gentleman you are in love with?"

There was a sudden burst of laughter from the card table and Thea reddened.

"Please forgive me," she said, jumping up and rushing from the room.

44

"I THOUGHT YOU WERE never going to come," Thea said breathlessly, taking her lips from Darius's for only a moment. "Hold me. Oh, hold me. I've been so worried."

Pacing up and down the hallway waiting for Gerald to leave, she'd been surprised how guilty she felt. But when he'd gone and the front door had shut behind him, she'd rushed back into the salon, and standing next to Darius's chair brazenly placed a proprietary hand on his shoulder.

Belle appeared bemused. Nancy however, was not, and had spat an angry *excuse me?* Though he was clearly enjoying the attention of all three women, Darius tactfully offered a polite nod to his card partners and stood.

Now she was safe in his arms.

"Thea, Thea," he murmured, caressing her hair, her shoulders, her breasts. "Of course I was going to come."

"It seemed like forever. Where have you been?"

"I've been around."

"But where?" she insisted.

He was frowning and looking uncomfortable, as if dismayed at the change in her and Thea hung her head.

"I'm sorry. I don't know what's wrong with me. I just can't seem to think straight anymore."

"My darling, you're anxious. That's all. And anyway, I'm here now."

"So do we have a plan? We only have two days left," she looked up hopefully.

"Heavens woman, give me a chance to get into the room." Then his mouth was on hers once more. "Oh God, I've missed you."

"I've missed you too," she managed.

"Darius…" she tried again when he'd leaned his forehead against hers.

"Yes?"

"I thought… I thought…"

"Well don't. You know how I feel about you," and parting her robe, he lowered his head to brush his lips against the curve of her breast.

Thea couldn't help the sigh that escaped, for the sensation was heavenly.

"You see. I know exactly how to make you happy," he said, easing her backwards towards the bed and lowering her down.

Afterwards they lay as always; his arm around her and her head on his shoulder. He was smoking a cigarette - a habit she'd tried to master but failed, since it didn't come as naturally to her as to others. In fact, it made her feel quite queasy, though thankfully she didn't suffer the same reaction when those around her smoked. Darius had a preference for foreign brands, Turkish and French in particular, and she'd discovered those aromas to be wonderfully heady. Now she closed her eyes and inhaled the fragrance.

"I've been so worried lately," she murmured.

Under her fingertips his skin was warm and just a little damp.

"My sweet, silly girl," he dropped a kiss onto the top of her head. "Everything's going to be fine. Just tell me what's happened. And why you didn't turn up to our last two meetings."

His tone was that little bit too flippant. Condescending even. Was he that oblivious to what she was going through? Didn't he realise her nerves were shot to pieces and she was seeing catastrophe around every corner.

Biting back an acid response she took a calming breath. Now was not the time for remonstrations.

"It's a strange thing, but when I said I was going to the lending library Belle insisted on coming with me. Lord knows why since she clearly had no intention of borrowing anything. And she's never done that before." "Is that all? Maybe she wanted the walk? Get some fresh air?"

"No. I don't think that was it," she said, this time a little more forcibly. "And, when I went to leave yesterday Kitty stopped me at the door."

"What reason did she give?"

"That it was raining, of all things. You know, I really think they're watching me."

"Are you sure you're not imagining things? Perhaps Kitty really did have your welfare at heart."

"No. Not her."

"Hmm. If that really is the case all I can say is it's not cricket."

"It won't make a difference will it?"

Raising herself up onto her elbow, Thea looked at him. Studied his eyes, the smooth plane of his cheek and the fullness of his lips.

"No. Of course not," he reassured her with a smile, "we'll just have to be clever. That's all."

"But we're running out of time."

"No, we're not. We've got two full days to get you out of here. Though," and now he paused to draw upon his cigarette, "you know, there is another option."

"Oh? What's that?"

Darius took a moment.

"Well, if things are becoming a little tricky around here, there's no God-given rule to say we have to make one of those two sailings. We could hold off and take a later one."

Thea was stunned.

"But those are the only ones while Silas is at sea," she said, horrified at the very idea.

"They're the only two destined for England," he corrected her, drawing on the cigarette for the last time. Rolling over to the bedside cabinet he stubbed it out in the ashtray.

"Who's to say we have to go there? In fact, who's to say we have to leave the country at all?"

He made to place his arm around her once more but Thea was having none of it. Unable to believe what she was hearing, she'd pulled herself up and was staring down at him.

"What? But that's the whole idea. Why on earth would we stay here? You hate New Zealand for one thing."

"I'm sure I could put up with it a little longer."

She shook her head, more in bewilderment than anything else. "But I don't understand…"

"Well," and he gave the slightest of shrugs, "maybe we were a little hasty in making such grand plans."

"Yes, but…"

"I'm just thinking about what you've just said about looking over your shoulder all the time that's all. Would it really hurt to hold off for another week or two? It might even take the heat off the situation. Then, at the last minute, when everyone's convinced they have nothing to worry about, we make our move. It would make life easier. Especially for you. It must be awful knowing you're not trusted, and I do worry for you darling."

"Do you?" Thea's voice was small, for she was overwhelmed with disappointment. Having been focused on their eloping - for wasn't that what they were doing - for weeks, she was at the point where she was prepared to risk anything to achieve her freedom. Even her safety. She had to make him realise that.

"Couldn't we still try, though? Please? I would much prefer us to be well away by the time Silas gets back."

"We could," he said hesitantly.

"Well, I'd like to keep to our plan. I want us to go to England."

She held her breath, for if he felt otherwise…

"My darling, if that's what you really want," he said, drawing her down to his chest, "then that's what we will do."

45

THEA WAS A BUNDLE OF nerves - fidgeting, pacing, wringing her hands - and every now and then perching awkwardly on the edge of the bed. After glancing at the door she would stand again, and on one occasion even grasped the brass rail at the end of the bedstead for support.

At the sound of light rapping she caught her breath until, as if suddenly remembering what was expected of her, she leapt forward, her palm moist and her fingers clammy on the polished brass doorknob. In an instant Daisy had slipped into the room and Thea was peering anxiously up and down the dimly lit hallway.

"It's alright. No one followed me."

"Did it work?" Thea said. Having closed the door, she was leaning hard against the panels.

"More than work! Yer should have seen me. Clutching me belly and rolling around groanin' like I was dyin'. Born for the stage I am!" and with a grin and a wink she struck a pose.

"So what happened?"

"I took me time. Started wiv a little moan, as you do. Held meself here…" Daisy had placed her hand on her stomach.

"Not that," Thea had grasped Daisy's shoulders. "I'm sure you were amazing, but did Belle suspect anything?"

"Nah, not 'er. I said it must be me monthlies arrivin' and she took one look and told me to get up stairs and lie down."

Thea gave a small *oh*, and then they were holding each other tight.

"Oh Daisy. I'm terrified."

"What on earf for? Yer getting' out ain't'cha?"

"Heavens! It looks like I am! Promise me you'll write."

"Course I bloomin' well will. Just you remember to send me yer address."

Now that the time had come there was little more to say yet each was as reluctant as the other to break away.

"Right," having finally eased herself upright, Daisy was straightening her shoulders in a workman-like manner. "You've about 'alf an 'our before yer expected downstairs again. Plenty of time to get away."

"And there was no one hanging around when you came up?"

"Not a soul. The place is a quiet as a church mouse."

"And it isn't even Sunday."

"Yer was always rubbish at jokes." After rolling her eyes Daisy turned away. But not before Thea had caught her stricken expression.

"I will never forget what you have done for me," and she flung her arms around her friend once more.

"I know. Just promise me yer'll 'ave a good life."

"I will. Tell Esme I said goodbye, and that I'm sorry I couldn't tell her myself."

"She'll understand."

"Yes. And the others too. Say goodbye to them too for me."

Thea held Daisy tight.

She was given a little push in the direction of the door.

"Will yer get goin'?" Daisy was untying her robe. "I ain't staying up 'ere all night," and she turned to the man propped up on the bed watching the proceedings with a strangely tender expression on his face. "No offense an' all that."

"None taken," he said, giving her a broad smile.

"Well then, shift over an' make room for me, lover-boy. Oh, and no 'anky-panky. Got it?"

"Absolutely. Wouldn't dream of it."

With another grin he held his hands up in mock surrender.

46

CLOSING THE DOOR AS QUIETLY as she could, Thea tiptoed along the hallway, across the landing and down the corridor to the bedroom she'd shared with Daisy and Nora these past four months. The usual hubbub floated up from the salon below; the jazzy notes of a gramophone record, subdued girlish chatter, the deeper base of a customer's voice and then a sharp and trilling laugh. For some reason she was acutely aware of something else too; that the air was saturated with the staleness of cigars and cheap perfume and the ripe tang of male sweat. Strange how she'd never really noticed how overwhelming it could be.

And then she was diving into the room and shutting the door behind her.

This was it, she told herself excitedly. In just a few minutes she would be free, and she gazed around wanting to imprint every detail on her memory. The cluttered surfaces, the rumpled beds, the dust motes rising and falling in the meagre light from the window; more than the rest of the house, this had been her home. The place she'd laughed and cried, endured hangovers and the odd sniffle and suffered the ignominy of the doctor's visit and his medical check. But there had been good times too. Celebrations that called for cheap booze and birthday cake or the scandalously delicious pastries from the French bakery on Ponsonby Road. But more than that, for the first time since her father and mother had died, she'd had friends. Good friends she would never forget.

It took only a moment to remove her scanty underwear and slip on the crepe-de-chine dress and coat, and after pulling on her hat and dragging out the small bag she'd packed that morning from its hiding place in the wardrobe, and with her purse containing the precious passport and all the money she'd managed to save, she was ready to go. Now she had to get down to the kitchen, through the scullery, out the back door, around the side of the house and through the gate. If she were lucky there would be a tram at the top of the road. If not, she'd enough cash to hail a taxicab.

Failing both of those, she had two legs and would walk.

The back stairs were treacherous since each squeaking, creaking tread had the potential to bring her down her. She trod lightly, careful where she put her weight. This was the part of the house never visited by customers, for unlike the gaudy promise of the foyer and the overdone opulence of the salon, here was only the drabness of dull green emulsion and linoleum floors. And instead of shocking photographs on the walls, there was only a print; a cheaply framed watercolour of an English cottage garden.

Reaching the bottom Thea held her breath and listened. A second passed. And then another. Satisfied there was no one about she peered into the kitchen. The pots and utensils set out on the large table in the middle of the room showed Huia's preparations for supper - a meal taken in shifts between customers - was well underway and that meant she would be close by. But right at that moment the place was deserted and skirting the enormous table she'd almost reached the scullery when the pantry door swung open and the last person she'd expected to see - hadn't Daisy told her she was busy in the salon - emerged with a loaf of bread in one hand and an earthenware dish of butter in the other.

Both froze and simply stared at each other. Clutching the handles of her portmanteau Thea thought she might faint - which could be a good thing given that at any moment Huia might walk in too. Even Frank could turn up. And then Belle would drop her impromptu meal on the table, rush upstairs to find Miss Kitty, and all hell would break loose.

She held her breath. Only feet away from freedom and so painfully close, it might as well be miles. Now she would be locked away until Silas returned. Shackled to a bed even; just as she'd been threatened. And Daisy! What would happen to her if anyone discovered the part she had played? It would be so much worse for her for she had no one coming to take her home. Why, she might even get thrown out. And then what? How would she ever get back to London?

Rooted to the spot she watched Belle place the loaf and butter down on a board and then, with deliberate casualness, pulled opened the table's shallow drawer. For an unbearably brief moment, no more than the blink of an eye, Belle glanced down, searching. Then her hand moved and her fingers closed around the item she wanted.

A large bone-handled knife.

Mouth dry, Thea stared in horror. Was she to be threatened and forced back upstairs at knifepoint? Or was it to be worse than that?

And then confusingly, Belle reached for the bread once more, and with her lips pressed together, began to saw into the crust of the loaf.

Wondering what was going on, Thea dared to shift her weight. Was she being toyed with? Was Belle waiting for her to make a move? And then what? Would she dash around the table and pin her to the wall, hold the knife to her throat? Stab her even? Who knew?

But with one slice of bread flat on the board, Belle seemed to be more interested on creating another of equal size.

Edging closer to the scullery Thea's eyes remained fixed on her opponent who, having pulled the dish closer, was now spreading a thick layer of yellow butter onto the topmost side of each slice as if nothing were amiss.

Thea couldn't believe it. Wouldn't believe it. It seemed Belle had no intention whatsoever of preventing her leaving.

But she would never let a girl get one over on her. It wasn't in her nature. Besides, she had to answer to Miss Kitty.

Just run, her brain ordered. Run! And so with her heart on the point of exploding, she threw herself at the back door and fumbled at the latch.

Behind her there was silence. No cry for help, no raising of any alarm. In fact, if her senses hadn't been so alert she would have missed what Belle said when she finally got the door open, for whilst the words were designed to carry towards her, they weren't overly loud.

"Good luck."

47

WHEN TWO WEEKS EARLIER DARIUS had appeared on what should have been her final night and told her that something unexpected had come up, Thea had been strangely unsurprised.

That is not to say she wasn't devastated because she was. Frightfully so. But if she were truthful she'd already started to question the depth of his commitment when she'd failed to make their meetings and he hadn't shown up at the bordello full of concern as to why.

After he'd left, making his way down the stairs and looking suitably chastened it must be said, she had clung to Daisy and wept.

"What am I going to do? Silas will be home soon and then I'll have no chance of getting away."

"Now, don't yer worry. We'll think of summit." Daisy was stroking her back as if she were a baby. "'E's a bastard that one, and no mistake."

"Don't say that."

"Well, look at yer. Yer a flamin' mess."

"It's not his fault."

"Yeah? Then whose fault is it, I'd like to know."

"Mine, in a way."

"And just 'ow d'yer work that out?"

"Oh Daisy, I've been such a fool."

Daisy made soothing noises. "No you ain't."

She carried on rubbing Thea's back.

"I thought he loved me."

Daisy nodded, as if therein lie the crux of the matter.

"I thought he would take me away. Get me out of this place." Lifting her head Thea stared around wildly, "I knew. I knew something wasn't quite right. Even you told me so. Why didn't I listen?"

"Shhh," Daisy murmured, pulling her back into her embrace.

"I can't go back to Silas. I just can't."

"And yer won't," she said quietly. "There's got to be anovver way."

"There isn't."

"Shhh," Daisy continued, "lemme think. The problem is, now that Darius 'as left you've got to get back downstairs and keep acting as if nuffink's wrong."

"Oh Daisy, I can't. Look at me."

"Yer've got to. No way round it."

"I'm a mess."

"Don't be daft. Yer've got a bit o' mascara down yer cheeks. That's all. Nip upstairs and tidy yerself up quick as yer can."

With a loud sniffle Thea eased herself from Daisy's arms. Even she knew it would take more than a dab of powder to cover her blotched cheeks.

"And then what?" she asked quietly.

"We'll have to come up wiv another plan, won't we?"

"I can't see how. Belle has her eye on me and now I can't even leave the house without someone wanting to know where I'm going. Even Frank is giving me funny looks."

"There 'as to be a way. We just 'ave to find it."

"It's not just that. Even if I can get away from here, where do I go? I've no money for lodgings. I couldn't even feed myself."

"Wot about yer earnings?"

Thea sighed. "Mostly gone."

She could hardly tell Daisy she'd spent it on lingerie to please and impress Darius.

"I could lend yer a bit."

"No. I won't take your money. How would I ever pay you back? Anyway, it's your escape fund."

"'Ow 'ad you planned it with Darius?"

"He was going to be waiting for me and we'd have gone straight down to the dock and got on the ship."

"Hmm," Daisy had lowered her head and her brow was puckered in thought. "Yer right. We don't only 'ave to get you out the 'ouse, we need to find someone to take you in."

"Oh Daisy, who would do that? We might as well give up. No matter where I go Silas will track me down eventually."

Thea had slumped down onto the bed.

"Come on, this ain't like you," Daisy said dropping down beside her and giving her a squeeze. "Thought you 'ad more gumption. Remember 'ow you stood up to Miss Kitty when you arrived. Ferocious, you were!"

Thea snorted and shook her head, but she did manage a tentative smile. "I was, wasn't I?"

"Frightened us all to death."

"I doubt that."

Suddenly Daisy looked up. "'Ere, 'ang on. Wot about yer friend?"

"What friend?"

"The scarred bloke."

"Gerald. What about him?"

"Seems 'e likes you. Reckon 'e might be game for a little subterfuge?"

"I have no idea." But Thea too was thinking.

"Well, wot d'yer reckon. Would 'e be up to helping yer? Yes or no."

"He might."

"Right then. 'Ow often does 'e come 'ere?'"

"I don't know. Every other week?"

"That's it then. Wait for 'im to turn up and then tell 'im wot's 'appened. If 'e's the sort of bloke you say 'e is, 'e might just 'ave an idea. And if nuffink else, he might know someone who could put yer up for a couple of nights."

48

IF THEA HAD THOUGHT WAITING for Darius to turn up at the bordello was stressful, waiting for Gerald turned out to be even more so.

"What if he doesn't come?" she demanded of Daisy one night.

"Then we'll 'ave to fink of summit else."

"Like what?"

"I dunno."

"If only I hadn't been so rude to him."

"When?"

"The evening Darius turned up and made a beeline for Nancy."

"Oh then. Yeah well, too late to worry about it now."

Mebbe 'e'll come tomorrow became Daisy's reoccurring phrase. Though as the days passed with no sign of him, and with Silas's return drawing closer and closer, Thea's spirits sank to rock bottom until, with just a few days left at the bordello, she realised she had to pull herself together. What other choice did she have? And so she took on the task of sorting through her clothes and other bits and bobs, deciding what might be suitable to take home with her and what to leave behind for the others, should they want it. Little of the former it was turning out, since the pile of rejects on her bed was growing rapidly. Seductive lingerie, paste jewellery and half-used cosmetics - Silas would have a fit if he saw it all!

Reaching to the very back of a drawer she pulled out the folded handkerchief containing her wedding band. If she had a choice, that too would be left behind.

"'E's back. 'E's downstairs." Daisy had burst through the door. "Quick. Hurry! Get yerself down there and welcome 'im."

"Oh my God!" Thea panicked. The ship must have docked sooner than expected. "I'm not ready. Where is he? Is he in the front room? Is he talking to Miss Kitty?"

Daisy stepped back, confusion on her face.

"Why would he be in wiv 'er?"

It was Thea's turn to frown. "Surely he's not in the salon?"

"Course 'e is. Where else would 'e be?"

Thea took a deep breath.

"Who's back, Daisy?"

"Gerald!"

"I thought you might have already gone," Gerald said, waiting politely until she'd lowered herself onto the sofa.

Thea's hands were shaking. Was that why he waited so long to return? He'd intended to avoid her? If that was the case, was she wasting her time expecting any help?

"You don't have to see me," she said, clasping her hands tightly. "In fact, I no longer work here. If work is the right word for all this."

It had been Kitty's idea.

Take a little time for yourself, she suggested. *Have a few beauty treatments. You'll want to look your best for your husband's return I'm sure.*

It was as if she'd known of Darius's betrayal.

Glancing around the room and meeting Daisy's questioning look from where she'd stationed herself behind the bar, Thea gave an imperceptible shrug.

"The other girls are very nice," she tried again.

"You don't understand. I came hoping to see you."

She held his gaze for a moment. And then turned away.

It was all too late. With little more than forty eight hours to go, how could she pin everything on this man? A man she'd never given any sign of encouragement. A man she'd treated no better than all the other faceless customers. A man she'd publicly rejected.

"I need your help," she said quietly.

"Tell me what you need me to do," he said the moment they were in the bedroom.

"I've been rather let down, I'm afraid."

"I see. Why don't you elaborate?"

"I thought we were going away together. I thought it was all arranged."

Thea burned with humiliation. Of course, Gerald would hardly know what she was talking about. Even so, he was nodding encouragingly.

"With...?"

"Yes." She couldn't utter Darius's name. It was too raw, too painful. Instead she lifted her chin and finished in a monotone, "It turned out I was wrong."

Gerald didn't move. "Go on."

"We were going to America," Thea tried to explain, as if it would make a difference, "by boat. First class, he said."

Turning, she reached for the corner of the dressing table. "It sounds quite dreadful, doesn't it?"

She wanted the floor to open up and swallow her. Why had she ever thought she deserved help?

"I will say you've never struck me as the flighty type."

"I'm not. You must think I'm such a fool."

"I don't think you're a fool."

"Gullible then," she insisted.

Gerald smiled. "Perhaps a little. So what is the problem?"

"My husband is coming to take me home in two days."

"And?"

"I don't want to go. I can't go."

"Why not?"

"Because I don't love him. And I don't think he loves me."

"You don't think you might be on the rebound from this other man?"

"No."

"So what are you going to do?"

"That's just it. I don't know. I want to get away. Start over somewhere else. Forget this part of my life."

"Then why don't you?"

Thea nodded towards the bed. "Can we sit down? I don't think I can do this standing up."

When Gerald sat at one end of the bed, she sat at the other, purposely creating a space between them.

"It would be so much easier if it were my choice to be here, but as you know, it's not. And that's why I simply can't walk out the door. I need your help. If you're agreeable," she added.

"What do you need me to do?"

"Everyone must think I'm still up here with you."

"Whilst in fact you're getting away?"

"Yes."

"And when do you want me to do this?"

"Right now. Daisy will be up soon. She'll wait with you and then, after thirty or forty minutes you can leave as if everything's normal."

"Can I ask what you will do? What your plans are?"

Thea offered a wry smile.

"That, unfortunately, is my second problem."

"Why?"

"I have none. At least not long-term."

"So where are you going to go?"

Thea said nothing. Her idea had been to get to the railway station and onto the next train. Regardless of where it was going. She would worry about everything else once she was away from Auckland.

"Look, I'm going to give you an address. It's across town but if you can make it there my sister will look after you until I arrive."

"What?"

"You can go to my sisters."

"But I can't just turn up."

"Yes you can," he said, his face transformed by a beaming smile. "Just tell her I sent you and that I'm meeting you there."

"But won't she wonder who I am?"

"Of course she will. She is a woman, after all. And that's why she'll take you in."

49

A mother of four of which two weren't yet of school age, Gerald's sister was tall, slender and unexpectedly attractive. She also had hair that reminded Thea of how hers had once been. Unfashionably long and wavy. Yet it suited her. It also seemed she was fairly unshockable, since over a pot of Lipton's tea she'd managed to drag almost every detail of the story from Thea and hadn't interrupted once.

"I can understand why my brother has chosen to help you," she said, sitting back with a smile.

"Do you? I wish I did. He hardly knows me."

"I'm sure that doesn't matter."

"What doesn't matter?" Closing the back door Gerald was pulling off his scarf.

"That you barely know Thea," his sister supplied from the kitchen.

Peeking in, Gerald looked from one woman to the other.

"I've told your sister everything," Thea said as he went to drape his coat on the hook behind the door.

That stopped him.

"Everything?" he said looking decidedly sheepish.

Emily slipped a hand over Thea's. "Everything."

"Ahh," coming over he dropped a light kiss on the top of his sister's head, "then my secret is out, I suppose."

"I'm afraid so."

"Not too upset with me?"

"As if you worried about what I thought," and she turned to Thea who was politely studying the table-cloth. "I spend a few hours a week at the hospital reading to the patients and such. I've done it ever since…" and she looked up at her brother. "Well, I've done it for a while. And because of that I've seen too much pain and suffering to condemn anyone for seeking out comfort, as he knows."

"She was about to say ever since I was laid up and covered in bandages."

"Yes well, you're not in a ward now are you? So sit down, I'll get you a cup and you can join us. You two need to work out what what's to be done next."

"You've been so very kind," Thea said as Emily took more crockery from a shelf, "but I really don't think I should impose on you, either of you."

"Rubbish!" Gerald was pulling out a chair. "I haven't enjoyed myself so much in a long time. Your friend Daisy's a card, isn't she?"

"She's amazing," Thea agreed, and then lowered her voice. "What did she do?"

"Absolutely nothing, at least nothing untoward. We sat and talked and when my time was up she left me at the top of the stairs. As far as I know after that, she followed the plan and went to lie down, ready to plead a pain in her stomach and say she'd been there the whole time. That is if anyone thought to question her. I'm guessing by now the whole place knows you're missing."

Thea's expression was troubled. "I hope she doesn't get in any trouble."

"She'll cope," Gerald's voice contained more than a hint of admiration.

"She will," she agreed with a smile. "She's been a brick the whole way through."

"So now what?" he said with a nod to Emily and the tea-pot.

"I have absolutely no idea. I do need to leave Auckland though."

"You do," Gerald agreed.

"I could always return to Canterbury."

"Is that where you lived as a child?"

"Yes."

"You don't think that might be the first place your husband might look?"

"I hadn't thought of that. And there's little point in going to Wellington. He's planning on moving his entire household down there once he's back," she explained to Emily.

"So your options are limited," she replied. "Do you have any skills?"

"None to speak of," Thea admitted and then coloured. "It was never thought to be necessary for girls like me. Of course, I can run a household, a small one at least."

Gerald was studying her, as if weighing up an idea.

"Have you considered Australia?"

"Australia?"

"If you're looking for a new beginning well away from all this then that might be the place."

Thea was silent. Even though it was New Zealand's closest neighbour, it was something she'd never considered and that made the idea both liberating and terrifying.

"You said you already have a passport," he reminded her over the rim of his cup.

"I have, haven't I?" and then she shook her head. "But my funds are too limited for that. Heavens, it will take all I have to find somewhere here."

"I'll lend you what you need."

Surprise turned to confusion on the faces of both women and while Emily made as if to speak, Thea got in first.

"You? But why would you do that for me?"

"Let's just say I would like to see you happy. And I'm sure there will be more opportunities for you over there. Think of the grand department stores in Sydney. No doubt they'd be pleased to have an assistant of your calibre. Or what about taking up employment in an office? Of course, you'd have to learn to type but I've no doubt that once you had the hang of it, you'd be a whizz."

"And there are always other places needing help. Hospitals or orphanages," Emily added, her eyes suddenly alive with the daring of it all.

"You see?" Gerald was grinning.

"You're both far too kind. And I have no idea what I would have done without you," she said, looking from one to the other. "But I really couldn't accept your offer."

"Why not?"

Thea looked across at Emily for help.

"Well, because…"

"Because what?" Gerald persisted.

"Because I've never been on my own before and to be in another country and have no one to turn to is rather frightening."

"I see. But you have no one here either."

"You're right. But I grew up here and that makes everything a little more familiar."

"Then why don't I go over with you? Help you settle in."

Thea stared from Gerald to Emily, who for the second time that evening was plainly as shocked as she was.

"Don't get me wrong," he said, "I'm not suggesting anything improper. Just that I could help you get started. After that I'd return here and you'd be on your own."

There was a long silence.

"I don't know what to say," Thea said quietly.

"Well, don't say anything. Hold off on any decision for now," he advised. "Sleep on it. Give yourself a couple of days to think it over."

He turned to his sister, "Is it all right if Thea stays here?"

"Of course it is," Emily was smiling once more, "I can make up a bed for her in with Alice. That is if you don't mind being around a noisy three year old?"

Thea looked over in gratitude. "It sounds rather fun."

"You haven't met Alice yet," Gerald said under his breath.

"Anyway," Emily continued, ignoring her brother's remark, "it'll be nice to have another woman about the place."

But Thea wasn't finished.

"I still don't understand why you would go to such lengths for me?"

Gerald looked at her for a long moment, and then shrugged.

"Why wouldn't I want to share your adventure? It's not as if I have anything better to do."

"But you must have employment here. Would you be able to take all that time off?"

The legs of Emily's chair scraped the linoleum as she got to her feet and started to remove the tea things from the table.

"Strangely enough, companies seem rather reluctant to employ someone like me," Gerald said, watching his sister's sudden burst of activity. "I believe they consider my appearance to be a little too upsetting. Have to think of the staff and all that."

"It's dreadful," the heavy teapot was set down on the draining board with a little too much force. "He's a hero. He was injured saving his men, for God's sake, and has a medal to prove it. But no one seems to care about that."

"Emily," he said mildly.

"But it's ridiculous. Your burns are on the surface. It shouldn't matter." The crockery was rattling ferociously. "You're intelligent. You're clever. Isn't it what you're capable of that counts not what you look like?"

"You would have thought so," he agreed.

Thea had sat quietly throughout the exchange, sensing this was not the first time the topic had been raised in this house.

"Well I think the idea of Australia is very exciting," Emily said as she turned back towards the kitchen sink. "They say it's streets ahead of us in so many ways and I hear Sydney is on a par with London for fashions. Just imagine that!"

Gerald was looking at Thea.

"Like I said," obviously trying for a casual tone, "why don't you sleep on it? No need for any quick decisions."

"But I've already made up my mind," she said.

December 1924

Sydney
Australia

50

THE VOYAGE ACROSS THE TASMAN Sea had been wonderful, and not only because the steamship was so well appointed. Calm seas and warm breezes meant time spent on deck playing quoits or shuffleboard, and when that became too strenuous they retired to quiet deckchairs to read newspapers or periodicals from the ships library. Later, after dining in the elegant restaurant, rather than make his way to the gentleman's smoking lounge, Gerald had promenaded her under the stars telling her of constellations and seafarers and discoveries of ancient worlds. Under any other circumstances it would have been so very romantic, and on one evening Thea had impetuously taken his arm. He'd laughed delightedly, though not before remarking it wouldn't do to get tongues wagging. For they'd introduced themselves to their fellow passengers as cousins - her a widow and him the son of an aunt on her mother's side - to all intents and purposes accompanying her to visit family on the other side of the Tasman.

Thea knew the three days at sea were merely a blissful interlude, and that once established in Sydney she would need to find employment quickly. She was even looking forward to that, for she would be standing on her on two feet. No more Silas, no more Kitty; she'd be free of all the shackles they'd imposed on her.

And it was all thanks to Gerald.

Arriving at Sydney's Circular Quay they established themselves in a nearby hotel. Not the very best but one that was clean and came highly recommended by others on board, and over the next few weeks or so Thea spent a considerable amount of time scouring the columns of newspaper advertisements hoping to spot a suitable employment opening.

Soon though she was worrying over the time and money Gerald was spending on her. They couldn't remain in their rooms all day long and he thought nothing of treating her to the theatre or cinema. Heavens, having left Kitty's with very little in the way of clothing he'd even taken her shopping!

"It is not that I'm ungrateful. In fact, quite the opposite."

They were strolling through the Botanical Gardens when she'd raised the subject.

"Then I can't see a problem."

"I feel it is all taking longer than expected and that is concerning me."

"Did you believe things would fall into place the moment we docked?"

"I rather think I did."

"Then you're being too hard on yourself. Starting over again takes time."

"But you can't support me forever," she'd laid a hand on his arm for clearly he was about to protest. "I think what is most troubling is that what we didn't consider. And that is with Christmas around the corner most employers have already taken on the staff they need to get them through the holiday."

"You could be right. But tell me, is that your only concern? That you may not find employment until the New Year? Or is it something else?"

Thea gazed around before replying. She had no wish to hurt his feelings, but it had to be said.

"It's both that and where we are living."

"The hotel?"

She nodded.

"Is it not to your liking?" he asked, clearly both perplexed and concerned.

"The hotel is lovely," she put in quickly, "but it's costing you far too much."

"Is that all?"

"What else could there be?" tucking her arm in his.

"Then why don't you let me worry about that?"

"Because you have done enough for me already."

"So are you suggesting you'd rather be in lodgings?"

"I believe I could just about manage if I were."

"But not without employment."

"No." Thea shook her head in frustration.

"So it would make you happy if we exchanged the hotel for rooms you might keep on later?"

"Provided they were affordable," she smiled.

"Thea," he'd stopped on the path, and taking her shoulders turned her to face him, "would you also prefer it if I returned to New Zealand?"

She didn't answer immediately, for another couple were enjoying the warm day and strolling towards them. She knew exactly what would happen. A few steps closer and both faces would be contorted in horror at Gerald's ruined features. Or else they would show a shocked sympathy. Worse were those who deliberately turned away, and like Emily, Thea had taken to raging against the injustice of his situation. Gerald would of course make light of it all, telling her he barely noticed anything amiss since the beautiful woman on his arm had all his attention.

And that was why, as the couple hastened by, she touched her hand to his jacket collar and smiled up at him.

He was searching her face.

"No. Don't answer that," he put in before she could speak, "at least, not yet. What have I got back there? Nothing. So please don't worry about me. In fact," and he leaned closer as if to impart a confidence, "I'm actually enjoying our little adventure."

"I can't believe I have to put it on again." Thea grimaced, fingering her wedding band. "I only brought it with me to sell. Otherwise I'd have thrown it overboard the first chance I had."

"I know," Gerald soothed, "but it's just for a short while."

"It brings everything back."

"Trust me. If there were any other way I wouldn't ask. But no one will rent us rooms if they have any inkling we're not man and wife."

"But why can't we be cousins again? It worked on the boat and at the hotel."

"Thea," he took her hand, "no decent landlord will allow us within five feet of his lodgings if he believes we're disreputable."

"It's what Daisy had to do too."

"Daisy?"

"Yes. She had to pretend she was married to get here. Society is so hypocritical"

"I guess it's moral standards. But I do have an idea. That is if you're willing?"

"What is it?"

"Let me buy you a new one."

Thea stared. "What?"

"A new wedding band. Don't look so shocked. I'm not proposing marriage or making an improper advance," though he was grinning, "but if it makes you uncomfortable wearing that one, let me buy you a new one. Then when I've gone you'll have two to sell. Though it may pay not to try to sell them both at the same time or to the same pawn-broker."

"Gerald!" Finding it hard not to giggle Thea snatched back her hand. "You make it sound as though I intend to collect them."

"Maybe you will. Maybe one day you'll be notorious. *Local woman collects husbands.* I can see the headlines now."

Thea's face clouded. "No. Rest assured I will never get married again. How could I? The moment I apply to the courts for a divorce Silas will know exactly where I am. And then he'll never let me go. His pride won't let him."

"He won't live forever, you know."

"So what are you suggesting? That I wait thirty odd years in the hope he has died of old age? Who would want to marry me then?"

"I'm sure someone would. Anyway, don't think about that now. Let's go into town instead and pretend for all the world that you are my fiancée, and having set the date and booked the church, we are in the market for the necessary ring. Would you like that?"

"Only if you don't get too carried away and tell everyone the marriage is to take place in St Andrews," she said, naming the oldest cathedral in the whole of Australia and one known for its Gothic splendour.

51

IF THEA HAD THOUGHT THE streets of Auckland busy, then Sydney's had to be three, four - no five times as bad she thought, stepping down into the gutter for the umpteenth time. Up ahead an omnibus was slowing and approaching the corner stop, picking up her pace she thought that if she were to work at Edith's Ladies Fashions, and in all honesty she wasn't at all sure she wanted to, she'd be making the hour-long journey five times a week.

And for eight shillings a day.

She hadn't taken to the manageress of the shop at all, thinking her a bit of a tyrant. Nor had the woman's comments about New Zealander's being the poor colonial cousins gone down well. No, and at this point as she was jostling to join the queue of waiting passengers, she decided it was not the position for her. Someone else could have the dubious honour of serving their customers.

She did wonder what Gerald would have to say, for this was yet another job she'd been thankful not to get and while it didn't help that those for which she *did* have a level of enthusiasm required skills she didn't possess, she couldn't believe how encouraging he remained; assuring her that the right opportunity was out there. They simply hadn't found it yet.

Since leaving the hotel they'd been living over a tobacconist and vintners and paying what she considered an exorbitant amount for what were in reality two very small rooms and a lean-to weatherboard outhouse in the backyard. Gerald seemed far less concerned, though even he complained at having to wash both himself and his clothes in the same galvanised tub, but it was central for all points north, east, south and west and close to public transportation. Later on he'd told her, if she planned to move she'd have to consider the location of her work when deciding where to live, perhaps even lodging with other girls from her place of employment. Or she might land a position that required her to live in.

That was all well and good, but in the meantime she was finding the lack of privacy a little trying. Twice now she'd caught him with his braces down and his undershirt unbuttoned at the neck. And while he'd been a touch embarrassed, she'd caught her breath and been, well... intrigued. Which was incredibly silly considering how often she'd seen him in varying states of undress when they had laid together at Kitty's.

Was he suffering too? Surely her being under his feet every waking hour was not what he'd been expecting when he'd made the suggestion of finding rooms? No, regardless of his continual assurance to the contrary, he would never have imagined it would take so long for her to settle.

Yet he'd shown no impatience, no irritation. In fact, he was the perfect companion and if she were truthful - and God help he never found out, for he would only feel even more obliged - she was enjoying his company perhaps a little too much. It was the little things. His ability to make her laugh, or when he pointed out things that might interest her. But with her taking the bedroom, at his instance it must be said, he was left to sleep on the truckle bed behind the table, and that was overwhelming her with guilt. For her very first thought when sitting at Emily's table had been that for as long as he was supporting her he would expect the same attentions he'd received at Kitty's. Why else would he have been so generous?

She'd tried to broach the subject back in New Zealand, when having boarded the steamship she'd seen he'd arranged two second-class cabins rather than one. Ignoring her protestations that she'd understood and accepted the full implications of their arrangement, he told her in no uncertain terms that the past was the past and this was her new beginning. Things were to be very different.

Now she was racing up the back stairs and calling out she was home.

"You've made good time. How did it go?"

With his sleeves rolled up and their small dining table covered in newspaper, he was brushing polish onto his shoes.

"All right," she replied, though a little evasively. "Are you going out?"

"Well, not knowing whether we might be celebrating or not, I thought *we* might go out. Though you might want to read your letter first."

His eyes were twinkling.

"A letter? Oh! Is it from Daisy?" and she made a grab for the envelope he was waving so tantalisingly.

"Who else knows where we are?"

"Emily?" Laughing and coming around the table she put her arms on his shoulders and leaned forward.

"It's not from Emily, though it is from New Zealand."

At that moment she snatched it from his grasp and inserting her finger behind the flap, dropped down into one of the two armchairs.

"Oh I'm so pleased. I thought she might not have got mine, even though I did send it weeks ago."

"Hardly weeks!"

"It seems that way."

She was unfolding the pages.

"How did the job interview go?"

"Oh so-so."

"Good money?"

"Not really."

"So I'm guessing you won't take it?"

She looked up and coloured. "I'd rather not. I know I'm being selfish, but the woman was just awful. Do you mind terribly?"

"Not at all. Plenty of time to find something else."

Visibly relieved Thea turned back to her letter.

"Uh huh," and then her tone changed.

"Oh... Oh... Gosh..."

"Is everything all right?"

"Oh, you won't believe it..." When she looked up again her funny eyes were as round as saucers.

"What?"

"Listen to this.

I know you are dying to hear what happened when your husband arrived. It was as if all hell broke loose. Cannon, artillery, the lot and as good a spectacular as I've ever seen. Frank showed him straight into Kitty's front room, and though he closed the door firmly, we could hear the yelling and carrying on from upstairs. As you can image Kitty wasn't going to give an inch and stood her ground. So between the two of them it was a right to-do! Anyway the upshot was he stormed out shouting for all the street to hear how he was going to close us down. Then it wasn't funny anymore as what would happen to us?"

Thea looked at Gerald. "It must have been dreadful and it's all my fault."

"No it's not," he said firmly. "Whatever happened was no more than your husband deserves. And you know Kitty. She's a survivor and so are her girls. Go on. What else does Daisy say?"

Thea looked down at the sheet again.

"Belle caught it too. Kitty dragged her off and gave her a piece of her mind. When she came back she was as white as a sheet. Then it was Frank's turn. I've never seen him so worried. More about his grog stash than anything else I bet. No idea what he'd do if she made him get rid of it, and afterwards even Huia gave him a tongue-lashing. She's the sensible one and knows they've got it made. And it's about time she stood up for herself, the bashings he's given her."

"That's true," Thea nodded. "You wouldn't like to see him when he's had a few too many."

"I've only ever seen him on his best behaviour. So when he's drunk he's obnoxious?"

"The worst kind."

"At least it means he's leaving us alone," Thea continued aloud, *"and that's not a bad thing."*

"I do feel sorry for Belle," she broke off again. "She could so easily have given me away in the kitchen and she didn't."

"She would have understood the consequences of helping you."

"I know. Even so…"

"Keep reading," he said, sitting back and folding his arms.

"And then I had to go in. You should have been there. You would have laughed so much. Of course I played the innocent. Told her I was as astonished as everyone else. Well, she didn't believe that. So I said that you did once mention running away to England with the fly-boy but I just thought it was the cocktails

talking. I never once thought you meant it. England, she said. Yes I said. And then she let me go.

Things are a lot quieter now, which is a shame really as we all need a bit of livening up every now and then.

Anyway, let's talk about more pleasant things. So how are you enjoying the high life? Is your Gerald…?"

"Oh!" Thea faltered, "I don't actually think I've referred to you as *my* Gerald. I have no idea what would have made her think that."

"What exactly does she say?"

Catching the gleam in his eye she found herself blushing again. "Hoping to hear good things about yourself?"

"Of course."

Rolling her eyes Thea picked up from where she'd left off.

"Is Gerald," she said deliberately, *"enjoying Australia? Do you think he'll come home? Or will he stay there a bit longer with you?"*

Now he was laughing. A deep and lusty belly-quivering sound. "Well that all depends on you finding your feet. Which I have to say, seems to be taking a while."

Thea dropped the letter to her lap.

"Are you suggesting I'm deliberately turning down employment just to keep you here? Because if you are…"

"Yes?"

Thea swallowed. For when he looked at her that way she almost melted. When he laughed, as he was doing again, his eyes crinkled in the corners, even the damaged one.

"I'm not going to lower myself to answer that," she said, shaking her head and turning away to hide her crimson cheeks.

52

THE NEXT LETTER FROM DAISY was folded inside a card arriving on Christmas Eve. After reading the first few sentences aloud Thea continued in silence.

You will never guess who showed up here the other night? Walked in as bold as brass as if nothing were amiss. Darius! Of course Ezz and I could barely manage a civil word. But you know what Nancy's like. She's always had a thing for him so she was all over him like a rash. Not that he seemed to mind.

But that wasn't all. No sooner had he arrived than Frank came over and whispered something in his ear and they disappeared off to see Miss Kitty. Well, of course I'd let everyone here think you'd gone off with him, so his turning up again really put the cat amongst the pigeons. I'd loved to have been a fly on the wall as I reckon he must have been pole-axed when she told him how you'd run away. Serves him right. I think he was waiting until you were safely back at home before showing his face again and that just shows what a piker he really is."

"Are you all right?" Gerald asked.

"Yes." Passing over the letter for him to read, she made space on the small mantelpiece for Daisy's card.

"I'm surprised he had the nerve," Gerald muttered darkly.

"Let's forget him," she was holding the red and green candle she'd bought for their Christmas table, "let's think of something more uplifting. Should we go to church in the morning?"

"Would you like to?"

"Yes. I rather think I would."

"Then that is what we will do."

"And later? We should have a proper dinner. We'll need to nip out now and buy what we need. How does a goose and all the trimmings sound?"

"And you intend cooking it in that?" Gerald was looking at the stove and the oven that would barely take a pigeon, only then with its legs removed.

"Can you suggest anything else?"

"I can."

"Oh?" Thea smiled. She could see he was enjoying himself.

"I thought we'd go to a restaurant."

"Oh yes! I'm sure their Christmas dinner will be far better than anything I could manage."

"And no washing up either," Gerald added. "So, if we don't have to go shopping today, shall we take the ferry over to Manly and stroll around Clifton Gardens? We could take a picnic even?"

Thea came over and took his arm affectionately. "You think of everything."

"Oh, I'm being selfish really. I would like to see a bit more of Sydney before I move on."

"Move on?" Thea managed. She was feeling horribly lightheaded all of a sudden. "What do you mean, move on? Where are you going?"

"Thea," and taking her arm from his he tipped up her chin, "we both know I can't stay here forever."

"But why not? All right, maybe not here," as she looked around wildly, "but somewhere close by."

"There's no reason for me to be here," he said gently.

"But I haven't found employment yet."

"You will."

"No. You said you'd stay until I did."

"I need to go."

"I don't understand. Why do you need to go? Aren't you happy here?" Thea was clasping and unclasping her hands.

"Of course. But it was only ever temporary."

"Then where are you going?"

"To find my fortune."

"Are you teasing me?"

"Not at all. I've been reading about the Queensland gold fields. It's all over the newspapers and I thought I'd try my luck."

"But that's the other end of Australia!"

"It is."

"But you can't!"

"Why ever not?"

"Because… well…"

He was looking at her. Gazing deep into her eyes as if trying to read what might be hidden there.

"Well…" she had no idea how she could tell him. Why couldn't he guess and put her out of her misery? Then she could crawl away and hide.

"You'll be fine," he said after a moment. "All right. I won't go until you have a job. You wait, by then you'll glad to see the back of me."

Turning away he lifted his jacket from the back of the chair.

"Shall I get something to take along this afternoon? Ginger beer? Or would you prefer lemonade."

Thea didn't want either. She was too miserable.

"I don't want you to go," she repeated.

He was looking strangely at her.

"Leave Sydney?" he asked softly.

"Leave me."

Standing in front of him she lifted herself up, and placing her arms around his neck touched her lips to his.

She felt his shock, felt it as a fleeting trembling that was there one moment and gone the next, then his arms were around her, holding her, crushing her almost and lifting her off the ground..

"Don't ever leave me," she begged, clinging to him. "Never."

"Say it."

His voice was rough. Demanding. And yet there was also a note of uncertainty. As if he couldn't believe what was happening.

"Say it," he repeated.

"I love you," she murmured, her lips against his.

"Say it again."

Leaning back she found only joy and wonderment on his face.

"I love you."

"Oh God Thea! Why didn't you tell me before?"

"I didn't know how to," she whispered. "Besides, you might not have felt the same way."

"Not felt the same way? My darling, I have adored you since the moment I set eyes on you."

"No, you didn't," still clinging to him Thea both hiccupped and giggled at the same time, "in fact, you were very rude."

"Only to hide my true feelings."

He swung her around.

"Rubbish!" she was laughing out loud and trying to catch her breath.

"How can you say that!" he too was laughing. "All right, it was the second time. The first time I thought you as bossy as any sergeant major."

"Oh really? Then I insist you kiss me again, trooper. Right now!"

His lips were divine. Greedy and assertive, wanting her all to himself.

"Does this mean we can be disreputable now?" she said happily.

Giddy with passion and intoxicated by love, Christmas 1924 was celebrated in style. Rather than simply dine out on the day, Gerald insisted they spend the entire holiday in the very best hotel in Sydney. He wanted to show her off he told her, and so nothing was spared. But it wasn't just that he admitted during one of their dinners in the hotel's premier dining room, it would be months if not years before they could indulge in such wild extravagance again. And that was because of where they were going.

"You have to know," he said, setting aside his knife and fork, "the northern part of Australia is nothing like New South Wales. It is hot, for one thing."

"I rather like the heat," she smiled.

"And the weather can be dramatic. Cyclones and torrential rain even."

"Are you worried?"

"Not at all."

'Then neither am I," she'd shrugged.

"There won't be any fashionable stores."

"Good. No one will know if I'm wearing the latest style or not."

He had chuckled at that, for the dress she was wearing was the very latest thing.

"You could stay here. Remain in the city until my return."

"And let you have all the fun? No thanks!"

"Does nothing deter you, my darling?" he said, reaching for his wineglass.

"Absolutely not," and she looked at him from under her lashes, "as long as I have you."

March 1926

Townsville
Australia

<h1 style="text-align:center">53</h1>

THE RED EARTH WAS LITTLE more than dust and the air so dry as to irritate the back of the throat. Two years ago the land had blazed. *Burning off* the Aborigines called it, nature's rebirth, and although seasons had passed since then, a hint of acrid smoke still lingered amongst the blackened tea-tree and eucalyptus.

Easing down from the saddle, Thea slipped the reins over the mare's head and unlatched the gate. It was good to stretch her legs after the long ride from her neighbours. With four children all under seven, Meggie was always grateful for some grown-up companionship - and for Thea's gifts of freshly harvested vegetables, or as on that day, a tin of baked goods. But making her way up the driveway alongside the horse, Thea soon released her grip on the bridle, for at such close quarters the tang of animal sweat was a little too overpowering, and as if needing no second bidding the animal immediately plodded over to the sparse verge edging of the fenced off paddock and lowered its head.

Knowing the mare would follow, Thea carried on around the bend. The single level Queenslander homestead stood in majestic resilience to the shimmering heat, though the same couldn't be said for the patch of garden in front of the long verandah. She had long given up on her dream of formal rose beds and brightly coloured annuals, for as much as she'd poured both labour and love into the venture, the planting had proved a dismal failure. Thankfully, and in no small part due to the constant irrigation from a bore, the lawn continued to thrive, as of course did the thick-leaved native shrubs and the small cluster of fragrant citrus trees.

Thea loved this place where tropical rainforest met dry savannah, though it was a million miles from anything she might have imagined back in New Zealand. Instead the parties and balls Darius had promised, she had calving and round-ups. And her friends weren't the ladies of leisure who might have been her set in England, but hardworking, gritty women with plenty to do and not enough time. Nonetheless, she wouldn't change her life for the world.

Clicking her tongue to encourage the horse, they walked the short distance to the stable block together. Once in the stall she rest her head against the horse's quivering neck.

"Give her plenty of water, and brush her down well," she instructed the Aboriginal station hand.

The house was just a short distance further, and stepping up onto the verandah she took off her hat, wiping a forearm across her brow and dropped gratefully into a wicker chair. Her check-up was due in a few days' time, and with the newly established baby clinic down on the coast and a decent drive away, that meant an overnight stay in a hotel. She was looking forward to that, and even more for the chance of a bit of shopping since she was fast outgrowing her clothes and needed at least two new dresses - and looser ones at that. They were also running short on some provisions and on top of everything else one of the farm vehicles needed a new part which hopefully had arrived on the last steamer.

Leaning back and closing her eyes against the shimmering heat, she stroked her swollen stomach.

They had left Sydney early in the New Year, sailing back out of the grand harbour and around the Heads to journey up the eastern coast of Australia. After a short stop in Brisbane they'd embarked on the last leg of the journey along with twelve other cabin passengers and a further twenty-five settler families travelling steerage class. Not to mention the two horses, three dogs and the large number of kegs, crates and bundles in the hold.

But their arrival in Townsville had brought her back down to earth, as with little in the way of luxuries, the place instead was a jumping off point for the booming gold field settlements in the hinterlands. After spending some months investigating the opportunities that might be found both in the mines and at places where alluvial gold could be panned from rivers and creeks, they'd continued north and put down almost all of their money on a cattle station offered as part of a deceased estate and at a knock down price at that.

And as Gerald had assured her, it had changed their fortunes.

Five thousand head of stock made for a lot of work but she didn't mind. If she had any regrets there was only the one. That as long as Silas Crawford lived - and she had no reason to think he did not - she and Gerald could never be husband and wife in the eyes of the law. Not that anyone else knew their circumstances, and for a long time, secure in their love for each other, it hadn't made a difference.

But now she was carrying his child.

They'd made a pact the day she'd found out she was pregnant. That they were unable to exchange vows would be a secret they'd take to the grave. No one would know. And if at any time they were challenged, they would say their documents were lost in a flood or a fire some years earlier.

Feeling the stirring of her unborn child, she smiled contentedly.

"Thea! Don't tell me you went riding today?"

Raising her arm against the intense glare she gazed up and with the sun behind him, his body was casting a welcome shadow.

"I did," she said dreamily, "but I didn't go far."

"What am I going to do with you woman?"

"Come and kiss me and then tell me how your day went. Did we have many cattle in the gully?"

"No, thank God!" leaning over, he lowered his lips to hers for a long and tender moment. Then, just as she had done, he swept the wide-brimmed hat from his head and wiped the sweat from his forehead.

"Damn, it's hot!" he exclaimed, dropping into the chair next to hers. "They're bringing more sheep down to the coast this week."

"Really? Where are they taking them?"

"Ayr and Collinsville. The boys are saying it's the driest conditions for ninety years."

"Then let me get you a beer."

Even before she could move, his hand was on her arm.

"You stay where you are. I'll get it," he said on rising. "Oh, and I saw in the Bulletin the Theatre Royal's having a concert this week. No idea what the programme is but since we're going to be in town would you like to go?"

"There might be something on at the Wintergarden instead."

"You and your American movies!" he shook his head and laughed.

Leaning down he kissed her again.

It wasn't Biarritz. It wasn't Morocco. It wasn't even England or America. Or any other place she and Darius had conjured up. But in this land of heat and drought and vivid colours and exotic sounds, she'd found the one thing she'd always wanted.

To be loved and to be loved well.

"Thank you," and lifting her hand she cupped the terribly scarred cheek of the man she loved with all her heart.

54

Ashford House,
Chichester
West Sussex
3rd October 1931

Dear, dear Thea

As you can see from the enclosed I am to be married! And to the Right Honourable James Melchamp. Who would have thought it! Me! Daisy. A girl from the East End. I can hardly believe it myself. He is a gent Thea, and while he is no Rudolph Valentino - oh do you remember how we used to swoon at the pictures - he is fine and upstanding and I am so grateful he has chosen me to be his wife.

Like your Gerald, he was hurt in the war. Not physically, but though he keeps himself busy, he has little turns when he is quiet and seems to prefer his own company. It doesn't bother me at all, just as my past doesn't bother him. Oh yes, he knows all about it. I didn't want anything to come out of the woodwork later so I told him everything. He didn't say much for a little while and I thought Daisy, that's it, you've lost the only chance you're ever likely to get. Then he turned to me and said that there are times in life when we all have to do things we otherwise wouldn't. Oh Thea, I could have got down on my knees in gratitude!

As you can see from the invitation we are to be married a week before Christmas. It will not be a grand affair. Just the two of us and a handful of guests. He has family, both older and younger brothers, but he is not one for fuss. And that suits me too. Not that I have changed much. No, I am still the Daisy of old! Even after all this time I miss our gin-slings and shopping trips! But between us, I think James will be happy with a more quiet life and I have come to realise, just as you did, that love doesn't necessarily arrive with all the hooting and tooting of a brass band. Sometimes it catches you unaware!

Oh Thea, I would so love it if you could be here on my big day. You would be able to tell me exactly what to do and say, just like always! Of course Australia is so far away and it is a long voyage.

Did I ever tell you how much I envied you your new life? Stopping off and seeing you both on my way home to England made me realise just how much I wanted such a life for myself! Not that anything would ever be as straightforward for me! But you were so happy with Gerald and your two darling boys that I was quite jealous! Even the idea of living in the untamed outback had a romantic ring about it. I can hear you laughing now!

I wonder what Kitty would say if she could see us. If she hadn't caught that terrible chill and wasn't already dead and buried, she'd probably have had a heart attack!

I wish I could pass on more news about Esme but as you know she sent only the one letter and that was to say she was content with her choice. Not that I would be happy being an old man's mistress, but for all that she will probably end up better off than both of us. Especially if he leaves her a little something in his will!

Well, I will close now my dearest friend. If it is not to be that you can be here for my marriage, then I will start dropping hints to my husband - and even writing the word brings me out in palpitations - that in the years to come we travel out to see you instead. That would be so wonderful.

Until then
With all my love
Daisy

There were no more letters, at least none in the box, and I had no reason to think there might be others hidden anywhere else. Gathering all the sheets of writing paper I carefully returned them to their respective envelopes. Then, with the pile of correspondence once again complete, I brought up the tails of soft pink ribbon and retied the bow.

It hadn't been hard to piece together the story since the correspondence had continued through Daisy's own escape from the bordello - not that hers had been anywhere near as dramatic. No, she had simply carried on working until she'd saved enough money for a passage home. But I couldn't help wondering if Thea and Gerald had ever made the long voyage to be at the wedding or if instead Daisy managed to persuade The Honourable James Melchamp to visit Australia.

Either way, just eight years later the world plunged once more into war, and then what became of Daisy and James? Assuming they remained in England, did they survive the bombings and rationing? And what of the austerity of the fifties and the optimism and sexual freedom of the swinging sixties? Did they live through those too?

It wouldn't be too difficult to find out.

And Darius? If I searched for news of him what would I find? A marriage? Children? Somehow I doubted it. Illicit liaisons with older women or heiresses seemed more likely given Daisy's scathing comments.

I might even turn up a scandal! That would be fun.

And Belle and Nancy and the rest of the girls? Surely they too were long dead. Or was there the slightest chance one remained, perhaps alone and in a rest home for the aged. Would she be found, shrunken and arthritic in a high-backed chair, locked away in her own world and reliving all her hopes and dreams while those around her carried on with their daily tasks, never dreaming that this woman would once have led the life she had?

I was being fanciful and my throat was closing in and burning. Unable to swallow, I fought back the luxury of tears.

Why, I wanted to ask my great aunt, why only now do you share your secret? Why couldn't I have known all of this whilst you were still alive?

The drapes over the French doors stirred a little. Beyond the small verandah a light breeze was bringing welcome relief to the late afternoon heat, and as I stretched out my legs, wincing as the blood rushed back into cramped muscles, I suddenly realised something else.

Unless it could be proved otherwise, and regardless of what might be on his birth certificate, Thea's son Bill was illegitimate, as had been his brother. Did he know? Perhaps he did and that was why he'd chosen to live elsewhere.

I already knew I wouldn't mention it. It wasn't my place for one thing. Nor would I tell him of the existence of the box or what was inside. Instead I would take it back to my apartment and keep Thea's precious memories safe, just as she had.

That was when I decided I'd stay the night. It wouldn't be the first time I'd done so and knew the spare room was already made up. In the morning I would ready the place for Bill's arrival by getting through some of the more mundane tasks before going out to the airport to collect him. Clearing out the refrigerator and store cupboards, cancelling the utilities. That sort of thing.

Meantime, with a crystal glass from her cabinet and a decent Barossa Valley Shiraz from her small wine cellar, I would spend what remained of the afternoon in the comfort of my great-aunt's cushion-clad wicker sofa on the verandah. The same one she had brought down from their home in the hinterland.

Then, having raised a toast or two to Thea and another to Daisy, I would watch the sun go down.

Somehow I knew both women would approve.

Originally from Sussex, England Hilary Murray now lives in Auckland New Zealand with her husband, grown up children and amazingly wonderful grandchildren.

If you have enjoyed this book and would like to keep up with her news and details of up and coming novels why not follow her on www.facebook.com/hilarymurrayauthor